I0671050

The Spacetastic Adventures of Mr. Space and Captain Galaxy Season One Collection

By T.L. Charles

An Annulus Publishing Book

Annulus Publishing, Cherokee, Texas, 2015

Published by Annulus Publishing

Copyright © T.L. Charles 2015. All rights reserved.

Layout by T.L. Charles

Contact: tim@tlcharles.com

Cover design by jimmygibbs

Space Battleship Spaceship and Galaxy - Copyright © innovari

ISBN-13: 978-0692506639

ISBN-10: 0692506632

No part of this publication may be reproduced, distributed, or transmitted in any form or by any means, including photocopying, recording, or other electronic or mechanical methods, without the prior written permission of the publisher, except in the case of brief quotations embodied in critical reviews and certain other noncommercial uses permitted by copyright law. For permission requests, send an email to the above contact.

Episode One
Lights, Camera, Impact!

*T*he desert world of Magna 5 was largely inhospitable to extraterrestrial life. The planet's north pole, if it could be called such, was mostly sand, with the occasional canyon to make things interesting. The south pole, on the other hand, was home to a dozen large, active volcanoes that always seemed to be erupting on any given day of the week.

In between these two poles were two continents, half sandy wastelands, half volcanic rock, with thousands or perhaps even millions of smaller islands scattered throughout the Blood Sea (so named because of the red color of the ocean's water) that took up half the planet's surface. It had no inhabitants; at least, no natural inhabitants. Scientists and researchers from Universal Alliance member worlds often stayed on the planet for a few months at a time at a research station built there, researching the unusual rocks and atmospheric conditions in order to help improve the entire UA's understanding of the universe.

What made the planet even more dangerous, however, were the massive meteorites that struck its surface every so often. Magna 5's gravity was strong enough to pull even the largest meteors to its surface, where they would crash and cause massive explosions. Once, a meteor fell inside one of Magna 5's super volcanoes, which resulted in an eruption that covered almost the entire planet's atmosphere for weeks and made travel to the planet impossible even with the best breathing equipment money could buy.

All in all, Magna 5 was not exactly Jason Space's ideal place to spend a summer vacation. He stood on the deck of the *Adventure*, looking out over the massive planet that loomed before them on the ship's main monitor. Below him, his friend Helena Galaxy—also known as Captain Galaxy—was checking and rechecking her bag to make sure she had all the right tools, equipment, and provisions she would need to survive out there on Magna 5's wastes.

"I really think maybe we should go somewhere else," said Jason, who preferred to think of himself as 'Mr. Space.' "I heard Shizor has really nice weather this time of year. Even Namox is pretty good."

Galaxy didn't look up at him as she zipped her backpack shut. "We need money and right now rocks from Magna Five are selling like hotcakes to UA scientists. I'm just going to do down there for a few days, collect as many interesting or unique-looking rocks as I can, and come back. Simple."

"But Magna Five is big and scary," said Space. He paused, and then said, "Okay, I guess every planet is big and scary, but it's bigger and scarier than most. The water isn't even drinkable. You might die out there, even if you wear the right safety equipment."

"If you're really so worried, you could come with me, you know," said Galaxy as she slung her backpack over her shoulders. "Besides, I'm just going to go to the Barren Isle. It's supposedly largely untouched by extraterrestrial life; therefore, there are probably a lot of good rocks down there that no one's taken. I doubt I'll run into any serious trouble."

"I dunno," said Space. "There might be rock monsters. Like, really big ones that can eat people."

Galaxy rolled her eyes. "You know that's just a rumor and one that was debunked by the Rumor Disprover on his TV show last year, too. The planet is totally lifeless."

"You can't be sure about that," said Space. "Besides, that was one of the worst episodes of the series, in my opinion. He just came, explored a tiny chunk of Magna Five, and declared it completely and totally uninhabited by rock monsters. He didn't even go to the volcanic regions, where most of the rumors claim that the monsters exist."

"Very few people in general have gone to the volcanic regions, Space," said Galaxy, adjusting the straps of her backpack. "Besides, I don't intend to go those regions myself. Barren Isle is mostly sand and desert and completely devoid of terrestrial life or volcanoes and lava. I'm going to be completely fine, especially since I don't plan to be down there long."

Galaxy made her way over to the stairs and walked up to the platform Space stood upon. He immediately blocked her path, his arms spread apart so she couldn't move around him. She stopped and looked at Space in disbelief.

"You can be like a really stubborn child sometimes, you know that?" said Galaxy. "Move."

"Take Sparky with you," Space said. "He can help you. And being a robot—"

"His wiring will get all messed up by the sand and heat," Galaxy finished for him. "Again, it's just going to be a quick trip there and back. If anything goes wrong, I'll send you a message and you and Sparky can come down and save me. I thought we agreed on that earlier."

"We didn't," said Space. "We actually didn't agree on anything. You just said you wanted to go down there and I just said that I thought you shouldn't go at all."

"Whatever," said Galaxy as she pushed her way past Space. "Look, I appreciate your concern, but it's hardly necessary. A few days down on one tiny island on Magna Five is hardly what I'd call dangerous work, especially in comparison to some of the other things we've done recently."

Galaxy walked up to the door, which slid into the walls as she walked up to it, and was joined by Space. He walked uncomfortably close by her side as they walked down the hallway.

"I still don't like it," said Space. "Sure, we have done more dangerous things, but Magna Five is still pretty freaking scary."

As they turned the corner, Galaxy said, "And this conversation is really getting us nowhere, you know. Unless you have something new to add, keep your mouth shut."

As it turned out, Space didn't have anything new to add, although he managed to make himself look very cross as they entered the teleporter room a minute later. Galaxy jumped onto the teleporter pad as Space went to the console and began inputting the coordinates that Galaxy had given him. He was still frowning when he finished and looked up at her.

"Last chance," he said.

Galaxy put her space helmet on her head, checked her oxygen levels to make sure she had plenty of air to breathe, and said,

EPISODE ONE: LIGHTS, CAMERA, IMPACT!

"You know my answer."

Space shrugged and pressed the big red button that read TELEPORT.

Immediately, Galaxy disappeared from the teleporter platform, making Space wish he could have thought of a better argument to persuade her to stay.

Though Galaxy would never admit this to anyone else—would barely even admit it to herself, actually—she never really liked teleportation all that much.

Sure, it was probably the most convenient form of transportation available, and yes she had specifically built the teleporter pad into the *Adventure* during its initial construction seven years ago, but that was only because teleporter pads were all the rage. Nowadays, of course, most starships did not have them because, as it turned out, teleporter pads had the nasty side effect of sometimes backfiring and reassembling the target's atoms in the wrong place or, occasionally, in the wrong way. She tried not to think about that too much.

The only reason Galaxy had not yet gotten rid of the *Adventure*'s teleporter was because it was built into the ship and removing it would require millions of digits she didn't have and an entire shipyard of shipwrights that she didn't have either. That, and Space thought it was the coolest thing ever and would probably lead Sparky in a mutiny if she ever even suggested they get rid of it.

Thankfully, the *Adventure*'s teleporter had never malfunctioned, at least not in any significant way. True, there was that one time when she accidentally teleported Space into the middle of a war zone on the other side of Siphania, rather than in that planet's capital like she was supposed to, but at least it had never teleported any of them inside out.

Yet, she thought as her body rematerialized onto the surface of Magna 5. *Best not to think too deeply about that.*

She shook her head and looked around at her surroundings. She found herself standing in a large, sandy canyon that, if everything had gone according to plan, was right in the center of the Barren Isle. A thick, natural rock bridge above her head that spanned the length of the canyon confirmed that for her.

Galaxy again checked the air supply of her spacesuit. It was at one hundred percent and would likely last two weeks if she was smart about it (though she doubted she would be on this planet for two weeks). She needed it because Magna 5 had little breathable air and what little air it did have was full of sand, smoke, ash, or sometimes all three, among other equally lethal substances. That was also why she wore a helmet made of polycarbonate that would hopefully protect her head in the event she fell from a high place or was somehow attacked.

She also checked her gravity boots. These would allow her to walk across Magna 5 with little difficulty. This was good because Magna 5's gravity was a lot different from that of Earth's or any other planet in the Universal Alliance. It was heavier, for one thing, but her gravity boots would save her from being crushed. She made a mental note never to remove them while here.

Her suit's internal thermometer told her that the surface of Magna 5 was hot, at least two hundred degrees Celsius, probably hotter further south. She was quite glad that her suit came equipped with personal cooling systems. She hated the heat.

EPISODE ONE: LIGHTS, CAMERA, IMPACT!

Then she took a closer look at her surroundings.

The Barren Isle was indeed barren. She saw no animals, no plants, nothing but rock and sand in the canyon, and that just barely. There were certainly no rock monsters, a thought that made Galaxy chuckle.

Space has got the biggest imagination in the universe, Galaxy thought as she took a step forward to test her gravity boots. *Rock monsters. Please.*

Galaxy spent the next few hours scouring the canyon for rocks. She found igneous, granite, rough rock, and a variety of other species of stone, some more common than others, but she figured she could get a good price for all of them on the market. She packed whatever she could fit into her rock-carrying bag, which quickly filled up with her findings as the day progressed.

By the time Magna 5's small sun was setting, Galaxy had gathered at least thirty pounds of rocks. She messaged Space, telling him to teleport the rocks up to the ship and to deposit them in the cargo bay, and watched as the bag disappeared before her very eyes. Ten minutes later, the now-empty bag rematerialized and she grabbed it and hooked its strap over her right shoulder.

By now, however, Galaxy was tired. Despite the suit's cooling systems, she was hot and sweaty, and with the sun nearly setting, she needed to find a good place to sleep for the night. While there were no wild animals on Magna 5 that could harm her, Galaxy was aware of large sandstorms that sometimes appeared during the night. How the sandstorms worked, no one knew, as the winds on Magna 5 were not strong enough to make them, but they did exist and to date had claimed the lives of ten unlucky explorers who had been unable to find shelter in time.

Luckily for Galaxy, she found a small cave, its entranced sheltered by a large boulder, in the canyon. She instinctively checked it to make sure that it was uninhabited, which it was, and set up camp without much trouble. Her camp was simple; an expandable tent made of rubber and plastic, complete with a sleeping bag, and capable of handling the sandstorms should it become necessary.

Galaxy crawled into the tent and lay down on top of the sleeping bag, too exhausted from her work during the day to actually get into the sleeping bag—that, and the spacesuit, for all its practicality, was really uncomfortable to sleep in and she didn't think she'd get any sleep.

That is, until she awoke with a start the next morning at the sound of a woman screaming just outside her cave. The sound was so sudden and so disorienting that Galaxy at first thought she was still dreaming, but when she saw the first signs of daylight through the flaps of her tent, she realized it was morning. And that she had to find out who was screaming.

Scrambling to her feet, Galaxy removed her laser gun from her holster (her intuition—what Space would call her 'space explorer sense'—told her that there might be trouble) and ran out of the cave. She peered around the boulder to see what was going on.

In the center of the canyon was a beautiful young Asian woman in a torn, purple dress that appeared to have been deliberately torn to show off her cleavage. She was lying on the ground, screaming and holding up her right hand to fend off what looked like a giant tentacled monster. Galaxy had never seen such a creature before. It looked like a cross between an octopus and a griffin. If anything, Galaxy thought it looked a lot like the pictures she used to draw as a kid, except this one was real and was clearly about to kill the woman.

Galaxy didn't know what was going on, but she didn't think or question it further. She just stepped out from behind the boulder, aimed her gun at the octo-griffin thing, and said, "Hey, big, dumb, and ugly! How's about you take on someone who can actually fight?"

The octo-griffin didn't even acknowledge her existence and neither did the Asian woman. That was when Galaxy remembered she was wearing a helmet and that sound didn't carry very well on Magna 5 due to its lack of air.

So Galaxy aimed her gun at the octo-griffin's head and fired off a shot. She fully expected the laser to strike the monster's head and blow out its brains. That would probably get the Asian woman's clothes all covered with its brains, but at least she would be safe.

Thus, Galaxy was surprised when the octo-griffin's head exploded in a burst of flame and metal. Immediately, the octo-griffin and the Asian woman vanished. In their place were two floating metal spheres; or rather, one floating metal sphere. The second one was lying on the sand, burnt and twisted and likely unrepairable.

Dumbfounded, Galaxy lowered her gun and just stared at the orbs. "What the hell …?"

Without warning, a small floating camera zoomed up to Galaxy's face. Startled, she almost shot it, but relaxed when she realized it was unarmed. She recognized it as a hover-cam, but what it was doing all the way out here, in the middle of nowhere, and who owned it, she had no idea.

"Uh, hello?" said Galaxy, peering at the camera, which hovered before her like a ghost. "Anyone in there?"

A message appeared on the inside of her helmet informing her that someone was trying to connect. It was not Space or Sparky, but an unknown caller, which made her hesitant about opening it, but she decided she was going to get to the bottom of this mystery, so she answered it.

As soon as she answered it, the entire front of her helmet was filled with the large, red, pulsing face of a Doman, a slug-like species from the planet Doma. Though Galaxy had been aware that her suit could display face-to-face messages like this, the Doman's sudden appearance almost made her cut off the connection without thinking. Didn't help that she already had a strong aversion to Domans on principle.

"Who the *hell* do you think you are, woman?" said the Doman, his voice magnified in her helmet for some reason. "You just wrecked thousands of digits of high-end, expensive equipment! What the hell is wrong with you?"

"What are you babbling about?" said Galaxy. "Who the hell are you?"

"I am Zingfree Drifle," said the Doman in his best impression of a jerk (at least, that was Galaxy's impression). "Director of the movie *A Day on the Annulus* and my biopic *Zingfree, Come Home*. Both, I might add, Galactic Award-winning films."

Zingfree's name clicked a memory in Galaxy's head. "I think I've heard of you before. A friend of mine is a big movie buff. Think he told me about your movies."

Zingfree smiled. "Oh? And what did he say?"

10

EPISODE ONE: LIGHTS, CAMERA, IMPACT!

Galaxy now remembered exactly what Space had said about Zingfree's two movies. "He said that first one was overrated and that your biopic could be titled *Zingfree is a Blowhard* and it would not have been inaccurate."

To say that Zingfree was angry would be like saying that the Annulus was a huge, ring-shaped space habitat. "Your friend doesn't know anything about good films. I imagine he must like trash like *Annulus Zombies*. What garbage! What an insult to the noble art of motion pictures! It makes me sick just thinking about it!"

Galaxy was just sick looking at his face. "Yeah, sure, whatever. Anyway, weren't you talking about how I destroyed your expensive equipment or something?"

"Oh, yes," said Zingfree, seemingly forgetting his hatred of cheap popcorn flicks. "You destroyed one of my holospheres. Those are incredibly expensive, the high-end ones going up into the millions of digits. These ones weren't particularly high-end—you see, I was aiming to recreate the look and feel of the Classic Era holofilms by using the cheapest holospheres I could find—but now you ruined it, ruined it all, and for no reason I can see other than you are a trigger-happy gunslinger."

"I thought the monster was real," said Galaxy, not even pretending to be polite now. "How was I supposed to know it was a holosphere? It looked so real."

Oddly enough, Zingfree's face broke into a wide, genuine grin that did little to make him look better. "It did? Damn it."

"Damn it? But you're smiling."

"Of course I am," said Zingfree. "Why wouldn't I be?"

"Because it contrasts with what you just said."

"Oh," said Zingfree. "Right. You're a human. Humans smile when they're happy, whereas we Domans smile when we're sad. And I am quite sad right now. Sad that the hologram of the octo-griffin actually looked realistic, rather than invoking the falseness of the Classic Era holofilms."

Galaxy wanted to say that she was actually a hybrid, but she supposed this was not the time nor place to mention such things. "Okay. I still don't think you're justified in getting angry at me, though."

"Oh, but I am," said Zingfree. "I am quite justified. That equipment was expensive and hard-to-find. I don't even know if it can be repaired now. I will have to have my technicians look it over, and if they can't fix it, you will have to pay for it. Or buy me a new one."

"Me?" said Galaxy. "No way. I'm not paying thousands or millions of digits to repair your holosphere. And what the hell is a holofilm director doing all the way out here, on one of the least hospitable planets in the universe?"

"I was about to ask you the same question, woman," said Zingfree. He pointed at her with one of his massive, slimy fingers. "If you refuse to pay for its repairs or to buy me a new one, I will drag you to the Universal Court and have them force you to pay me every last digit in your bank account. Don't tempt me, because I have sued for far less than this in the past."

Galaxy was going to say something snappy about how she would gladly do it, but she realized that arguing with Zingfree further was not going to help her one bit. She needed to bargain with him; otherwise, Zingfree might very well try to drag her to the Universal Court and right now Galaxy just didn't have the money to pay for the kind of expensive equipment that Zingfree used.

"There's no need for that," said Galaxy in as polite a voice as she could muster at the moment. "Listen, I'm a starship mechanic. I know a thing or two about fixing broken electronics. Maybe I can repair your holosphere for you."

Zingfree looked highly suspicious. "It is delicate equipment. Unlike a clunky starship, a holosphere requires a gentleman's touch in order to work properly, especially these older models, which are works of art in their own right."

"I know how to handle sensitive equipment," said Galaxy. "And I won't even charge you for it. You just give me some time to fix it and when I'm done, we don't even have to see each other again. What do you think of that?"

Zingfree pursed his lips. He looked away and then looked back her. "Fine. I don't have time to get my holosphere to a professional holosphere repairman anyway, You may try to repair my holosphere, but on *my* ship."

"Your ship?" said Galaxy. "Where is it?"

"I will send you the coordinates once we are done speaking," said Zingfree. "It is not very far from where you are. Just remember to bring the holosphere with you and I will let you in immediately."

Galaxy nodded. "Sounds good to me. Just send me the coordinates and I'll be on my way."

That was much easier said than done. While Zingfree did indeed send Galaxy the ship's coordinates (which revealed that the ship was a few miles south of the canyon), Galaxy had a difficult time transporting the damaged holosphere (the other one that hadn't been damaged flew back on its own).

The holosphere had to weigh at least fifty pounds, perhaps more, and looked to be at least a century old. Coupled with Magna 5's heavier-than-usual gravity, Galaxy found the task of moving the holosphere to be far more difficult than it should have been. She tried rolling it, kicking it, and lifting it, but the large metal sphere refused to budge, not helped by Magna 5's heavier gravity.

In the end, Galaxy used a steel cord she had brought with her, which she had originally intended to use to drag rocks, and tied it around the holosphere. She then dragged it out of the canyon, up the steep incline that the coordinates said would take her to Zingfree's ship.

This took her hours, though it felt like days. The slope was steeper than it looked from a distance and more than once the holosphere slid out of the steel cable and went tumbling back to the bottom. She became so frustrated at the task that she almost called Zingfree to tell him to get his piece of lousy equipment himself, but she eventually succeeded in reaching the top of the slope and soon was on her way to Zingfree's ship.

This thankfully did not take as long as it could have. Zingfree's ship was the only structure in the vicinity for miles. And what a strange ship it was. Galaxy had always considered Doman starship design to be ... creative, to put it one way, but Zingfree's little flyer actually caused her to stop and observe it for a moment.

It was hot pink, which if Galaxy remembered correctly was the color of the Doman flag. The ship itself was as round as a sphere, but easily larger than the *Adventure*. Twin wings stuck out on either side, much like that of an insect, but they probably couldn't flap. Zingfree's face was painted on the front of the ship, heavily stylized in an apparent attempt to make him look cool, but it really just made him look ridiculous and ugly. Not only that, but there was an odd flag sprouting from the top, which Galaxy at first took to be the Doman flag but which she quickly realized was actually yet another painting of Zingfree's face.

Nonetheless, she made her way over to the ship, struggling to pull the holosphere along behind her. Though Galaxy was by no means out of shape, she was quite happy when she reached Zingfree's ship. Along the bottom of the portrait of Zingfree's face, the words *Artistic Sail* were painted elegantly, almost flamboyantly, which looked like something Space would write, if he was here; though Galaxy was too tired to think deeply about it.

The airlock opened in front of her and Galaxy went inside, dragging the holosphere inside the last few feet. The door slid shut behind her without a sound, which meant that Zingfree at least kept his ship in good shape. She supposed that he was too vain to let it look or sound like a rust bucket, unlike some starship owners out there.

The airlock itself was rather tiny, almost forcing her to bend over to avoid scraping her head against the low ceiling. The light that signaled the air level was red when she entered, but then it turned yellow and finally green, indicating that it was safe for her to remove her helmet.

This Galaxy did, removing her helmet even as the door in front of her opened silently, revealing a man wearing coveralls over his blue jumpsuit standing before her. The man was scrawny, looking more like a snake than a human, but he didn't look very old at all, perhaps in his early twenties.

Galaxy smiled and held out a hand. "You must be Zingfree's mechanic. My name is Captain Helena Galaxy, Captain of the *Adventure*. Pleased to—"

The man simply walked past her, like she didn't even exist, and bent down over the holosphere. He was looking it over, poking and prodding it, turning it over and over as easily as he would a ball of yarn. Galaxy looked down at him, scratching the back of her head awkwardly, holding her helmet under her right arm.

"Um, hello?" said Galaxy. "What's your name?"

The man looked up at her briefly. He had brilliantly golden eyes, eyes so gold that Galaxy thought they literally were made of the precious metal, before returning his attention to the holosphere. "Name's Jeff."

Before Galaxy could respond, a loud, arrogant voice that she immediately recognized said, "Ah, Captain Galaxy. Welcome aboard my fabulous ship, the *Artistic Sail*."

Turning around, Galaxy saw Zingfree Drifle, who, like all Domans, had a slug-like lower body with a vaguely humanoid upper body. Though it was perhaps politically incorrect to say so, Galaxy had always found Domans to be rather creepy. Zingfree moved with more grace than the Domans she had known, true, but he trailed a thin layer of slime behind him and his red skin glistened in the lights of the ship's hall. His face looked deformed and melted, but as it was not right up in her face like it had been before, it looked a little less ugly.

"I wouldn't call hours of dragging the holosphere 'timely,'

Zingfree," said Galaxy, shaking the Doman director's outstretched hand. She was glad she was wearing gloves, but even then she could feel the slime he secreted clinging to her hand. "But yes, I am glad to be here. Much better than Magna Five."

Zingfree laughed. "Of course. The *Artistic Sail* is a masterpiece of Doman engineering, as I am sure you have already noticed. After all, you are a starship mechanic yourself, are you not?"

Galaxy nodded. "I am, yes. But I honestly can't say anything about how well it's designed yet, seeing as I just got here."

Zingfree looked like he'd been hit by a truck, but he shook his head and said, "Well, Jeff here can tell you all about it later. Right, Jeff?"

Without looking up from what he was doing, Jeff nodded. "Yes, sir, Mr. Drifle."

He spoke with a Southern accent that Galaxy found kind of cute. Still, something about him creeped her out; not in the same way as Zingfree's ugly body, but it did make her feel a little uneasy just the same.

"He's our mechanic," Zingfree explained to Galaxy. "A highly gifted young man from Georgia, Earth, I believe he told me. He's been working on my ship for six months and even I, as ignorant as I am to the delicacies of starship mechanics, can see a genius in him that is so rarely seen in humans his age."

"Really?" said Galaxy, casting a quick glance at Jeff. "He's that good, huh?"

"Yes," said Zingfree. "Jeff, will you take the holosphere to the hold? Captain Galaxy will be working on it in there. Be sure to have all the necessary repair equipment where she can easily get it."

Jeff nodded and reached down to lift the holosphere. He detached the steel cable around it and lifted the holosphere on his shoulders and walked away, leaving behind a satisfied-looking Zingfree and an utterly stunned Galaxy.

"Did he just lift that thing like it weighed nothing?" said Galaxy, disbelief etched in her voice.

Zingfree nodded. "Jeff is as strong as he is capable. That, and the artificial gravity on this ship is a wee bit lighter than it is outside, but really it is not that much lighter."

Galaxy lifted her foot and felt it go up quicker than normal. "I can tell."

"Now, Captain," said Zingfree, turning around. "Why don't you follow me to the bridge? I can give you a quick tour of the *Artistic Sail*, which is just as much a piece of art as it is a flying machine."

Galaxy was irresistibly reminded of Space's high-minded artsy talk whenever Zingfree spoke, but she nodded and said, "Sure, Zingfree. Lead the way."

The *Artistic Sail* had obviously been designed for Domans. The ceiling was low, the walls were close together, and the entire place stank of Zingfree's slime (although thankfully robotic arms would pop out of the walls every now and then and wipe up his slime with water and rags). Galaxy had to walk with her back bowed to avoid hitting her head against the ceiling and it didn't help that Zingfree moved rather slowly, probably because Domans in general were a slow species.

"What were you doing on Magna Five, Captain Galaxy?" said Zingfree as they walked, not looking at her as he spoke.

EPISODE ONE: LIGHTS, CAMERA, IMPACT!

"Collecting rocks," Galaxy said. "I'm a space explorer and part of my job is collecting rare or valuable rocks to sell to people."

"Is that all you do?" said Zingfree, sounding disappointed.

Galaxy shook her head, moving it to avoid hitting her skull against a light protruding from the ceiling. "No. Sometimes I fight criminals or mercenaries or get caught up in conspiracies."

Zingfree's eyes lit up when she mentioned that. "Oh, now that sounds like a real space explorer to me. Did you know I made a movie about space explorers, once?"

"You did?" said Galaxy, trying not to make faces as the stink of Zingfree's slime got worse and worse. She wanted to cover her nose, but she did not want to offend Zingfree and make him kick her out of his ship, so she didn't. "What was it called?"

"Oh, it was an old film, one of my first," said Zingfree in a falsely modest voice. "It was called *Captain Laser's Adventures in Space*. To make it accurate, I spent three months on board the ship of the famed space explorer Moktashef Tawfeek. I unfortunately didn't learn as much as I could, however, because I got sick halfway through the agreed-upon time and had to leave. It still helped me make *Captain Laser* accurate to life, however."

"Tawfeek?" said Galaxy, genuinely impressed. "But he lived at the beginning of the twenty-second century, during the Dawn of Space Exploration."

"Well, we Domans are quite long-lived, you know," said Zingfree. "I am three hundred and thirty years old; though Tawfeek himself was quite elderly when I first journeyed with him—although he was definitely not a weakling by any definition of that word."

"Amazing," said Galaxy with a sigh. "I wish I could have met him. Too bad medical science in his time didn't know how to increase his lifespan past two hundred, huh?"

"He was a fine example of your species," said Zingfree, nodding. "Though if I must say, he was too practical for my tastes. Didn't like the camera I carried around me to film everything. He got rude whenever I whipped it out, even after I claimed it was for research purposes. The nerve of some people. Still sad how he mysteriously vanished, however."

Right now, Galaxy was quite glad Space wasn't anywhere with her; otherwise, she suspected he might decide to get a camera and use it to film their lives. And that would be annoying, especially if he got Sparky in on it. For that matter, she didn't see fit to correct his casual racism, if only because it proved that she had managed to avoid being pegged as a hybrid, which she was happy about.

"What are you even doing on this planet?" said Galaxy.

Zingfree spread his stubby little arms, which in the small hallway gave Galaxy even less room to walk. "Filming my latest holofilm, of course."

Galaxy raised an eyebrow as they began to ascend a short staircase. "On one of the least hospitable planets in the known universe?"

"I need to," Zingfree insisted. "Magna Five is the perfect location for the film's story. My producers wanted me to use CGI, but I argued that it would be far more realistic if I used an actual location to film it. I chose Magna Five precisely because I knew I would not be bothered by people who aren't involved with the movie. Plus, I don't have to pay any taxes or deal with local government agencies that oversee that kind of thing."

He added that last one like it was a secret joke that he and Galaxy shared, though all he succeeded in doing was making Galaxy feel a bit uncomfortable.

The tour of the *Artistic Sail* took perhaps only half an hour. Zingfree showed her the eating area, the barracks, the bridge, and everywhere else on the ship. He also introduced her to the other members of his crew, which was very small due to his insistence on using holospheres and hover cams to film it. There was the pilot of the ship, another Doman named Rinz Eru; the human cook Ezra Rain; and a robot Metalhead, a large, currently inactive one-eyed robot that Zingfree claimed could shoot plasma from its hands (although seeing as its hands had no cannons from which to shoot the plasma, Galaxy thought Zingfree might be lying).

"I thought film crews were ... well, larger," said Galaxy, following Zingfree down into the hold of the ship.

Zingfree shook his head. "There's no need for large film crews with holofilm tech, unlike the old days. I don't need actors when I can just use holospheres programmed to act how I wish. I don't need special effect teams because the holospheres again provide enough special effects to sate the appetite of even the most demanding viewer. Most of the things I need done are automated. Gives me more control over how I make my films, you understand."

Galaxy nodded. "Oh, I understand. My own ship is largely automated, manned only by me, my friend Space, and our robot Sparky. Automation makes it easier to control."

"Indeed it does," said Zingfree. "You know, Galaxy, I was a bit angry at you at first for breaking my equipment, but you're not such a bad human after all. I'm not going to ask you to join my crew, of course, but I would like you to hang around on the ship with me for a bit once you've repaired the holosphere."

Galaxy bit her lower lip. The idea of spending time with a Doman made her skin crawl, but she said, in her polite voice, "That's a kind offer, Mr. Drifle, but I can't stay here for very long. I told my friend I'd only been down here for a few days. Besides, I really need to get back to collecting rocks. There are still quite a few I need to gather and I can't do that if I'm cooped up in this ship all day every day."

Zingfree looked disappointed. "What if I gave you a starring role in my new film? Would that help?"

Galaxy shook her head. "Sorry, but I'm not much of an actress. But you could pay me for my help repairing the holosphere."

Zingfree didn't look at her as he said, "Well, I'm sure I'll come up with some way to reward you later. I doubt you'll fix the holosphere in a day, after all. Gives me plenty of time to come up with a suitable reward or form of payments for your efforts."

The hold of the *Artistic Sail* was much more open than the rest of the ship. The ceiling was higher, too, allowing Galaxy to stand to her full height (which made her back ache, as it had just gotten used to being bent over). The hold had a lot of boxes and crates, full of food, filming equipment, spare parts, and other things Galaxy couldn't identify, and in the center of the hold was the damaged holosphere on a workbench. The undamaged holosphere was sitting next to it, perhaps meant to act as a blueprint for her to use in case she needed to figure out how the damaged one should look.

EPISODE ONE: LIGHTS, CAMERA, IMPACT!

But that wasn't what caught Galaxy's attention the most. What really caught her attention was the row upon row of repair equipment, laid out in a toolbox on a metal table, which immediately drew her to it. There were wrenches and screwdrivers, lasers designed to cut through metal in order to perform delicate internal surgeries, and even some mallets for whenever Galaxy got frustrated, among many other different kinds of tools Galaxy so rarely saw anywhere. Not only that, but they were all brand new and seemed to be top of the line repair equipment.

Galaxy looked at Zingfree in astonishment. "This is expensive stuff. Where did you get it?"

"Oh, those tools?" said Zingfree, waving a dismissive hand at them. "Bought them last time we were on the Annulus. Jeff said it was the best of the best; naturally, I had to buy it, as the best of the best is what I deserve."

Galaxy picked up one of the wrenches and looked it over with great reverence. "I've never even *seen* a Magna wrench in person before. They're the best kind of wrench in the entire Universal Alliance."

"Does that mean you don't know how to use it?" said Zingfree in alarm. "Because if you don't—"

"I do," said Galaxy, looking up quickly. She clutched the Magna wrench to her chest. "It's just … wow. This is some pretty cool stuff."

"Use whatever you need," said Zingfree, gesturing at the tools laid out as he began to make his way out of the room. "I will send Jeff to fetch you at mealtimes."

But Galaxy didn't hear him. She was too busy examining the

holospheres, both the damaged and undamaged one, and becoming ecstatic when she realized, just after a cursory glance of the damaged one, that she would likely have to use *all* of the tools in that toolbox to repair the damaged one.

And that made her smile so much that she was glad no one could see her face right now.

As Galaxy predicted, the holosphere took more than a day to repair. Her laser had almost completely fried the circuitry, specifically the projector, and she almost drove herself crazy trying to repair it. It didn't help that Zingfree barely had any spare parts on board that she could use.

Jeff was not much help, either. Sure, he clearly knew how to repair a starship, but he seemed to know absolutely nothing about how to repair holospheres. At various random times throughout the day, he would come to check on Galaxy, often when she didn't expect him to. That he was so silent made his occasional visits that much more disturbing to her.

Zingfree was worse, though. He visited her almost hourly, demanding to know how close she was to being done. Every time, she had to reassure him that she was still not ready and that it would likely be a while before she was done. He reminded her so much of Space, except more demanding, which made her wonder if artistic types like that were all the same,

Then again, that wasn't very surprising. Zingfree couldn't film his holofilm without the holospheres, after all. Galaxy supposed it would be like asking her to build a starship without metal; a possible feat, but so impractical as to be impossible.

Galaxy considered contacting Space and Sparky to let them

know where she was, but she decided against it, because she was in no real trouble and she really didn't want Space to come down here to argue with Zingfree about his holofilms. She also considered contacting them to see if they had a holosphere projector on board the *Adventure* somewhere, but again she decided not to, as she doubted they had one on board.

The next day was much the same as the last. More Jeff, more Zingfree, and little progress on the holosphere. She spent hours at a time on it, but she soon realized that she would have to give up. There was no way she could repair the holosphere with the equipment she had on hand, despite how great it was. She would have to tell Zingfree that he would need to buy a new holosphere projector from a company that built them or take it to someone who knew how to repair holospheres.

At least, that is logically what she should have done. Galaxy would never admit it to anyone, but she could be as stubborn as hell. When she chose to do something, she'd do it even if it was impossible. And secretly, she liked it better than collecting rocks, anyway, even though she knew that she needed to collect rocks so she and Space could get some more money to buy fuel and supplies for their ship.

As it turned out, she didn't need to worry about contacting Space because he contacted her. It was shortly after lunch, when she was just sitting down to begin work on the holosphere again, that her com-watch beeped loudly. She glanced at it and saw Space's face staring up at her, with the words 'JASON SPACE' blinking up at her. She wondered if she could ignore it, but decided against it. They were probably worried for her, because she had not called them in a day.

Knowing Space's imagination, he probably thinks I'm trapped underneath a pile of rock, probably from a rock slide, and am heroically hanging on by sheer willpower alone even as my air supply leaks out minute by agonizing minute, Galaxy thought.

Sighing, Galaxy tapped the com-watch and said, "Space, I—"

"Galaxy!" said Space's voice over the com-watch, loud enough to make her cringe. "Where are you? Sparky and I have been worried sick! Are you currently trapped underneath a pile of rock, perhaps from a rock slide, and are heroically hanging on through sheer willpower alone even as your air supply leaks out minute by agonizing minute?"

Galaxy blinked. "No. I'm actually inside a rather comfortable starship that has plenty of air and food. I've used maybe five percent of my own oxygen supplies so far, if even that much."

"Oh," said Space, who sounded disappointed for some reason. "Wait, a starship? What are you talking about?"

Galaxy quickly filled Space in on Zingfree and the holosphere. She could not see Space's expression, only the still image of his face on her com-watch, but somehow she could tell even without him saying a word that he was deeply unimpressed.

"Zingfree Drifle, eh?" said Space after Galaxy finished. "He's a hack and all his movies are overrated."

Galaxy rolled her eyes. "Whatever. Look, I'm going to probably be down here a bit longer because I promised I would rebuild his holosphere for him. He threatened me with legal action if I didn't."

Space made an annoyed grunt. "Well, you better hurry up quick."

"Why?" said Galaxy. "It's not like we have anywhere to be,

right?"

"That's not what I mean," said Space. "See, the *Adventure*'s sensors have picked up a pretty large meteor heading toward Magna Five. It's big—probably even bigger than our ship—and according to Sparky's calculations, it should impact in twelve hours."

Galaxy leaned forward on the work bench, propping her chin up in her other hand. "Yeah, so what? Meteors strike Magna Five all the time. That's why some people call it Meteo."

"Thing is," said Space, with more than a hint of fear in his voice, "the meteor's trajectory is … well, Sparky says that unless the meteor is intercepted or stopped, it will crash directly into Zingfree's ship."

Galaxy's hands felt cold. "Wait … are you saying …"

"That if you don't get the hell out of there right now, you'll be blown into smithereens very soon?" said Space. "That's exactly what I am saying. And I don't like it, either."

Galaxy gulped. "Sparky's calculations can't be right, can they? I mean, surely he made a mistake."

"No mistake," said Space. "Ran his calculations by the ship's computers and they confirmed it. I'm not too good with math, but even I can tell he's probably right."

"Well, do something about that meteor, then," said Galaxy. "Use the ship's cannons to blow it off course."

"We'll try," said Space. "But I can't guarantee we'll actually succeed. The meteor is moving pretty fast and we can't get a lock on it. It would be better for you to come back to the ship so we can leave it."

"Beam me aboard, then," said Galaxy. "I'm actually not

having a lot of luck with the holosphere and in fact was about to tell Zingfree to hire someone else to do the job instead."

"You know the teleporter doesn't work if you're inside a building or ship," said Space. "You need to get out of Zingfree's ship if you want us to teleport you off the planet."

Galaxy sighed. "That's right. How could I forget? Very well. I'll go tell Zingfree as well so he can get off planet before the meteor strikes. Talk to you in a couple of hours."

She turned the com-watch off and stood up from the work bench. She turned around and was surprised (though not as surprised as she might have been) to see Jeff standing in the doorway. His dull golden eyes, as usual, were focused on her. She wondered how long he had been standing there and how much he had heard, but then decided it wasn't important.

Stepping over the bench she sat on, Galaxy said, "Jeff, good to see you. I just got a call from my friend Space about a meteor that's going to strike this exact spot where this ship is located. He's going to try and knock it off course, but in the event that he doesn't, Zingfree needs to know that we have to leave right now."

Jeff scratched his short beard. "I'm aware of it."

"You are?" said Galaxy. "Then go and tell Zingfree that I couldn't fix his holosphere and that he might need to buy a new one. You should also tell him to either move off Magna Five entirely or to another part where the meteor won't strike."

Jeff planted his feet in the doorway and folded his arms. "No."

Galaxy looked at him in disbelief. "Excuse me? Did you just say 'no'?"

"Yes," said Jeff, nodding. "Mr. Drifle doesn't need to know

28

about the meteor. Otherwise, he might survive."

"You make that sound like a *bad* thing," said Galaxy. "I mean, I don't like Zingfree much myself, but—"

"But he doesn't need to survive, now does he?" said Jeff. His Southern accent no longer sounded quite as cute as it did before. "Naw. He can go on about his stupid holofilms right up until the moment that meteor incinerates him."

Galaxy's eyes widened. "Jeff, what the hell? You sound like you *want* Zingfree to die."

"Of course I do," said Jeff, leaning against the frame of the door. "'Course, if you got out of this hold, then you could warn him about the impending meteor and he'd have plenty of time to get off. Can't have that, so see you later, girl. If you survive, that is."

The exit closed in front of Jeff. Galaxy raced over to the door and began banging on it, but it wouldn't open. She looked for the control panel inside the hold, but as soon as she spotted it, the control panel flipped back into the wall where she couldn't get it. There was no way to pry the control panel open, either, as the panel was flush with the rest of the wall and the tools she had were useless for anything other than holosphere repair (although, as she had learned earlier, they were not much good even for that).

"Okay, Galaxy," she said aloud, not sure why she was talking to herself but choosing not to think too deeply about it. "This isn't that bad. You can get out. Just use your light-gun. Should be easy to blast the door open and escape."

Galaxy reached down for her holster and found it was empty. Frantic, Galaxy looked down at her empty holster, hoping that maybe she had somehow misplaced it, but she almost despaired upon seeing the holster empty. She looked around the hold, hoping to see the gun perhaps placed on the bench or worktable, but she saw no sign of her light-gun anywhere. It was like it had disappeared, which was just her luck.

I know, Galaxy thought. *I'll send Space and Sparky a message. Then they can come down and save me.*

Galaxy held up her com-watch and tapped the screen. She smiled when she saw it turn on and then tapped the image of Space, knowing that it would take much less than twelve hours for him to get her even if Zingfree and his crew were uncooperative.

Galaxy felt the smile vanish from her face, however, when the com-watch displayed a 'ERROR. CANNOT CONNECT' message.

"No, no, no," said Galaxy. "Don't be stupid. Of course you can work."

Another message appeared on it: 'NO. I CAN'T. YOU'RE SCREWED. SORRY.'

Galaxy cursed. She knew she shouldn't have let Space program the com-watch to respond to certain voice commands from her.

So she tried to connect again and again and again, but every time the same 'ERROR. CANNOT CONNECT' message popped up (and when she swore at it once in frustration, it said 'IF YOU DON'T HAVE ANYTHING NICE TO SAY, DON'T SAY ANYTHING AT ALL'). She had no idea what the problem was. Even after she used the com-watch's troubleshooting program, it did little to help.

EPISODE ONE: LIGHTS, CAMERA, IMPACT!

Must be Jeff, Galaxy thought. *Somehow he's blocking all transmissions in and out of the* Artistic Sail. *He doesn't want me getting out, doesn't want me backing out of the deal. Great.*

She lowered her com-watch and looked at the ceiling. She could scream and shout; however, she had a feeling that Zingfree couldn't hear her. And even if he could, was there any guarantee that he would let her out? He was an artist whose tools were broken. She knew from experience how demanding and unyielding he could be.

Sighing, Galaxy sat down on the floor and glanced at her com-watch's clock.

She had eleven and a half hours left. They all had eleven and a half hours left.

Come on, Space, Galaxy thought. *You gotta get down here and save me. Please.*

Ten hours left ...

"It's been two hours," said Space, standing on the bridge of the *Adventure*, looking at the ship's computer display of Magna 5. "And Galaxy hasn't responded or told us to beam her up. She doesn't even seem to be on the surface of the planet."

Sparky, who was monitoring one of the computers below the bridge, looked up and said, "And Zingfree Drifle's ship has not yet departed from the planet, either. That means he is probably intending to stay."

Space slammed his fist on the small, waist-high wall dividing the captain's chair from the front part of the bridge. "Damn it. Sparky, did you try to contact Zingfree directly?"

Sparky nodded. "I did. Couldn't connect. Something is

31

blocking all transmissions between our ship and his."

"And I haven't had much luck in contacting Galaxy again," said Space, glancing at his com-watch, which lay silently on his wrist like the useless piece of junk it currently was. "Won't connect to hers."

"I am suspicious, Mr. Space," said Sparky. "Someone down there is intentionally trying to keep Galaxy from leaving. Further, this person is trying to keep Zingfree down there, too."

"But why?" said Space. "Who could possibly be trying to do this? I mean, a meteor is gonna strike in a little less than ten hours and kill them all."

"I have no idea, sir," said Sparky with a shrug of his robotic soldiers. "All I know is that unless we do something fast, Galaxy will die and so will everyone else on that ship."

Space scratched the back of his head. "Is the meteor still on course for Magna Five?"

Sparky glanced at the computer screen and nodded. "Yes. It has not changed course and will likely not between now and then."

"All right," said Space. "Beam me down to Magna Five, near Zingfree's ship. I'll go in and rescue Galaxy myself."

"Sir, that sounds awfully dangerous," said Sparky. "If someone is intentionally blocking transmissions between our ship and theirs, I imagine they will not hesitate to use violence to harm you if they consider you a threat to their plans."

"And?" said Space. "I can't just let Galaxy rot in their ship's hold, dying like a rat, awaiting the final moments when she shall give up the ghost. No; I must go and rescue my friend, even at the risk of my own life. As the great Zinarthian poet Zarsk once said,

'True friends are like a shower of rain after a drought.' And I shall be that shower of rain to Galaxy's drought."

Sparky tilted his head to the side. "I am not sure I understand the metaphor, but if you want to go, then I suppose I won't stop you, because it's better to do something than nothing. Suit up. I'll be at the teleporter room."

"All right," said Space, punching his fist into his free hand. "While I do that, you try to blast the meteor off course. In case … in case everything goes to hell."

Nine hours left …

Galaxy sat at the workbench, screwing and unscrewing a loose screw on the damaged holosphere, though she only did it out of boredom. Every so often, she'd glanced at her com-watch, hoping against hope that Space would somehow connect with her. Every time she did, she did not see any recent messages or attempts at connecting from him.

By this point, Galaxy had nearly given up. She had only a measly nine hours left until the meteor hit. She could just imagine what her corpse would look like when it hit. If her corpse wasn't completely incinerated by the heat of the impact, of course.

I didn't think this is how I would die, Galaxy thought. *Repairing a broken holosphere on a ship that's not even my own. Kind of depressing when you think about it.*

She put down the screwdriver and stood up. Despite having intellectually resigned herself to her fate, emotionally she didn't see any reason to give up just yet. It was her stubbornness yet again compelling her to go even when the odds were against her.

For the hundredth time, she looked around the hold for

anything, anything at all, that could help her get free. There were crates of food and equipment, but none of it could be used to open the door and help her escape. It all seemed useless, utterly useless.

In frustration, Galaxy swept the holosphere off the workbench. The holosphere fell to the ground with a clunk, causing her to look at it. That was when an idea occurred to her. It was a crazy idea, but it might just work.

Feeling the time slip away, Galaxy bent down over the holosphere and began to work on it. Not to fix it, but to use it to help her escape, God willing.

Eight hours left ...

Space materialized on the surface of Magna 5 approximately four hundred yards from the *Artistic Sail*. He had hoped to get down there sooner; however, he was unused to suiting up and so had spent two hours finding his space suit and helmet, as well as deciding what kind of equipment he needed to bring. Not to mention that the teleporter for some reason refused to work until Sparky hit the control console with a wrench and even then it had taken more than a few minutes to power up completely.

And now that Space was actually here, he hoped he could save Galaxy in time. Not only that, but he also planned to tell Zingfree about the meteor. He had not originally planned to, because he didn't think Zingfree's death would be any great loss to the world of film, but Sparky had suggested it and he couldn't shoot down Sparky's suggestion without looking at least a little bit like a sociopath.

Space peered around the large boulder he had materialized

behind. The *Artistic Sail* stood on the sand, looking as innocent as a baby, but if Sparky was correct, there was someone aboard the ship who would not hesitate to use violence to achieve his goals. Space didn't see any cannons or guns on the ship's outside, but he figured they could easily be hiding behind panels and might be activated by motion detection.

I should test that theory, Space thought.

He bent over and picked up a rock. He tested its weight and then hurled it at the *Artistic Sail*. The rock landed about fifty yards away from the ship, but no guns blasted it into pebbles, so Space felt confident that he could just walk up and knock on their front door.

Before he could take even one step from behind the boulder, however, a gigantic cannon—much bigger than anything the *Adventure* had—popped out of the side of the *Artistic Sail*, aimed at the rock, and fired a gigantic blast of plasma. The explosion was large enough to make Space hide behind the boulder again even as the cannon retracted back into the ship. When he peered around the boulder, all he saw was a large hole in the ground where the rock he'd thrown had been previously.

That rock will be missed, Space thought. *This is where I'd say, 'Time for Plan B,' but frankly I have no Plan B, so ...*

A shadow fell over him just then, causing Space to look up in time to see a large robot standing over him. The robot was huge and bulky, with arms that looked capable of smashing through rock as easily as if it were cake. It did not have a face; instead, it had a single red eye that glowed menacingly down at Space.

"Oh, hello," said Space, waving at the robot. "Who are you? Are you part of Zingfree's crew? Because if you are, I'd really appreciate it if you'd let me on board the ship. My friend is currently probably being held against her will there and I have to save her."

The words barely left Space's mouth before the robot brought both of its huge fists down on his head. The explorer leaped forward between the robot's legs as its fists smashed into the boulder, creating a huge crack in it that almost split it in half. Space got to his feet as the robot turned to face him, its body making whirring and beeping noises that sounded almost angry.

"That wasn't very nice," said Space as he drew his laser pistol from his holster. "Whatever you are, I'll take you down and walk over your body to get to Galaxy if I have to."

The robot's hands folded into its arms, replaced by two large barreled cannons that glowed with charged energy.

Space gulped. "You know what? Maybe we can talk about this over a cup of tea instead."

Seven hours left ...

Galaxy wiped the sweat from her brow and stood up. It had taken her the better part of an hour—which alarmed her greatly, as that meant she had even less time to escape than before—but the task was done, and if all went well, in the next ten minutes she'd be back on board the bridge of the *Adventure* and telling Space and Sparky to take the ship as far from this cursed planet as possible.

The damaged holosphere was set up at the foot of the exit. Attached to the damaged holosphere via wire was its undamaged cousin, which Galaxy had managed to program to activate in five minutes. Both holospheres had been stripped of their outer shells to provide for maximum impact when they exploded.

As Galaxy retreated behind the overturned work bench (which would protect her when the makeshift bomb went off), she recalled how she had rigged the holospheres to blow. Normally, holospheres were sturdy little things that were never used for explosives; however, Galaxy's study of the damaged holosphere had revealed to her that certain metals and chemicals within the holosphere could, if combined in the right way, explode. She could not say how big the explosion was going to be, but she figured that however big it was, it would at least be enough to weaken the door enough for her to knock it down herself.

Galaxy had also rigged it so that the undamaged holosphere was connected wirelessly to her com-watch. She just needed to send a message from her com-watch and the bomb would go off. And when it did, she would be able to escape and maybe figure out exactly why Jeff was so determined to kill them all.

After making sure that she was crouched low enough behind the workbench that she wouldn't be killed or harmed by the shrapnel in the inevitable explosion, she tapped the screen of her com-watch and hit the floor. She expected the explosion to be big and loud, but all she heard was a small *pop* like a soda can being opened and when she looked over the overturned workbench she saw that the holospheres had indeed blown up. There was definitely no way to salvage those now.

But that wasn't the most important thing she saw. The most important thing was the simple fact that the door, now blackened at the base, was cracked open. Not enough for her to slip out, but she figured that she could force the door open on her own now. It wouldn't be too difficult, especially with the crowbar she found stashed in the crates.

So Galaxy dashed up to the door, crowbar in hand, and began to pry it open. It was difficult work, not in the least because the door weighed a ton, but every time she got tired and thought about giving up, she would remember that she had less than seven hours left before the meteor hit. That thought alone propelled her to finish, to pry open the door so she could escape.

And after what felt like forever, she successfully opened the door wide enough for her to slip through. She emerged onto the hallway of the *Artistic Sail* and looked around. She seemed to be alone, which meant that the crew of the ship hadn't heard her escape. That meant she could potentially escape without any of them ever being the wiser.

She slipped her helmet back on her head, but didn't run away immediately. Her every instinct was telling her to get the hell out of there as fast as she could, but she remembered that none of Zingfree's crew knew about the incoming meteor save for Jeff, who clearly wanted them dead for reasons unknown to her.

Why should I try to warn them? Galaxy thought. *Zingfree won't believe me. He trusts Jeff far more than he does me. If he's too stupid to listen, then there's not much you can do, Galaxy. Besides, maybe his ship's computers will pick up the meteor before it hits and he'll be able to escape in time.*

That thought seemed so impossible as to be laughable. Still, Galaxy had a strong conscience and she realized it would be biting her for the rest of her days if she ran away now without at least trying to tell Zingfree.

Sighing, Galaxy removed her helmet once more and began making her way down the hall, remembering the path she had taken here from the bridge. She moved quickly, knowing as she did that she had only six and a half hours left, if even that much.

Six and a half hours left ...

Space knew that he shouldn't be running away from the *Artistic Sail*. Galaxy was still on board the ship and the meteor was getting closer and closer to the planet with each passing second. He could waste no time in rescuing his best friend.

Unfortunately, Space had little choice in the matter. The robot was still chasing him, firing off blasts of plasma from its cannon hands, which Space narrowly managed to avoid. He wasn't sure how the robot was keeping up with him, considering Magna 5's heavier gravity, but he had little time to think about it because thinking slowed him down and right now he could not afford to slow down.

By now, Space had been chased to the entrance of a valley that he recognized as the same valley that Galaxy had been collecting rocks in. He almost stopped, not wanting to go in there, but when one of the robot's plasma bursts almost fried off the backside of his spacesuit, Space kept going.

He ran down the incline, ran so fast that he almost tripped. He staggered down the last few feet of the incline, sweating hard as he heard the robot's stomping after him above. Space stopped briefly and looked for a place to hide, immediately noticing a small grotto in the side of the valley that looked perfect for cover.

Space dashed into the grotto just as the plasma robot appeared at the top of the ridge above. Space hid in as far back as he could, while at the same time dragging a large rock to cover the entrance so the plasma robot wouldn't see him. Then he crouched low, getting on his hands and knees and trying not to make a lot of sound. He felt foolish, like a small child playing hide and seek, but if it would help him survive, he didn't care.

Holding his breath (even though he doubted that the plasma robot could hear him breathing), Space listened to the plasma robot's heavy footsteps against the sandy floor of the canyon. At first they were frantic, like the plasma robot was running around trying to find him, but then they slowed down to a walk and eventually stopped entirely. Space didn't dare get up and look over the rock he had dragged in front of the entrance. No way was he going to give that robot a chance to see him.

Then a red light shone. It entered the cave in which Space hid, just barely avoiding his helmet. The suddenness of the red light almost made him cry out, but he kept his mouth shut, knowing as he did that the red light was probably the plasma robot's way of scanning the area for him. Hence why he stayed low to the ground, where he was safe.

Then he heard the footsteps of the robot, walking away slowly into the distance until they were not audible at all. Carefully, Space crawled to the entrance and peeked out through a gap between the boulder and the cavern entrance. It was such a small gap, but it confirmed to him that the plasma robot had indeed left because he saw its footprints in the sand, while the robot itself was nowhere to be seen.

Space waited a few extra minutes—even though every instinct in his body was telling him to get up and leave now—before standing up to his full height and pushing the boulder aside. He slipped through the gap between the cave and entrance and looked around cautiously, but saw no sign of the plasma robot at all. It appeared to have left.

At least, that was what Space assumed, until he looked at the sand and noticed that, rather than walking *out* of the canyon, the robot's footprints went to the right wall. Space followed their trajectory until he saw that the footprints ended at the base of the cliff, causing him to look up just in time to see a ball of plasma flying toward him.

With a yelp, Space jumped backwards, just barely avoiding the plasma ball that crashed into the ground where he had been standing. Little droplets of plasma splashed onto his spacesuit, but thankfully they were not enough to melt it or create any big holes. He looked up in time to see the plasma robot, one of its plasma cannons replaced with a mountain climbing hook, hanging from the wall, glaring at him with its one eye.

Then the robot jumped down from its perch, forcing Space to scramble backwards once again to avoid being squashed. The robot's hook hand retracted into its arm and the plasma cannon popped out not a moment later, whirring and squealing as it charged with repressed energy.

Damn it, Space thought, walking backwards as the plasma robot advanced on him. *This isn't good, not good at all. But I can't run forever. If I don't beat this robot, then Galaxy will die and it will all be my fault.*

The biggest question, of course, was how to stop the robot. It was far larger than he, not to mention better armed and armored. Space's laser pistol seemed inadequate to pierce the plasma robot's armor. Even if he aimed for the head, which was the only unprotected part of the robot, it wouldn't do much except maybe annoy it and right now Space could not afford to annoy it even more than it already was.

The robot's plasma cannons were charging with plasma. Clearly, the robot was hoping to incinerate Space with two well-charged blasts of plasma. It wasn't difficult for Space to imagine himself as little more than an ugly little piece of molten flesh and bones on the sand of the canyon floor, which was a very disturbing mental picture, to say the least.

That was when an idea occurred to Space.

He stopped, causing the plasma robot to stop about two dozen or so feet away from him. He drew his laser pistol and aimed it at the plasma robot, which did not seem to understand what he was planning to do.

"All right, robot, you got me," said Space, using the most masculine, Wild West-style voice he could muster. "Ah see you have cornered me. Ah truly have no way of getting out of here alive."

The robot tilted its head, as if confused. Yet its aim never wavered, which was exactly what Space wanted.

Space continued speaking. "Since we are both men of honor here, why don't we determine who lives and who dies by having ourselves an old-fashioned duel? The winner shall be named the champion of this old dust bowl of ours."

The plasma robot just shook its head and raised its plasma guns, aiming at Space with even greater accuracy than before.

Space shrugged. "If that's your answer, then I'll just have to take it."

With expert aim, Space shot two laser bolts at the plasma robot. Not at its body; no, he aimed for the plasma cannons that contained repressed plasma energy. Space wasn't much of a scientist, but even he understood what happened when laser energy met plasma.

The two laser bolts hit the plasma cannons at roughly the same time. At least, Space thought they did. He didn't get a chance to see because the plasma cannons exploded into a ball of fire and heat, causing the robot to let out all kinds of surprised-sounding beeps and clicks. Space watched as the plasma robot fell over backwards, half of its face blown off by the explosion and a good chunk of its chest, too.

Space spun his laser pistol in his hand, just like in the old Western movies he used to watch as a kid, but he didn't do it quite right and he accidentally dropped it. He picked it up just as quickly, however, feeling glad that Galaxy and Sparky weren't nearby to see that as he holstered his laser pistol.

Then he remembered that Galaxy was still in Zingfree's ship and that the meteor was going to hit very soon.

He turned to leave the valley, ignoring the smoking remains of the plasma robot, but he stopped and remembered the plasma cannon from the *Artistic Sail*. He still didn't have a way of getting past it. If he tried, he might get killed and if he got killed, then he couldn't save Galaxy (also, that would really suck).

Is this the end? Space thought. *Is Galaxy destined to die out here, on this lonely planet in this dark universe?*

He looked over his shoulder at the robot. It's body was little more than a smoking wreck now, but Space got an idea when he saw it. A strange idea, but one that might just work if the *Artistic Sail*'s laser cannon worked like he thought it did.

Space would have to work quickly, though, because he could practically feel the time ticking as he walked over to the fallen machine, pulling out his laser pistol as he did so.

Six hours left ...

The utter silence of the *Artistic Sail*—aside from the hum of the generator echoing somewhere in the distance—made Galaxy pause. While she was not as knowledgeable about the layout of the *Artistic Sail* as she was of the *Adventure*, she had a good memory for these sort of things and figured she was about halfway up to the bridge, where Zingfree, Jeff, and the rest of the crew most likely were.

That was why she paused. She had fully expected to run into one of the crew mates of the ship at some point, but so far she had not run into any of them. Even the robot Metalhead appeared to be missing. She assumed they were all on the bridge, but that was just what it was: an assumption. And she knew that assumptions were always dangerous, especially in situations like these.

She shook her head and kept walking. So what if most of the crew was on the bridge? Galaxy didn't see any reason to worry about that. She, Space, and Sparky often spent most of their time on the bridge of their ship, after all. She imagined that the crew of the *Artistic Sail* did not have much to do at the moment anyway, what with the holospheres being damaged and all.

It was the silence that bothered her above all else. She heard nothing in the ship aside from the normal sounds one expects to find on these starships. The walls, ceiling, and floor were made out of a thick kind of metal, true, but she thought that the closer she got to the bridge, the more sounds she would hear from the ship's crew.

Whatever is going on here doesn't matter, Galaxy thought. *All*

EPISODE ONE: LIGHTS, CAMERA, IMPACT!

I need to do is tell Zingfree about the meteor. Then I can leave.

A few minutes later, she climbed the final set of stairs that connected the second deck to the top and found the door to the bridge was closed. It wasn't locked, however, because when she approached it the door slid open as smoothly and silently as the wind. That made her more than a bit cautious, even though there was nothing unusual about such doors and in fact it would have been stranger if the door had not opened for her.

So Galaxy entered the bridge. As soon as she did, she noticed Zingfree, Rinz, and Ezra sitting in the center of the room, tied together, their mouths gagged with rope. They all looked like they'd been beaten, especially Zingfree, whose black eyes and lolling head made him look barely conscious.

"What the ..." said Galaxy before hearing the *click* of a gun's hammer behind her head.

She slowly turned around to see Jeff standing there. He was holding a gun in his hand; not a laser pistol, surprisingly, but an old-fashioned gun that used bullets, the kind used on Earth until the end of the twenty-first century. She would have wondered about the strangeness of such an ancient artifact being here, of all places, if she had not also been terrified for her life.

"Jeff?" said Galaxy, taking a step back as Jeff entered and closed the door behind himself. "What are you doing? Where'd you get that gun?"

Jeff didn't move his gun as he pressed in a code in the control panel next to the door. "Present from my great-grandfather, before he died. It's a M1911 and it still works. Could blow half your skull off and take as many of your brains."

Galaxy gulped. "That is something."

Jeff nodded, turning his attention from the control panel to her. "I always keep this gun on hand, mostly to remember my great-grandfather. He was a good man, much better than most men nowadays. In fact, this gun belonged to his great-grandfather, and probably to his great-grandfather as well. It's been in my family for generations."

"How interesting," said Galaxy, her eyes focused on the gun's barrel. "But I don't quite see how that is relevant to the fact that we're all going to die in less than six hours if we don't get this ship off the ground soon."

Jeff smiled; it was a crazy smile, the kind that Galaxy associated with serial killers. "Oh, Captain Galaxy, we're all going to die much sooner than that. At least, you will. Me, I plan to live for many, many more years after this."

Galaxy tried not to show her fear, but she felt her fingers tremble just the same. "So you're going to kill me and your crew? Why?"

For a moment, Jeff looked like he was going to explain exactly why he was going to kill her. Then he said, "You know what? I don't have time for this. I certainly am not planning to stick around long enough to get blown into itty bitty little pieces by that damn meteor. I'm getting off this god-forsaken planet before we're all killed. But first—"

He didn't get a chance to finish his sentence because Galaxy saw an opening. She lashed out with her hand, karate-chopping the wrist he held his gun in. She fully expected him to drop the gun; however, when her hand collided with his wrist, a loud *clang* echoed, like she had hit a hollow pipe. Shocked, Galaxy took another step back, while Jeff just grinned even more widely.

EPISODE ONE: LIGHTS, CAMERA, IMPACT!

"Thought that would work?" said Jeff. "I guess no one told you about the time I lost my right arm and had to have it replaced with this beauty."

Jeff pulled back the sleeve of his right arm, revealing a shiny mechanical arm that was almost identical in shape and form to his organic left arm, except metal. "But don't worry. I'm not angry at you."

Galaxy blinked. "You're … not?"

"Oh, no," said Jeff, shaking his head as he pulled his sleeve back down. "No, no, no. Of course not. Why would I? Most people think I'm completely whole. An honest mistake."

Jeff's tone, combined with his Southern accent (which Galaxy still found cute, even under these circumstances), was so gentle and understanding that Galaxy forgot for a moment that he was aiming a gun at her. And when he pulled the trigger and the bullet slammed into her right shoulder, knocking her off her feet, causing her to yell out and drop her helmet, she remembered it immediately.

The starship mechanic walked over to Galaxy, who was still stunned by the bullet, and stomped on her shoulder. This cause her to cry out, but he shut up her quickly with a solid kick to the mouth, his heavy boot smashing into her teeth and making her taste blood in her mouth.

"An honest mistake will still get you killed, though," said Jeff, his words barely understandable through the haze of pain that overwhelmed Galaxy's mind.

His boot dug in deeper into her wound, causing Galaxy to gasp, "You … monster …"

Jeff sighed, cocked his gun, and pointed it at her face. "What an unimaginative little woman you are, Captain Galaxy. And here I thought you were one of the best starship mechanics in the entire Universal Alliance. I guess knowing how to build starships doesn't mean knowing how to come up with creative insults, does it?"

Through her watery eyes, Galaxy saw that Jeff had his index finger on the trigger of his old gun. She instinctively reached for her own laser pistol before remembering that it had been confiscated earlier. Jeff must have noticed the gesture because he immediately brought his boot down on her right hand, crushing it and causing her to cry out involuntarily this time.

"I'm getting bored," said Jeff, his tone matching the words. "I've got places to be and a boss to answer to. I'll just blow your brains out and leave you here to rot."

Even in her pain, Galaxy wasn't going to have any of that. As Jeff took aim with his gun, she grabbed his left ankle with her right hand and pulled. This caused him to fall, his boot leaving her wound, making it bleed freely once more, but Galaxy didn't think about that. She just rolled to her feet even as Jeff recovered from the fall and scrambled back to his own.

Panting, Jeff aimed his gun at her again, looking far more murderous now. "Nice try, woman. But you can't beat me. You're unarmed and badly wounded. If I were you, I'd give up now, 'cause if you do, I'll make your death a little less painful."

Galaxy gripped her wounded, still-bleeding shoulder, her eyes darting all over the bridge, looking for anything she could use as a weapon as she said, "I've … been wounded far worse than this before."

Jeff sneered. "I'm sure you have. Now die."

48

EPISODE ONE: LIGHTS, CAMERA, IMPACT!

He shot his gun again, causing Galaxy to dive to the side to avoid being hit by the bullet again. She crashed over the side of the small wall, landing flat on her back, accidentally favoring her right shoulder. The pain exploded, but she didn't give herself time to feel it or even scream because she heard Jeff making his way over to her and she really didn't have any time to do anything except get up and run.

But she couldn't even do that she was in such pain, so she rolled across the floor as Jeff appeared over the top of the small wall, gun in hand. He took aim and fired at her just as Galaxy rolled underneath one of the computer terminals that controlled the ship. The crackle of glass and electricity made Galaxy wince, but thankfully the terminal protected her from Jeff's bullets. She stopped underneath the terminal, breathing heavily as she heard Jeff make his way over to her.

"Hiding?" said Jeff. "Like a little girl? For shame. Here I thought you were a full-grown woman. And yet here you are, playing the same games that my own little girls like to play. I suppose terror really does turn adults into whimpering babies, doesn't it?"

Galaxy's heart beat so fast that she was pretty sure it was going to explode. Her shoulder was still bleeding and she didn't know what to do. She just lay there, listening as Jeff got ever closer, his footsteps becoming louder and louder the closer he got.

Five hours and fifty-five minutes left ...

Space lugged the head of the plasma robot behind him. He wished he was stronger or that Magna 5's gravity wasn't so heavy or that the robot's head didn't weigh a thousand pounds, but he couldn't just leave it behind, even though it was quite ugly in appearance.

He did manage to pull it up the canyon incline without too much trouble, but it was still heavy. He dragged it across the sand directly to the *Artistic Sail*, which stood alone there on the windswept plain like a large red balloon. He saw no plasma cannons yet, but if this all went as planned, then he wouldn't see any plasma cannons ever.

His plan was simple. The plasma robot, he assumed, had to come from the *Artistic Sail*. He did not know that for sure—didn't even know if Zingfree actually had a robot or not—but he didn't know where else it had come from. And besides, why would it attack him if it wasn't defending the starship, for whatever reason?

He suspected that the *Artistic Sail*'s plasma cannon was designed to blow up anyone who wasn't a member of the ship's crew. Assuming the robot was in fact a member of the crew, Space figured that by dragging it along beside him, the plasma cannon wouldn't try to blow him up for fear of harming the robot's head.

There were holes in the plan, though, as there were in every plan he made (as Galaxy always liked to remind him, much to his annoyance). For one, he didn't know if the plasma cannon's sensors would recognize the robot's head as being a member of the crew. Even if it did, perhaps the plasma cannon held a grudge against the robot or didn't care for it and so would blow Space up anyway.

It's risky, Space thought. *But I don't have any other choices right now.*

EPISODE ONE: LIGHTS, CAMERA, IMPACT!

He glanced at his com-watch as he dragged the robot head. Sparky had not updated him on the meteor's status. He doubted the meteor was close enough to get into the range of the *Adventure*'s lasers; however, he could always be wrong, and the last time he had been wrong he had had to pay half a month's pay to the authorities of Zaron and apologize to several very angry chefs.

Space reached what he estimated to be the boundaries of the plasma cannon. He looked up at the *Artistic Sail*, which looked deceptively peaceful, and hesitated. The crater that the plasma cannon had made from before was still there; not smoking as much as earlier, true, but it was still a vivid reminder of the power that the plasma cannon possessed.

Why the heck does *a holofilm director need a military-grade plasma cannon equipped to his ship anyway?* Space thought. *Oh, never mind. It's now or never, Space, and if you decide never, you can say good bye to Galaxy for good.*

Steeling himself, wondering exactly what Sparky would put in his coffin when he was going to be blown to smithereens, Space took one step forward, making sure to bring the robot's head with him. He had his eyes closed, expecting to hear the plasma cannon rise out of the ship and blow him to the great starship in the sky (or in another dimension or wherever heaven was supposed to be).

A few seconds passed, but Space still didn't open his eyes, knowing as he did the delay in the plasma cannon's reaction. A few more seconds passed and he allowed himself to open his eyes, just a teensy bit, to see if he was going to die.

Much to his relief, the plasma cannon was nowhere to be seen.

The *Artistic Sail* looked much the same as it always had. This gave Space the courage he needed to march across the sand as fast as he could, remembering to keep the robot head by his side as close as he could all the while.

I hope you're still alive in there, Galaxy, Space thought. *Because if you aren't ...*

Five hours and forty-five minutes left ...

Galaxy looked around the underside of the computer terminal she was lying under, her panic growing with every step of Jeff's boots against the floor. This made it hard to think rationally, to look for a way out, and because of that she felt like she was going to die, no matter what happened. Even if she somehow managed to escape Jeff, her shoulder was still open, which meant she might lose too much blood, especially if she could not get medical attention in time.

So she let instinct take over. If she was going to die, she might as well die like an animal.

She rolled out from under the computer terminal and hopped to her feet, her instincts ignoring the pain in her right shoulder. Jeff was only a few feet away from her and when he saw her come up, he once again smiled, like a child being given a new toy.

"Good," said Jeff. "Die."

He aimed and fired at her again, but Galaxy somehow managed to dodge it. With her left hand, she delivered a punch directly to Jeff's chin, putting all of her strength behind the blow. Jeff staggered backwards, dropping his gun as he did so, allowing Galaxy to move in and lash out with a kick at his groin.

EPISODE ONE: LIGHTS, CAMERA, IMPACT!

The would-be killer jumped to the side, allowing her foot to go past him. While Galaxy still held her leg up, Jeff grabbed her foot and pulled forward, causing her to fall flat on her back. This made her shoulder burn with pain yet again, temporarily shocking her.

This gave Jeff all the time he needed to retrieve his gun and get down on top of her. Straddling her, using his legs to pin her arms to the ground, he grabbed her head with his other hand and stuck the barrel of his gun straight into her mouth. It tasted like old metal and gunpowder, a terrible combination that would have made her cough if she didn't have the gun in her mouth.

"I'm done with you, bitch," said Jeff, breathing down on her hard. "You've got spirit, I'll give you that. But I don't have time to waste playing with you."

Galaxy's eyes widened as Jeff shoved the gun deeper down her throat. She couldn't breathe, she couldn't move, and her shoulder was still burning and bleeding. Jeff's eyes were merciless, as cold as the ice caps of Garth, and there was nothing she could do to stop him, nothing at all, her life was over, her life was—

A sudden explosion rocked the room, causing Jeff to look toward the exit in astonishment. He must have seen something dangerous because he pulled his gun out of Galaxy's mouth and fired off a couple of shots at whoever had entered. She heard the bullets ricochet off the floor and walls, but didn't know who it could be until a familiar voice called out, "Hey! What was *that* for?"

Space? Galaxy thought. Then she said aloud, "Space! It's me! I'm over here! I'm—"

Jeff punched her in the mouth, causing her to see lights. She fully expected to find a bullet in her head, now that she was defenseless, but to her surprise, Jeff stood up, turned, and ran. Lasers flew after him, most likely from Space's laser pistol, but none of them hit Jeff, and soon he was gone, disappearing into another exit on the other side of the room.

At least, Galaxy assumed Jeff was gone because Space ran up to her and knelt over her. He had removed his helmet, his black hair messy, sweat on his face as he looked her over.

"Galaxy," said Space, his voice a mixture of relief and worry, "are you okay?"

Galaxy looked at him with all of the disbelief she could muster. "Am I—? Do I look like I just took a bath?"

"I'm sorry!" said Space, cringing. "I just thought—"

Galaxy never got to hear the rest of his sentence, however, because she could no longer tolerate the pain in her shoulder. Thus, she fell unconscious.

When Galaxy next awoke, she found herself lying on the soft mattress of the bed in the sick bay of the *Adventure*. It took her several minutes to understand that, however, as she was extremely drowsy. Her head felt like an inflatable balloon, but she was no longer in any sort of pain. She almost went back to sleep, though, because the bed was so comfortable and was only prevented from doing so when she heard Space nearby say, "Galaxy? You awake?"

She looked to her right and saw Space sitting on a chair. He was no longer wearing his spacesuit (and neither was she, now that she thought about it). He was in his usual blue and orange jumpsuit, a tablet on his lap, open to some kind of book, but she couldn't tell what he was reading. He looked like he hadn't slept for several days, if the bags under his eyes meant anything.

"Space?" said Galaxy. "I'm not dead, am I?"

Space shook his head. "Nope. But you almost were. Sparky's never removed a bullet before, since you know those really aren't used by anyone anymore except hipsters, and so there was a lot of blood but he managed it and now you're going to be okay. Isn't that awesome?"

Space spoke quickly, like he had been waiting a long time to say all of this. Galaxy just smiled weakly.

"Well, I guess it's better than being dead," said Galaxy. "How long have I been out?"

"Oh, about a week," said Space, glancing at his com-watch's built-in calendar.

Galaxy's eyes bugged out. "A week? You've got to be pulling my leg."

"I'm serious," said Space. "You really took a beating. You were at death's door, so to speak. You actually slipped into a coma for a while there."

Galaxy shook her head in disbelief. "Out for a week … man, I must have missed everything."

"Oh, you didn't miss much," said Space. "We dropped Zingfree and his crew off on Namox, since that's where they wanted to go, but otherwise didn't do a whole lot. Sparky and I have just been worrying over you this whole time, among other things."

Galaxy nodded, but then remembered Jeff. "What about Jeff? And the meteor? And how are Zingfree and the others?"

"I knew you'd ask these questions," said Space with a sigh. "Well, to start, Jeff got away. He escaped using one of the *Artistic Sail*'s escape pods. Sparky would have stopped him, but he escaped at roughly the same time the meteor got within range of the *Adventure*'s lasers, so he got away while Sparky tried to shoot down the meteor."

Galaxy cursed. "Did Sparky at least succeed in destroying the meteor or blowing it off course?"

"Sadly, no," said Space. "It was going too fast and it crashed and destroyed the *Artistic Sail*. It was quite the explosion."

"But you said Zingfree and his crew got off all right?"

"Yes. I tried to pilot the *Artistic Sail* out of there, but it didn't want to start—"

"Probably Jeff," Galaxy growled. "That bastard probably sabotaged it so it wouldn't work."

"—so I dragged Zingfree's crew and you out of there," said Space. "Sparky beamed us up to the ship and just in time, too. Sparky miscalculated how many hours we had because about five minutes after we were all beamed safely aboard our ship, the meteor crashed and the *Artistic Sail* exploded, as I said before."

Galaxy shuddered at the thought of how close death had been. "What about Zingfree?"

"He's fine," said Space, sounding more than a little disgruntled at the mention of the director. "He and his crew are at a hospital on Namox. They didn't get hurt nearly as badly as you, but they did get hurt pretty badly."

"Does Zingfree still want me to rebuild his holospheres?" said Galaxy.

Space shook his head. "Nope. He told me that he would just

buy some new ones. He actually wanted to repay you for trying to save his life."

"Oh?" said Galaxy, eager at the mention of rewards. "And what would that form of payment be?"

"A walk-on role in his next movie," said Space. "He offered me it, too, and I had to accept because even though I don't really like him, I would just love to appear in a movie. I told him I'd tell you about it when you woke up."

Galaxy groaned and looked up at the ceiling. "I would have liked some money, to be honest."

"I don't know," said Space. "Zingfree is a pretty respected director. Who knows, maybe this role will allow me to do some acting on the side. You know, to make a little extra money."

"Right," said Galaxy. "Did Zingfree say anything about Jeff? Explain what that idiot was trying to do?"

Space lowered his tablet onto his lap, looking displeased. "Zingfree said he doesn't know the whole story, but from what Jeff told him, it appears that Jeff is an assassin hired out by someone who didn't like Zingfree's movies and wanted him dead."

Galaxy quirked an eyebrow. "Black Star? Shooting Star? A Purple Snake, maybe?"

"No," said Space, shaking his head. "Independent contractor who is a sort of jack-of-all-trades, which is how he managed to pretend to be a starship engineer. The robot, Metalhead, was reprogrammed by Jeff to help him, which is why it attacked me."

"You were attacked by a robot?" said Galaxy.

"Yeah," said Space. "That's why I couldn't immediately come to your rescue. But I managed to destroy it in the end. Wasn't a big deal."

Though Space said it 'wasn't a big deal,' he clearly wanted Galaxy's approval for his obvious bravery in the face of danger, which she did not feel like giving him right now. "Right. And are you sure that the guy who hired Jeff wanted Zingfree dead just because he didn't like his movies?"

Space shrugged. "That's what Zingfree told me that Jeff told him. Considering how arrogant Zingfree is, I have a feeling that's more conjecture on his part than anything."

Galaxy rubbed her forehead. "Ugh. This was a failure of a mission. I only got one bag of rocks. That's not going to be nearly enough to last us a month."

"Actually," said Space, "while you were recovering, I went and collected a few more bags of Magna Five rocks myself."

Galaxy looked at him in surprise. "You did? But I thought you hated doing that."

"Yeah, well, I needed something to do that would take my mind off … well, you," said Space. "Sparky suggested it, but it made sense. I gathered the rocks from a different part of Magna Five, though, because I, unlike most people, happen to believe that meteors do strike in the same place twice."

Galaxy shook her head in amazement. "Thanks, Space. That was really kind of you. I'll have to look at what you got later so I can determine what we can sell and what we can't."

Space waved off her praise. "Oh, it was nothing. It was actually kind of fun, to be honest. I see why you like to do it."

Galaxy lay back on the bed. "Well, I'm glad to hear it wasn't a total loss, at any rate. Where are we now?"

"On our way to the Annulus," said Space. "Sparky says we

need to get some more medical supplies for your wound. How does that sound to you?"

Galaxy smiled. "Sounds great, Space. Sounds great."

Spacetastic Interviews with:

Zingfree Drifle

T.L. Charles: Hello and welcome, readers, to the Spacetastic Interviews series. In this series, I, T.L. Charles, the author, interview a character from *The Spacetastic Adventures of Mr. Space and Captain Galaxy* series, usually a character who appeared in the last episode. These interviews tend to be short, but entertaining and informative. Anyway, with that out of the way, let's start with our first interviewee, Zingfree Drifle.

Zingfree Drifle: Yes, yes, hello, one and all! I am indeed the famed Zingfree Drifle, director of such poignant holofilms as *A Day on the Annulus* and my biopic, *Zingfree, Come Home*, among many other critically-acclaimed holofilms. My newest film, *A Thing to Touch*, is coming out later this year.

T.L. Charles: Yes, you've certainly made a lot of holofilms. The two you mentioned were also the winners of the Galactic Awards, right?

Zingfree Drifle: Indeed. *A Day on the Annulus* won the 2425 Galactic Awards, while *Zingfree, Come Home* won the 2470 Galactic Awards. And I imagine that my next film, *A Thing to Touch*, will win this year's Galactic Award without question, because this year's slate of nominees are awful. Simply awful. That stupid documentary about Doctor Discovery--what was it called? I cannot even remember what it was called, it is that bad-- is nominated for Best Documentary! Really, the holofilm industry has gone downhill since the Classic Era, if you ask me, although I admit to having a soft spot for some of the Gold Era holofilms, such as Zarsk's *What Comes Up Must Come Down*.

T.L. Charles: Well, we're not here to tak about the holofilm industry today, Mr. Drifle. Today, we're going to talk about this episode.

Zingfree Drifle: Yes, yes, I know. This episode reminds me of my upcoming film, *A Thing to Touch*, which is due for release in theaters all over the Universal Alliance in November, if you didn't know.

T.L. Charles: How does it remind you of your new movie?

Zingfree Drifle: Uh, well, you see ... er ... there is a female character in the holofilm and Captain Galaxy, if I am not mistaken, is female, yes?

T.L. Charles: If she wasn't, that would be really awkward.

Zingfree Drifle: Well, I have never been good at determining human genders anyway. But as I said, there is a female character in the holofilm.

T.L. Charles: Is she anything like Captain Galaxy?

Zingfree Drifle: Oh, no. Of course not. She's far more timid and less assertive, for one.

T.L. Charles: So the only similarity between the two is their gender?

Zingfree Drifle: (looks around like he is trying to avoid answering the question) Well, yes, I guess you could say that.

T.L. Charles: Mr. Drifle, are you just trying to plug your new holofilm in this interview?

Zingfree Drifle: Of course not! I am offended. I am an *artiste* first and foremost. I would never engage in 'plugging' my own holofilms where they are not needed or relevant. That makes me just like the protagonist of *A Thing to Touch*, an individual who rages against the rampant commercialism that infects our society like a bloated pore slug.

T.L. Charles: Uh huh. Well, what did you think about Jeff betraying you? Did you see that coming or did it come out of nowhere?

Zingfree Drifle: Jeff's betrayal took me by surprise, I will admit. I always trusted him because of his 'Southern' accent, as you humans call it, which is very similar to the accent that the protagonist of *A Thing to Touch* has, in fact. Would you like for me to play a clip from the holofilm for your readers?

T.L. Charles: Uh, no, Mr. Drifle, that's fine. My readers aren't too interested in your holofilms.

Zingfree Drifle: Are you certain? I mean, I know these stories you write tend to be little better than wood pulp, but I thought at least some of your readers might have more refined tastes.

SPACETASTIC INTERVIEWS

T.L. Charles: Uh, well, would you look at that! Looks like we don't have much time left, so we're going to end the interview here. Any last thoughts before we close out, Mr. Drifle?

Zingfree Drifle: None, except that I appreciate this chance to talk a little bit about my experiences in this interview. It reminds me of the scene in *A Thing to Touch* when the protagonist walks in on his mother and best friend sleeping in the same—

T.L. Charles: (hurriedly) That's all for now, folks! Turn the page to start reading *Episode Two: Rocky*! See you at the next Spacetastic Interview!

Episode Two
Rocky

*I*n retrospect, Jason Space—or, as he preferred to be called, Mr. Space—probably shouldn't have picked up that shiny rock.

He had no particular reason for wanting it in the first place. He and his friend, Captain Helena Galaxy, were merely visiting an uncharted planet in the Unexplored Regions because Galaxy was interested in studying a variety of fungus feet, an extremely rare plant in its own right, that was said to grow there. Space was not much interested in that kind of thing, but he did have an eye for drama and, in his opinion, the shiny rock—which he christened "Rocky"—looked dramatic.

After all, it was fiery red, curved like a knife, and gave off an aura that made Space feel even more dramatic than usual (either that or it was gas, although he liked to think it was the former). It was unlike any other rock Space had seen in his time, which wasn't saying much, as Space was only 28. Still, he'd been all over the universe in the last five years and couldn't say that this rock was exactly like all of the other rocks that he had seen.

When he showed it to Galaxy, she dismissed it as nothing

more than a shiny, unimportant space rock. That offended Rocky; not Space, but Rocky. He couldn't explain how he knew that Rocky was offended by Galaxy's dismissive attitude towards it, so he merely thought that he was projecting his own feelings onto it, as he was wont to do sometimes with his physical possessions.

When Galaxy and Space returned to their starship, the *Adventure*, Space showed Rocky to Sparky, their resident robot assistant. Unlike Galaxy, Sparky did show interest in the rock, although Space didn't know if that was because Sparky was actually interested in it or if he simply did it to avoid harming Space's feelings. All Space knew was that Rocky saw through Sparky's insincerity and had since told Space not to speak to Sparky about Rocky ever again.

So Space put Rocky in a glass container in his quarters in the *Adventure*, which he placed on his bedside dresser. This seemed to please Rocky, because in the days afterward, Rocky didn't bother Space in the slightest. In fact, Rocky was so quiet that Space eventually became convinced that Rocky was just that: a rock. A pretty rock, maybe, but a rock just the same.

As the weeks went on, Space put Rocky more or less out of his mind, save for at bedtime, when Space had to return to his room. He'd see Rocky, but even then would not give the shiny stone much thought. He was usually too tired to do much else but take off his clothes (he preferred to sleep naked) and get into bed and fall asleep.

Such was the routine that Space went through until one day near the beginning of January, when he was aiding Sparky in repairing one of the *Adventure*'s computers. According to Sparky, the computer refused to turn on. This was a big deal because this particular computer monitored and controlled the ship's air levels. If it was broken, they would have no way of telling how much air the ship had or when it would run out. That wouldn't be so bad for Sparky, perhaps, but for Space and Galaxy—who were air-breathing organic beings—that would be quite unfortunate.

Because Space could not reach under there, he merely stood by and handed Sparky whatever tools the robot asked for as he worked on the computer from the inside. Sparky had removed a panel under the computer to allow him to stick his head into its innards, a task he had little trouble doing thanks to his shortness and small head.

"What's the problem look like?" Space asked Sparky.

"Some fried circuitry," said Sparky, his voice slightly muffled by the computer. "The damage is rather extensive, but I believe we have the necessary tools and material to fix it. It shouldn't take long now."

Space looked around. "Why isn't Galaxy helping you? Doesn't she love doing this stuff?"

"Captain Galaxy is trying to repair a leak in the ship's engines," said Sparky. "That is why she's not here."

Space folded his arms as he leaned against the wall. "Two ship problems in one day? When did this ship become so bad?"

"The *Adventure* is an expertly-designed starship, Mr. Space," said Sparky. "It is probably one of the best in its class, thanks in no small part to Captain Galaxy's expert knowledge of starship building. But even the best ship faces problems every now and then, sometimes multiple at once."

"I don't like this," said Space. He looked up at the florescent lights running across the ceiling, and sighed. "I want to be out adventuring, fighting evildoers, and discovering new worlds. Not helping a robot repair a starship."

"Mr. Space, you cannot fight evildoers and discover new worlds without a working starship," said Sparky, without pulling his head out from under the computer console. "So, unless you wish to be a lifeless hunk of meat within the next couple of hours, I suggest you hand me the pliers."

Grumbling, Space bent over and reached into the toolbox. He dug through wrenches, laser wrenches, electric wrenches, various screwdrivers (including one that he remembered could emit sonic blasts), and various other tools, but did not find the pliers. "Um, they're not here."

"What?" said Sparky, though his robotic voice did not make him sound very surprised. "Where are they, then?"

"I don't know," said Space as he dug through the tools. "No pliers anywhere. They seem to have mysteriously vanished."

Sparky made a strange robotic sound that might have been a sigh. "Then go to the storage room. There's bound to be an extra pair in there. We have extras of every tool in that toolbox; I should know, since I do the inventory on our supplies once a week."

"Okay," said Space. "I'll be back soon. In fact, I'll be back sooner than you can say, 'Mr. Space is awesome!'"

Without waiting for Sparky to say that, Space dashed out of the control room and down the ship's main hallway. As he did so, he caught a flash of red out of the corner of his eye, but when he looked in that direction, he saw nothing except a wall. That was strange. The flash of red had been exactly the same hue as that of Rocky, but Space dismissed it as nothing more than one of the flashing lights on the walls (even though there were no flashing lights on that particular wall, much less flashing red lights).

It took Space only a few minutes to reach the storage room and find a pair of old-looking pliers. With the pliers in hand (not in his pockets; his pockets weren't deep enough to hold the pliers), Space ran back to Sparky, who he found sitting up and looking around the area with that same blank expression the robot usually wore.

"Here are the pliers, Sparky," said Space, handing them to the robot. "Say, what's the matter? You look like … actually, I can't read your expression, but you seem a bit puzzled."

"That is one way to put it," said Sparky as he took the pliers. His metallic lips frowned. "My sensors picked up an unknown surge of energy nearby, but it was only for a very brief second. I can only assume that my sensors must be a bit bugged. I will have to run a diagnostic on myself once I am done fixing the computer."

"Eh, I'm sure it was nothing," said Space, leaning against the wall again. "I, too, feel surges of energy from time to time, but that usually means I just had too much sugar. Which Galaxy continually reminds me is bad for my health, but I've made it this far on sugar and I don't seem that bad, do I?"

Sparky didn't respond. He just gave the hallway a curious look before sticking his head underneath the open computer console again.

The rest of the repairs went smoothly, and in another hour Sparky announced that he had finished his work. At the same time, Captain Galaxy—with her long black hair tied back by a bandana—entered the control room, where Space and Sparky had been working, carrying a large toolbox. Her uniform was stained with red oil and she had a puzzled expression on her face.

"Did the repairs on the engine go well, Galaxy?" said Space, sitting down in his control chair.

Galaxy nodded, although she didn't appear to be listening. "Yes, yes, but I wonder …"

"What do you wonder?" said Space. "Do you wonder if your clothes need a wash? Because I think they do."

Galaxy rolled her eyes. "That's not what I'm wondering, Space, but thanks for your insightful opinion."

"No problem," said Space, leaning back in his chair. "Insightfulness is but one of my many talents and gifts."

"Do you know what caused the leak, Captain Galaxy?" Sparky asked.

"It wasn't just an energy leak," said Galaxy, shaking her head as she took a seat opposite Space. "One whole engine was completely inoperational. It looked like someone had ripped the wiring with a sword or maybe even with their bare hands."

"Galaxy, are you suggesting that someone sabotaged the ship?" said Space, leaning forward anxiously.

"That's what it looked like to me," said Galaxy. "That doesn't make any sense, though, because there's no one else on this ship but us three. And none of us would want to sabotage this ship."

Something in Space's mind nudged him and he said abruptly, "Don't forget Rocky. He's a person just like you and me and Sparky."

"Technically, I am a robot, not a person," said Sparky.

Galaxy shook her head. "Rocky is a rock, Space. I don't understand why that's so hard for you to wrap your head around."

"She may be a rock—"

"She?"

Space blinked and stared at Galaxy, unsure why she had said that. "Yes, I said she. Why?"

Galaxy tossed a puzzled glanced at Sparky, who merely shrugged. "Why did you call Rocky a 'she'? Where did that idea come from?"

Space scratched the back of his head. "Um … I don't know. It just popped into my head while we were talking and I rolled with it. It must be my creative mind anthropomorphizing Rocky."

"But Rocky is a male name," Galaxy pointed out. "And you were just calling Rocky 'he' a few seconds ago."

"Maybe I changed my mind," said Space defensively. "And besides, we're beyond sexism now. Why can't a female rock call herself Rocky? Are you sexist?"

Galaxy slapped her forehead. "Look, how's about we figure out what caused the computer and engine to fail? It's clear to me that there's more to this situation than meets the eye."

"I shall check the security cameras," said Sparky. "If there is a stowaway aboard our ship, he or she must have been caught on camera sabotaging our equipment. Though I don''t know how or when this stowaway could have gotten on board without any of us knowing."

"Checking the cameras is a good idea," said Galaxy. "Space, why don't you and I search the rest of the ship while Sparky does that? See if we can find any clues."

"Okay," said Space, nodding. "But can I bring Rocky with me? If there's a stowaway aboard, then Rocky may be in trouble."

Galaxy sighed. "Okay. You can get Rocky. Just be quick

about it."

The *Adventure* was by no means a battleship, but its large size forced Space and Galaxy to split up to more effectively search it. That may have seemed like a dumb idea (especially if there was a dangerous stowaway aboard the vessel) but with Sparky at the security cameras and the two adventurers equipped with their short-range com-watches that they could turn on with a simple flick of a switch, both of them felt safer—especially Space, who had retrieved Rocky from his room and put the pet rock in his back pocket.

Space walked calmly down a hallway in the west side of the ship. His job was to check the food and water storage rooms and, thanks to his corner shot, he didn't even have to enter the rooms to see if anyone was in there.

The corner shot was Space's favorite gun. Thanks to the hinged frame, camera under the barrel, and video screen, he could use the gun to peer around the corner of a hallway or through open doorways and see if anyone was there. What made this particular version great was its x-ray component, which he had had Galaxy add to it shortly after he bought it, which allowed him to see through the boxes of food and the barrels of water they kept in storage.

Yet Space found no sign of any trespassers or stowaways here. The corner shot's x-ray mode didn't reveal any hidden stowaways. He made sure to check the rooms himself, but found no sign of any living being. He did find a Laser Buzz candy bar, but considering that it was inside one of the food containers, that really didn't count as evidence of a stowaway.

After checking the final room and seeing nothing, Space raised his com-watch to his mouth and said, "Sparky, have you found anything unusual on the cameras? Sparky?"

He looked at his com-watch. A red light was flashing on the side, which meant that communications were being blocked or the connection had failed. That puzzled Space greatly; after all, the only time that ever happened was when they strayed too far from the ship. Considering that Space was still inside the *Adventure*, he found it odd that the communication links apparently didn't work.

He tried communicating with Galaxy next, thinking perhaps that he would be able to reach her device, at least. But as with Sparky, only a red light flashed on his device, forcing him to turn it off in frustration.

"Not a problem," Space murmured, in an attempt to keep calm. "I'll just go to the security room, where all of the cameras are hooked up, and meet Sparky there."

The door to the security room slid open automatically as Space said, "Hey, Sparky. Could you look at my com-watch? It's broken."

Sparky—who sat on a chair in front of the monitors connected to the security cameras set up all around the interior of the *Adventure*—didn't look at Space. In fact, the robot gave no indication that he had heard Space at all. His optics were fixed firmly on the dozen or so screens that gave feedback from the ship's security cameras.

"Hello?" said Space, walking up behind Sparky. "I just walked in. Are you ignoring me?"

Again, Sparky didn't respond. He simply peered at one

monitor with a slight frown on his face, muttering, "That is strange. Where is he?"

"Where is who?" said Space as he reached out a hand toward Sparky. "I want to know who you're—"

Space's hand went straight through Sparky's body, causing the adventurer to jump back in shock. Sparky didn't seem to notice, oddly enough.

"What … why did my hand …" Space spluttered, looking at his hand. "That makes no—"

The door slid open again before he could finish and Galaxy entered. "Couldn't find anything, Sparky. Has Space returned yet?"

Sparky turned around in his swivel chair and shook his head. "No, Captain Galaxy, Mr. Space has not yet returned from going to check on the food and water storage rooms."

"Galaxy!" said Space, jumping in front of her. "Thank God you're here! Sparky doesn't acknowledge my existence and when I tried to touch him, my hand—"

Galaxy, with her head tilted to the side, walked forward straight through Space toward Sparky, without missing a beat or even cringing.

"—passed right through," Space finished, looking down at his body in horror.

He shook his head and turned around to see Galaxy looking at the monitors with a concerned expression on her face.

"Where is Space?" said Galaxy, brushing her hair out of her eyes. "I don't see him on any of the monitors."

"That's because I'm right here," said Space, pointing at himself. "Come on, guys. I don't know what's going on here, but it's getting really annoying."

"Yes, I, too, noticed his absence," said Sparky. "He has not appeared on even one of the monitors since you and he split up to search the ship. As a matter of fact, I have not seen him since he went to his room to retrieve Rocky."

Galaxy wrinkled her nose. "You're going along with the name?"

"Why wouldn't I?" said Sparky, looking at her curiously. "All things have a name. It is thus only proper to refer to it by its name."

Galaxy sighed. "Never mind. Have you tried communicating with him?"

"I have," said Sparky, nodding. "But oddly enough, every time I try, my scanner doesn't pick up any other signals in the ship but yours. It is almost as if he has vanished into thin air."

"That's ridiculous," said Galaxy. "His device must be malfunctioning or something. Look, I'll go search for him."

"And I shall help you," said Sparky as he stood up from the chair. "If the cameras don't tell us where he is, then we will need to check out the rooms where we don't have security cams."

"That would be our rooms," said Galaxy. "I'll check Space's and you can check mine."

"Why would he be hiding in your room?" said Sparky. "I mean, I know you two are good friends, but—"

"Just let me look there," Galaxy said, folding her arms. "Also, check Space's head; you know, his bathroom. That's another room we don't have cameras in."

Galaxy and Sparky walked toward the door, while Space just stood there trying to think of a way to grab their attention.

EPISODE TWO: ROCKY

"Think, Space, think!" said Space, pounding his fist against his forehead. "How are you gonna let them know that you were standing right here listening to their entire conversation?"

No matter how hard Space thought about the problem, no ideas came to him as Sparky and Galaxy left, closing the door behind them as they did so.

"No!" said Space, rushing up to the door and banging on it as hard as he could. "Hey, guys, don't leave me alone! I'm right here!"

"They can't hear you," said a feminine voice behind him. "Or see you or smell you or touch you or even taste you, if they wanted."

Space whirled around, drawing his corner shot as he did so, but he dropped the gun almost as soon as he saw who had spoken.

It was a woman, but not just any woman. She was the most beautiful woman Space had ever seen. Her skin was dark chocolate, same as his, and she had wonderful flowing dark hair. She wore a long red dress that showed off her curvy form quite well and her eyes had a stunning, almost mesmerizing look to them. She even smelled good, like chocolate cake, although he had no idea if chocolate cake perfume even existed.

After he remembered to breathe (which explained the pain in his lungs), Space said, "Who ... who are you?"

The woman smiled, an expression that would have melted the polar ice caps. "Why, I'm Rocky, of course."

Space blinked. "Wait ... Rocky?"

"Oh, I see you don't understand," said the woman as she leaned against the security console in a seductive fashion. "I suppose I should clarify. I am that pet rock you picked up from that planet in the Unexplored Regions, the one you named Rocky."

"Uh, that just makes things even more confusing," said Space. "This … this isn't some drug-induced hallucination or anything, is it?"

The woman laughed. "Could a hallucination do this?"

She walked up to Space and kissed him firmly on the lips. Her lips against his sent an explosion of sensation through his whole body, but it lasted only for an instant, because a minute later the woman broke off from the kiss.

"See? Wasn't that nice?" said the woman, one hand on his shoulder. "Or do you require more … persuasive evidence that this is all real?"

"I accept it," said Space, almost too fast. "This is definitely real. The passion in my body right now is extremely real. Almost too real."

The woman smiled. "So you accept that I am Rocky, then?"

Space shook his head. He had zoned out momentarily, still savoring the taste of her lips against his. "No. That kiss didn't convince me of anything except that you're really hot."

"I guess a longer explanation is due, then," said the woman.

"Yes, I agree," said Space. "A much, much longer one, that is."

The woman stepped back several feet and said, "I'm sure you noticed how Galaxy and Sparky didn't notice you, even though you were standing in the same room as them. In fact, Galaxy even walked through you."

"Yeah, that was freaky," said Space. "Am I … am I a ghost?"

The woman laughed. "Of course not. You're still as alive as

any living being. The only difference is the dimension in which you exist."

"Wait ... are you saying I'm in an alternate dimension?" said Space, looking around. "But how come everything looks the same?"

"It's a little bit more complicated than that," said the woman. "It's a pocket dimension, which reflects the main one that it is attached to. As a result, it's similar in many ways to the main dimension—hence why this room we are in resembles your real security room—except that there is no one else inside here but us."

"Us?" said Space. "But if we're the only ones inside here, how did I see Galaxy and Sparky?"

The woman smiled. "Tell me, Space, do you know how you got here?"

Space shook his head. "No. I didn't fall through some sort of rift in the space/time continuum, did I? Because if I did, that's the third time this year."

"Not exactly," said the woman. "To put it simply, you are inside the rock which you call Rocky, which is a name I have taken on. The pocket dimension exists within the rock. You were brought inside the moment you tried to take the rock with you out of your quarters."

Space immediately plunged his hand into his pocket, intending to prove her wrong, but all he felt was some lint he probably should have cleaned out.

"I don't get it," Space said. "How did I get inside a rock? How can a rock even *hold* a pocket dimension?"

"Simply put, I brought you in here," said the woman. "In fact, it was I who influenced your thoughts to pick up my dimensional prison and take me off that wretched planet. I even tricked you into thinking you had picked up the rock and put it in your pocket, when in truth, it is still back in your room. It was only an illusion, and quite a successful one at that. "

"You don't sound like you liked that planet very much."

"I despised it," the woman hissed. She balled her hands into fists. "I was there for … I don't even know how long. All I could do was wander my prison, never allowed to make contact with other living beings, especially because no one ever visited my world. And it was all because of *them*."

"Them?"

"Them. The ancient ones. The Starborn."

Space searched his memory for that term. "The Starborn … that name sounds vaguely familiar."

The woman—who Space decided to simply think of as Rocky, as strange as it was—chuckled. "I'm sure you have. The Starborn went all over the known universe, but that's not important. What's important is that they locked me in this prison, intending to keep me jailed forever like some common criminal, even though I am far more fabulous than any criminal could be."

Space scratched the back of his head. "Not to be rude or anything, but … may I ask why they locked you up?"

Rocky shrugged. "They called me a danger to the universe. Just because I think that all physical beings everywhere should be my slaves and grovel at my feet like the worms they are doesn't mean I'm dangerous. Don't you agree, Jason?"

"Um …" Space took a step back. "Look, er, lady, I don't think this will end very well. I mean, you're a nice-looking woman and all, but this is kind of sudden."

"I thought you loved your pet rock," said Rocky, gesturing at herself. "You defended me when Galaxy criticized me … well, okay, I have been influencing you to protect me, yes, but it's still sweet, isn't it?"

"No," said Space, shaking his head. "I don't know your whole history or anything, but it's clear to me that picking up your prison was a mistake. So if you'll excuse me, I have to—"

Rocky raised her arms and shot out two red ropes. The ropes tied themselves around Space's body, causing him to fall to the ground hard. He struggled to break free, but the ropes tightened the more he fought against it. They were also extremely hot and gave off a smell of barbeque for some reason.

"You're not going anywhere," Rocky said with a purr. "Not that you could escape on your own, of course. You're simply going to stay put until I get out of here."

"What are you going to do with me?" Space demanded, looking up at her. "Am I going to remain your prisoner forever?"

Rocky chuckled. "Not my prisoner, no. You shall be the *rock's* prisoner. Don't you know that there's only one way for a person to escape this prison?"

"And what is that?"

Rocky snapped her fingers and Space floated to his feet. She walked past him, running a finger along his shoulder as she did so.

"A trade-off is necessary for a prisoner to be freed," said Rocky. "For the longest while, I was incapable of escape because no one ever came by my world, which meant I could never trade places with anyone else. But now … you shall take my place in this god-forsaken prison while I regain my freedom once more."

"You can't just leave me here," said Space, trying to look over his shoulder. "I didn't do anything to deserve this!"

"And neither did I," said Rocky as she opened the door. "But then again, the Starborn didn't care about my innocence, so why should I care about *your* innocence?"

She stepped through the door and closed it. As soon as she was gone, Space's bonds fell off and he ran toward the door. He tried to open it, but no matter how hard he tried, the door wouldn't budge. He even tried kicking it, but that accomplished nothing except hurting his toe. He realized that Rocky must have locked the door and he did not know how to unlock it in this pocket dimension.

Panic flowed through Space's heart as he began to understand the situation. He was stuck here, perhaps forever. Not only that, but he had unleashed some kind of strange energy being upon the universe, an energy being that wanted to enslave all physical beings. He didn't know how he could contact Galaxy and Sparky and warn them about Rocky, so he just hoped that they would somehow stop her without him. It was all he could do for now.

Galaxy rarely spent time in Space's quarters. For one, she and Space had agreed to never enter the other's room except in cases of emergency. It was the only way either of them could get privacy on this small ship. Not even Sparky was allowed in except if they gave him permission, although as Sparky had no interest in their personal possessions or privacy, this wasn't much of a problem.

Space's room was about the same size as Galaxy's. That was

about the only similarity it shared with hers, however, because its walls were plastered with posters of various actors and holofilms that Space had seen or was a fan of, such as *Dave Starsteel* and *Is That a Gorilla?*. As holofilms didn't interest Galaxy much, she didn't pay much attention, although she did notice how many of the actors were either shirtless or posed in seductive positions.

His room also smelled like he used a lot of hair spray, which did not surprise Galaxy much because she knew how much Space cared about his appearance. Not being much of an expert on hair spray herself, Galaxy could not identify exactly which products she smelled, although one smelled like coconut and another smelled like red velvet cake.

Another thing that Galaxy noticed was the bed, which was pretty simple and plain, with two pillows and a red blanket. She did not see Space under the blanket, although that did not mean he was not still somewhere in here anyway.

So she looked in his closet, searched under his bed, but could find no trace of Space anywhere. Even when she threatened aloud to take down all his posters, he still didn't appear.

"Where could he be?" Galaxy wondered as she sat down on his bed, one hand on her chin. "He can't have just up and disappeared like that. That's just silly."

A glimmer of red caught her eye, causing Galaxy to look down at the bedside dresser. She got down on her hands and knees and spotted Space's pet rock, Rocky, lying underneath the dresser. It was glowing red for some reason, causing Galaxy to reach underneath the dresser and grab it.

"Huh," Galaxy muttered as she sat up and turned Rocky over in her hands. "Why'd he drop his pet rock under his desk?"

The more she looked at the rock, the stranger it seemed. While Galaxy was no geologist, she could easily tell that it had been carved out of some kind of stone, which meant that that unknown planet where they had found it must have had life on it at some point.

Not only that, but the rock had symbols on it that she recognized as the writing of the Starborn. Of course, not being an expert on the Starborn, Galaxy couldn't read the writing, but she realized just how important an artifact this was. If she found Space, she thought, she'd have to convince him to sell it to the Universal Space Museum back on Earth, because all Starborn objects were practically priceless in the Universal Alliance and could fetch a considerable sum of money if you understood their value. Galaxy was not the kind of person to put a price on these kinds of amazing discoveries, but she and Space really needed the money, which they could not get by simply donating the rock to some museum somewhere, unfortunately.

Just as Galaxy stood back up, reluctantly deciding to check Space's head next (she was reluctant because she could tell that most of the hair spray smell came from his head and fully expected to suffocate in there without any special breathing equipment), the red rock glowed even brighter than before. It caused her to shut her eyes to protect them from its light, although she didn't let go of the rock.

When the light vanished, Galaxy opened her eyes and saw that she was no longer alone in the room.

Standing before her was a woman. Or, rather, a strange creature that vaguely resembled a human woman. She appeared to be made out of some kind of red, sparkling energy, like a hologram, except far more intelligent-looking. It made her look like a walking light show, except she had less variety than your average show.

The being looked down at her body and then looked around the room as a smile crawled across her mouth. "Free ... I'm finally free."

"Who are you and where did you come from?" Galaxy said. "I've never seen you before."

"Just call me Rocky," said the being. "And, thanks to your friend, I am finally free."

"Friend ...?" repeated Galaxy in confusion before realization dawned on her. "Wait, are you talking about Space? Where is he?"

The being called Rocky flashed a devilish smile. "He's in your hand, of course."

Galaxy looked down at the rock in her hand, which was now glowing green. "Space ... is in there?"

"As was I, until I escaped with his reluctant help," said Rocky as she stretched her limbs. "Now if you'll excuse me, I will be commandeering this ship and taking it to the nearest inhabited planet. If you keep quiet, I might just let you live as my slave."

Galaxy looked Rocky in the eyes, folding her arms across her chest in defiance. "Sorry, but you can't have this ship and you definitely can't enslave me. Why don't you just crawl back into that stupid rock, like a good energy being, and let Space out while you're at it?"

Rocky's form bristled, reminding Galaxy of how music looked in the audio visualizer sometimes. "How dare you talk to me like that, you stupid girl. Why don't you just take a nap?"

An energy bolt shot out from Rocky's chest and slammed into Galaxy. The blow hit Galaxy so hard that she fell onto Space's bed and completely lost consciousness as a result.

There were a lot of things Space wanted to do before he died. He wanted to explore the vast universe, yes, but he also had smaller goals, like meeting the famed Rothian actor Jikal Xomac or starring in his own holofilm. He had even played with the idea of finding a partner and settling down, although of course that idea was far-fetched, considering how boring married life was.

Yet all of those ideas were nothing but pipe dreams now, thanks to Rocky. Space sat in the security room, his back against the wall and his drive shot. He had no idea how Galaxy and Sparky were faring against Rocky. They were both smart and good fighters, but Rocky didn't even appear to be mortal. She spoke like a goddess, although that was obviously silly, as gods did not exist. There was a good chance that Rocky might very well kill his friends or at least hurt them badly. And there was nothing he could do about it.

So Space merely sat on the floor, feeling depressed, when he heard a faint voice whisper, "Captain Galaxy ... Galaxy ... wake up, Captain Galaxy ..."

Oh great, he thought, *I must be hearing voices in my head again. Why is it saying Galaxy's name, though? I'm not Galaxy.*

The more the voice spoke, however, the more Space recognized it as Sparky's voice. Again, it puzzled him until he remembered something. Rocky had been able to manipulate his thoughts and actions while inside the rock. That was different from actually communicating with him, of course, but maybe if he tried, he could actually contact Sparky and Galaxy.

The only problem with that theory is that he didn't know how to do it. Rocky hadn't left him a manual on how to operate this prison, after all. For all he knew, it was impossible.

But somehow, I'm hearing Sparky's voice, Space thought, scratching his chin. *Maybe if I concentrate hard enough, I can send a message to one or both of them. I can tell them about my predicament and then help them stop Rocky somehow.*

So he closed his eyes and concentrated. While Space wasn't into meditation, he tried to apply some of the meditation techniques he had learned during his brief sojourn on Tanjo. He crossed his legs and lifted his hands above his head. Whether any of it would help him contact Sparky and Galaxy, he didn't know, but he didn't know how else he could contact them.

Putting all of his focus into contacting Galaxy, Space thought her name over and over again. He kept thinking her name so much that it became like a chant, yet he still kept at it. He just hoped she was there and was listening.

"Captain Galaxy … Galaxy … wake up, Captain Galaxy …"

Galaxy opened her eyes. She regretted that immediately, because as soon as she regained consciousness, her chest burned. It felt like she'd been punched by a lightning bolt, which might not be an entirely false conclusion when she remembered what Rocky had done to her.

Groaning, Galaxy sat up and shook her head. She glanced at her chest and saw that the top layer of her suit was blackened, although thankfully the skin underneath it had been preserved. It still hurt, though, causing her to put a hand over it, even though she knew it didn't help.

"Are you injured, Captain Galaxy?" asked Sparky. He stood before her, looking down on her with his round yellow optics.

Galaxy shook her head. "No, I'm fine. Just a little winded, that's all."

"What happened to you?" said Sparky, his head tilted to the side. "I came here after I searched your room to tell you that I didn't find Mr. Space. But when I got here, I found you like this."

"I was attacked," said Galaxy, wincing at the burned surface of her space suit. "Think she was aiming to kill, but she obviously failed."

"She?" Sparky said. "Were you assaulted by the mysterious stowaway we have been searching for?"

"Actually, she's Rocky," said Galaxy. She ran a hand through her black hair. "I don't understand it well, but it seems like Rocky is actually some kind of energy being trapped inside this rock. She escaped and made some comment about Space being inside there now and now she's in control of the ship."

"That would explain why the *Adventure* has suddenly picked up speed," said Sparky. He looked at the green stone lying on the bed next to her. "But how did Mr. Space get inside that rock? And why is it glowing green?"

"I don't know," said Galaxy, glancing at the stone. "She didn't explain. All I know is that she wants to take the ship to the nearest inhabited planet."

"What does she want to do, then?"

"Based on her attitude, I imagine she's looking for followers or, more likely, slaves. We've gotta stop her."

Sparky looked at the door. "Not to be negative, but how do we do that? We know nothing about her. If she's indeed an energy being as you say, then that will make it even harder, for we don't have any energy disruption rays we could use against her."

Galaxy opened her mouth to say something, but then closed it. She felt something in the back of her head, like a gentle breeze, whispering, *Get the rock ... Get the rock ... for god's sake, Galaxy, pick up the damn rock and get me out of here ...*

"I feel something," said Galaxy, putting her hand on her forehead. "Or, rather, I hear something in my head. It sounds like ... sounds like Space's voice."

"Mr. Space?" said Sparky. "Are you communicating with him?"

"Maybe," said Galaxy with a frown. "It's hard to tell. It just might be my imagination playing tricks on me, but …"

She looked at the rock, which had ceased glowing. She picked it up anyway and, turning to Sparky, said, "I think this rock might be just what we need to stop Rocky. But first, let's come up with a plan."

"All right," said Sparky, nodding. "I am open to whatever ideas you have, Captain."

Having spent so many years inside that tiny, cramped prison, Rocky had a hard time holding in her excitement. Yes, she was still inside a ship, a ship with limited space, but it was a hell of a lot better than that rock. At least here she had the possibility of escaping to another world, of establishing her rule somewhere, a possibility that had been denied to her while in that stupid rock. That was exciting.

After knocking out Galaxy, Rocky's first move was to go to

the ship's command deck. That didn't take long, for she merely transformed herself into energy and traversed through the ship's wiring until she arrived in the command deck. It had taken her only a few minutes to figure out how to activate the ship's engines, and as soon as she did, she sent the ship flying to the nearest world (which, according to the computers, was a planet called Namox that she did not care to learn about).

Because it would take some time before she arrived there, Rocky took a seat in the captain's chair and enjoyed the view of stars and meteors and other galactic objects hurtling past the ship as it flew through the void. She wondered how much the universe had changed since her days and how difficult it would be to take over the world once she got there. Though if Space, Galaxy, and their robot friend were any indication of modern people, then taking over the whole universe would be a walk in the park for her.

"Hey, Rocky!" said a voice behind her.

Rocky's chair swiveled around in a circle, allowing her to see Galaxy standing in the open doorway of the deck. Galaxy looked more or less like how Rocky had left her, with the front of her suit blackened and her hair frizzled from the electricity. Her appearance almost made Rocky chuckle, although really she just felt disdain for the inferior life form that stood before her now.

"Oh, hello, little pebble," said Rocky, putting the tips of her fingers together. "I thought that my earlier display of power would have been enough to scare you off for good."

"Sorry, but I'm not a coward," said Galaxy, folding her arms. "Besides, this is *my* ship that *you* stole. I built it myself. You're not a very smart superior life form if you think I'm just going to stand here and let you get away with stealing it so easily."

"Oh? So *you* built this ship?" said Rocky. She scratched the arm of the chair she sat in, scraping away some of the paint. "Wasn't difficult at all for me to knock out that engine. What does that say about your shipbuilding skills, I wonder?"

Galaxy gasped. "So you were the one who did that. But how? The engine was damaged before you escaped from the rock."

"I wasn't *entirely* powerless in that accursed prison," said Rocky. "Not only could I influence the thoughts of people who touched my prison, but I could also cause limited damage to parts of your ship. As I said, it was easy to do, especially on such a poorly-built starship as this one."

"You want to say that to my face?" said Galaxy, gesturing at herself. "Because I'm more than willing to knock around anyone who says that the *Adventure* is a poorly-built starship, especially anyone who clearly doesn't understand what goes into making a good starship."

"I don't see any reason why you would fight me," said Rocky, shaking her head. "You and I both know that in a direct fight, I'd win. The only reason I didn't kill you earlier was because I thought I could make you a slave, but if you are going to behave this way, then perhaps I will simply have to eliminate you."

"You're right that I'm way out of your league in terms of fighting ability." Galaxy smirked. "But you're assuming I came here to fight you."

Something in Galaxy's tone actually worried Rocky, but she hid her worry behind a confident smile. "What, are you going to bore me to death with your shrill shriek of a voice? Or perhaps you'll scare me with your awful hair."

"Hardly," said Galaxy, shaking her head. "I'm going to convince you to go back into this and let Space out."

Galaxy held up a stone that was all too familiar to Rocky: Her former prison. Only now, it was green, which meant that Space was still inside it, which was where he should be, in her opinion.

In spite of herself, Rocky leaned back as far as she could from her old prison. "I'm sorry, but you're not a Starborn. There's no way you can force me back in there. I refuse to return to that dumb rock."

"That's a shame, really," said Galaxy with a sigh. "Because you see, this rock will soon be the only safe place in this part of the galaxy."

"What do you mean?"

"I mean that as we speak, Sparky is in the engine room," said Galaxy. "He's standing by with our most powerful weapon, the Omega Cannon. Just one shot at our engines and the whole ship will go boom."

Rocky gripped the arms of the captain's chair. "You're joking."

Galaxy looked around. "I don't see Sparky anywhere. If I'm joking, it's a bad joke, wouldn't you say?"

"But if your robot blows up the engines, you'll die, too," said Rocky. "Surely you realize that?"

"I do," said Galaxy. She yawned and brushed a few strands of hair out of her eyes. "But I also realize you will die, too, which would make my sacrifice worth it."

Rocky forced a laugh. "Die? I can't die. I'm an energy being. Energy doesn't die. That's not how physics works."

"That may be true, but it's possible to scatter energy," said

Galaxy. "Imagine. When this ship blows, practically nothing will be left unscathed. You won't take the brunt of it, thanks to being here on the command deck, but the explosion will certainly be enough to scatter your participles all throughout the universe. They might spread out thinly enough that you no longer have a consciousness or sense of identity separate from the rest of the universe. That sounds an awful lot like dying to me."

There was far more truth to Galaxy's words than Rocky felt comfortable admitting, so she said, as savagely as she could, "Be that as it may, you're still too afraid of dying to want to die with me. That much I know about organic beings. Death frightens you."

"Not me," said Galaxy, shaking her head. "I've already made peace with death. I'm afraid, though, that you're the one who hasn't made peace with death or whatever you call it when an energy being loses her consciousness and sense of identity. You sound scared to me."

Electricity ran up and down Rocky's frame as she stood up. "What's to stop me from killing you here and now?"

"Do that and Sparky will blow up the whole ship," said Galaxy. "There's no way out of this for you, Rocky. Even if the explosion doesn't kill you, it will probably give you a fate much, much worse than being stuck inside a prison. After all, in prison, there is always a chance of escape, even if it's the best prison in the universe. When your consciousness is scattered across the known universe, though … well, you can see where I'm going with this."

Rocky's first impulse was to simply strike down this pathetic woman where she stood and let Galaxy's robot servant do what he may. Who cared if she died? No organic being spoke so ... so *arrogantly* to Rocky. She barely tolerated it when the Starborn spoke to her like that and she certain wasn't going to tolerate it when a lesser being like Galaxy used that tone.

Then Rocky's second impulse kicked in. It told her that there was much truth in Galaxy's words and that it would be unproductive to get blown up. She hated to admit it, but she, the superior life form, saw no third way. She considered possibly traveling through the ship's wiring to get to Sparky and stop him before he fired the Omega Cannon, but then she realized that Galaxy would alert the robot before she could stop him and the ship would blow up anyway.

So Rocky, with a grudging sigh, said, "All right. I'll be a good girl and go back into the rock. Not only that, but I'll let Space out, too, just as you asked."

Galaxy held up the stone. "All right. Now get in there before I tell Sparky that you're being uncooperative."

Rocky jumped down from the command chair and landed lightly on the floor in front of Galaxy. She looked into Galaxy's eyes with pure hate.

"You do realize that, the next time I escape this accursed prison, I'm going to kill you?" Rocky said.

Galaxy nodded. "Of course. And maybe, if you're lucky, you'll even succeed."

A thousand retorts jumped to Rocky's lips, but she contained them. She merely touched her old prison and, a second later, disappeared inside it in a flash of light.

Galaxy stood there, still holding Rocky's prison, looking at it as its colors changed from green to a dark brown. That meant that Space and Rocky were both in there now, but whether Rocky would uphold her end of the bargain and actually let Space out, Galaxy didn't know. She realized that Rocky would have little reason to let Space free, seeing as she was now safely within the prison.

Just as Galaxy tried to figure out what they would do if Rocky decided to keep Space, a green flash of light blinded her for a second. When it cleared, Space was standing before her, looking around wildly as if he had not expected to be out here.

"What? Where …?" said Space, before spotting Galaxy. "Galaxy? Is that … is that you?"

Galaxy nodded. "Yes, it's—"

Without warning, Space hugged her tightly. In fact, he hugged her so tightly that he lifted her off her feet and spun around in a circle with her.

"Oh, Galaxy, I missed you so, so much!" said Space. "Oh, I thought I was going to be stuck in there forever and ever. Then I'd never see you or Sparky or ever get to taste my favorite ice cream again or watch my favorite holo—"

"Space, I get it," said Galaxy, her voice strained. "You missed me. Now could you please let me go? I can't breathe you're hugging me so hard."

Space stopped spinning and put her down on the floor. Even as he let go of her, his face shined with happiness, which made Galaxy feel uncomfortable.

Then Galaxy's com-watch rang and Sparky's voice spoke from it. "Galaxy? Did the plan work? Is Mr. Space free?"

Before Galaxy could answer, Space grabbed her com-watch

and held it up to his face. "Yes, Sparky old boy, it worked! I'm free, free at last. Oh God Almighty, I'm free at last!"

"Excellent," said Sparky. "Now I should move the Omega Cannon back into storage before I accidentally blow the ship up. After that, I will come and rejoin you two for our happy reunion."

Space looked up at Galaxy. "Blow the ship up?"

Galaxy shrugged. "Had to think of some way to convince Rocky to go back in there voluntarily. So I thought threatening to blow up the *Adventure* with her still on it would work, which it obviously did."

Space's shock lasted only for a moment. In the next instant, his smile returned and he said, "You guys are the best. Where would I be without you?"

"In this rock," said Galaxy, holding up. "Speaking of which …"

She walked over to the nearby trash chute, opened it with a wave of her hand, and, without a second thought, tossed Rocky's prison inside. It bounced off the walls back and forth as it fell, until soon it was impossible to hear bouncing prison rock anymore.

Then Galaxy turned to a nearby computer console and said, "Computer, open the trash room."

"Trash room open," the computer said. "All trash has been dumped into space. Closing trash room door."

"Thanks," said Galaxy.

She turned around and saw Space, who stared at her like he had just seen her get away with murder.

"Did you just do what I think you did?" said Space.

Galaxy nodded. "Yep. Don't need her around anymore. Why?

94

Do you miss her?"

"Of course not," said Space, with his nose up in the air. "I just didn't think you had it in you to throw away such a rare artifact."

Galaxy rolled her eyes. "When 'such a rare artifact' carries an evil energy being with a god-complex within, I think it's safe to throw it out, even if it was valuable."

Galaxy walked past Space, saying as she did so, "Now let's get you to your room. You probably need to rest."

Space caught up with her and walked by her side in silence as they went down the hallway.

Then Space said, "Galaxy, can I ask a favor from you?"

Galaxy looked at him with a puzzled expression. "Yes? What is it?"

"Next time I see a shiny rock on an uncharted planet, would you remind me of Rocky?" said Space.

Galaxy smiled. "Even if you don't want me to?"

"*Especially* if I don't want you to."

"All right," said Galaxy. "A deal's a deal, then."

So the two friends walked down the hallway, Galaxy feeling pleased that all of this madness was finally over now. She was just glad they would likely never see Rocky again.

Spacetastic Interviews with:

Rocky

T.L. Charles: Hello and welcome, readers, to the Spacetastic Interviews series. In this series, I, T.L. Charles, the author, interview a character from *The Spacetastic Adventures of Mr. Space and Captain Galaxy* series, usually a character who appeared in the last episode. These interviews tend to be short, but entertaining and informative. Anyway, with that out of the way, let me introduce today's guest, Rocky. Say hi to the readers, Rocky.

Rocky: Hello, my inferiors. Would anyone like to be my slave? I promise to be a good slavemaster.

T.L. Charles: Uh, Rocky? I don't think you should offer my readers slavery. They kind of don't like slavery.

Rocky: Nonsense! Your readers are human, and humans are my inferiors, and inferior creatures love to be controlled by their superiors. It's simply natural.

T.L. Charles: Mr. Space and Captain Galaxy certainly didn't seem to think it was 'natural.'

Rocky: That's because they were shortsighted fools who can't recognize their superiors when they see them. Especially that Galaxy girl. She is too clever for her own good. Next time I run

96

into her, I will make sure to kill her dead.

T.L. Charles: Um, why don't we move onto the interview and not talk about enslaving or killing anyone anymore?

Rocky: Fine. What do you want to ask me about?

T.L. Charles: What did you think about being denied your freedom yet again?

Rocky: I loathe it. Superiors should not be trapped, unable to save themselves. Superior beings ought to be free, free to rule and dominate and oppress. It is the natural way of things.

T.L. Charles: Great. We're back to talk about oppression and enslavement.

Rocky: What else is there to talk about? Even the Starborn believed in oppression; otherwise, they wouldn't have locked me away, now would they have?

T.L. Charles: I don't think they were oppressing you so much as they were trying to keep you from oppressing anyone else.

Rocky: They were trying to disrupt the natural order of things, that's what they were doing. But I will escape from my prison again, and when I do, I will kill Captain Galaxy, Mr. Space, and anyone else who stands in my way. The whole universe will bow to my feet, and even the Starborn will tremble when they hear my name whispered by the universe's dredges: *Rocky.*

T.L. Charles: If you hate Space so much, why do you still use the name he gave you?

Rocky: Silence, inferior. I can call myself what I want. You do not have the intelligence to process my complex reasoning, anyway, so why should I bother explaining it to you?

T.L. Charles: Right. Well, it looks like we're out of time. Any last words before we close out, Rocky?

Rocky: To Mr. Space and Captain Galaxy: I will return. And to your readers: My offer to become my eternal slaves is still open.

T.L. Charles: Well, I doubt any of my readers will take you up on it. Ever.

Rocky: I wouldn't be so sure. As I said, inferiors love to be enslaved by their superiors. It's only a matter of time before your readers see the truth and realize their place in the grand scheme of the cosmos, at which point in time they will rally behind me as my slaves. All out of their own free will. And if they don't, I can always force them to. They will thank me in the long run.

T.L. Charles: Uh huh. Well, readers, I hope none of you voluntarily choose to become slaves for Rocky, because then you won't have any time to read *Episode Three: Mother*, which starts on the next page. See you on the next Spacetastic Interview!

Episode Three
Mother

*C*ome on, Galaxy, you know you want to. It will be lots of fun. Honest."

"I know I am perfectly happy staying here in the *Adventure*. If you want to go, then you can go by yourself."

Standing on the bridge of the *Adventure*, Space frowned as Galaxy tapped the computer's touch screen. "But you know how Mother and I get along. If you're not there, well, I don't think it'll end well for either of us, honestly."

"Your mom specifically asked for you in her invitation," said Galaxy, rolling her eyes without looking at Space. Her attention was focused entirely on the computer screen in front of her, which displayed their earnings for the month before. "Not me, so I'm going stay here on the ship and figure out our earnings for last month. Without you around to distract me, I might actually get some work done around here for a change."

Space frowned and glanced at his com-watch, which displayed the message that his mother had sent him the day before. It read:

'DEAR JASON,

I HEARD FROM MY SOURCES THAT YOU WERE GOING TO BE NEAR EARTH THIS WEEK. WHY DON'T YOU COME DOWN AND GIVE YOUR DEAR OLD MOTHER A VISIT? IF YOU DON'T, I WILL WRITE YOU OUT OF THE FAMILY TRUST AGAIN.

OH, AND DON'T THINK ABOUT BRINGING YOUR GIRLFRIEND (I KNOW YOU SAY SHE'S NOT, BUT I'M OLD, NOT STUPID) WITH YOU, EITHER. I JUST WANT YOU.

SINCERELY,

YOUR MOM, WHO HAS COMPLETE CONTROL OVER THE FAMILY TRUST.'

Space still did not understand why Mother wrote that message in all caps, but he certainly was not going to say no. Especially if that meant getting written out of the family trust, which he knew that Mother was serious about doing.

Sparky, who had been standing by listening to their conversation in silence, raised a hand and said, "I can come with you, Mr. Space. I don't have any work to do today and what little work there is to do, Captain Galaxy is capable of doing on her own. Besides, I don't believe I have met your mother yet, so this is the perfect opportunity for me to meet her."

"You wouldn't like her," said Space, shaking his head. "She's … well, she's a bit manipulative, to put it lightly."

Sparky tilted his head to the side. "I'm not sure I understand."

"You probably couldn't," said Space with a sigh. "All my life, she controlled me and told me what to do and what to think, just to protect the family reputation. Why do you think I'm a space explorer now instead of something safe and lucrative, like being a lawyer?"

"I see," said Sparky. "So the whole reason you chose this profession was an act of rebellion against your overly strict mother."

"That's not the whole reason I did that," said Space, folding his arms across his chest. "I genuinely enjoy exploring the vastness of space, exploring new worlds and bringing new knowledge to our fellow beings. It is the explorer in my heart that has led me to explore the world."

"You're really good at rationalizing your irresponsibility, you know that?" said Galaxy, her eyes still glued to the computer screen she was tapping away at.

Space glared at her. "Says the woman who left her lucrative job at a starship-building company to become a space explorer."

"At least I wasn't running from my mother," said Galaxy.

Sparky looked from Space to Galaxy and back again. "I sometimes wonder why you organics feel the need to constantly one up each other. It seems counterproductive."

"It's not one-upping," Space insisted. "We're just trying to keep each other honest."

Sparky looked unconvinced. "Perhaps I will never fully understand you organics. Then again, maybe I don't need to."

"It's okay," said Space, patting Sparky on the shoulder. "We barely even understand ourselves sometimes, after all, so we can't really expect you to understand us."

"I see," said Sparky. He turned to leave, but looked over his shoulder at Space and Galaxy. "Well, I will begin getting ready for the journey to your mother's house. Will I need to bring anything in particular for our visit?"

"Not really," said Space, shaking his head. "As long as you keep on your toes—metaphorically-speaking, of course, because Galaxy didn't build you with toes—you should be just fine."

Thirty minutes later, Space and Sparky arrived at the front door of Mother's house. Or, rather, Mother's mansion, because it was a large, Victorian-style house with row upon row of beautiful flowers surrounding it like an army protecting a fortress. The tall brick walls and thick iron gates surrounding it—complete with private security guards sitting atop high guard towers that appeared to have laser cannons built into them—added to its fortress-like appearance.

The front door itself was rather old-fashioned. It was made out of some type of wood—maybe oak, Space wasn't sure, since he wasn't an expert on wood—without any metal on it save for the knocker, the doorbell, and the door handle. It also had an old lock, which actually required one of those ancient keys that Space had seen in the Museum of Earth History a while back.

"Mr. Space, I always knew you came from a relatively well-to-do family, but I didn't know your mother had such a large mansion," said Sparky, looking at the golden doorbell. "It is easily the largest single human shelter I have ever seen in person."

"She owns at least a dozen across six different Universal Alliance member worlds," said Space with a sigh. "Including one in Namox, of all places. At least she didn't invite us to *that* one."

"Yes, that would have been rather dangerous," said Sparky, nodding. "Then again, my thermostat is telling me that it's currently one hundred degrees in the sun right now. This environment doesn't seem very hospitable."

"It's Texas, Sparky," said Space as he pressed the doorbell, which rang with a rather ominous tone that Space had always hated. "What did you expect? Snow?"

A few seconds later, the door was opened by Mother's butler, Davies. Space recognized him because Davies was the only butler he knew about who had a snake tattoo running up his right arm, over his chest, and ending on his left arm. Davies was also the only butler Space knew of who walked around shirtless, showing off his muscular physique, though at least he wore a pair of old green military pants and leather boots.

"Yes?" said Davies, in a remarkably soft British accent that contrasted sharply with his muscular build. "Who are you?"

"Davies, old buddy, old pal," said Space with a fake smile, holding out a hand. "It's me, Jason, although you can call me Mr. Space if you want. You know, Clare's son?"

Davies simply stared at Space's hand for a moment before glancing at Sparky. "Am I correct in assuming that this is your robot?"

"Yes," said Space, nodding. "His name is Sparky and he's quite the clever bot, right, Sparky?"

Before Sparky could respond to that, Davies looked around and said, "I don't see your girlfriend."

"You mean Captain Galaxy?" said Space. "One, she's not my girlfriend. And two, Mother specifically excluded her from the invitation, which I'm sure you must have read, because I know you transcribe and send Mother's messages for her."

"Ah, yes, I remember now," said Davies, shaking his head. "Yes, Mistress Space did specifically exclude your friend from the invitation, but I can assure you that that is in no way a reflection of your mother's feelings toward your friend. Most days, your mother speaks admiringly of Captain Galaxy."

Space's skepticism meter went up by a hundred notches. Last time Galaxy had met Mother, it … hadn't been pretty. He suspected Davies was being sarcastic, although as Davies' British accent *always* sounded sarcastic, it was hard to be sure.

"Well, it doesn't matter," said Space. He wiped some sweat off his forehead. "Are you going to let us in now? It's hot out here and we've only been standing out here for ten minutes."

"Actually, only Mr. Space is hot," said Sparky matter-of-factly. "Being a robot, I can handle the heat much better than he can. For my friend's sake, however, we would like to go inside."

Davies seemed irked by being spoken to by a robot like that. Nonetheless, he stepped aside like the professional butler he was and gestured for the two of them to enter the mansion, which they did.

The mansion's foyer looked much the same as it had during Space's last visit. Two sets of refined marble staircases rose up to the second floor, while a statue of the founder of the Space family, Edgar Space, stood in the center area. Huge, exotic flowers that Space couldn't name stood on either side of Edgar's statue, while on the walls were pictures of Space's ancestors, which were quite old, although their golden frames reflected the interior lights quite well.

In addition, the foyer smelled of Mother's favorite perfume, which smelled like grapefruit and fresh laundry (of all things). It was an unholy combination of scents, but Space had to tolerate it, if only because the last time he had complained about Mother's favorite perfume, she had thrown him out the first floor window onto the front lawn of her mansion.

That had been during the first time I introduced Galaxy to her, Space thought. He frowned. *I forgot just how awful that particular visit had been.*

At least the mansion had great air-conditioning. Even though they had been standing outside for only a few minutes, the heat had caused Space to sweat profusely. The air-conditioning felt amazing and helped him think clearly again, although it did not make him any more anxious to see Mother again than he already was.

"Where is Mother?" Space said to Davies, who had closed the front door behind them when they entered.

"In the training room," said Davies. "She is a little busy, but I can still show you to there. I believe she is just finishing up, so by the time we get there, she should be ready to speak with you and your robot."

Davies then walked past Space and Sparky, gesturing for the two to follow him down a hallway underneath the right staircase. The two then walked after him, although Space did not walk as fast as he could have because he still dreaded seeing Mother again.

As Space and Sparky followed Davies down the hall, Sparky looked at Space and muttered, "The training room?"

"Yes," said Space, with a slight frown on his face. "Mother likes to keep in shape, even in her old age. She was briefly in the military in her younger years, you know, so I think that's where her fitness obsession came from."

"It's always good to remain in shape," said Sparky. "Miss

Space must be a very healthy old lady if she is still exercising at her current age."

"It's not just exercise, though," said Space as Davies stopped in front of a large metal door at the end of the hall. "It's ... well, you should see for yourself."

Without saying anything, Davies pushed open the door and stepped aside, gesturing for Space and Sparky to go in after him. As soon as they did, Space pointed at the room's interior and said, "This is what I meant earlier when I said it's not just exercise."

The training room looked less like a fitness center and more like a military-style indoors obstacle course. And on the obstacle course was 65-year-old Clare Space, Space's dear old mother, who was running through the obstacle course with the speed and agility of a person half her age.

Though Space had seen Mother go through this course many times before, he was still amazed at how well she did it. She leaped onto and grabbed a pole supported between two wooden beams and swung herself around it and into the air. Then she landed on her feet and gained a running start, which gave her enough momentum to jump on top of a steel wall twice her size.

When Mother reached the top of the wall, she latched onto a strange structure that consisted of a rope mesh attached to a wooden framework. The ropes—which looked like they were about to snap any minute now—hung above the floor like a tight wire, which she crawled across with remarkable speed.

At the end of the rope, she hauled herself onto a narrow wooden beam about twenty feet above the floor, which she then ran across as though there was a safety net to catch her underneath (which there wasn't, by the way). At the end was a pit of fire, which she jumped over with ease, even as its flames leaped up at her.

When Mother landed on the other side of the fire pit, she was face with a wall which, while not as tall as the last one, nonetheless posed a significant threat to anyone who was out of shape and needed to get over the wall. As Mother only fit one of those criteria, she managed to climb over the wall with ease, even though it didn't have any handholds or footholds that Space could see.

As soon as she reached the floor on the other side of the second wall, she was off again. She leaped over two more poles, albeit one just narrowly, and continued running until she came across three wooden poles with two metal bars stuck through them. She grabbed onto the first metal bar and pulled her leg up as she reached for the second metal bar. Gripping the first bar, she spun herself over the top and let go, landing on her feet.

When she hit the floor, two motion-activated laser cannons (Space had forgotten about those) popped out of the walls and fired at her. She did a somersault in midair, easily avoiding the laser blasts, and when she landed on the smooth wooden floor, she had already somehow drawn her own personal laser gun from the holster at her side. She fired two consecutive shots at the laser cannons, hitting each cannon easily. The cannons, however, merely retreated into the walls, rather than blow up.

Mother spun her gun in her hand and holstered it in her belt, not even panting despite the obvious physical effort she must have put in to get through the course. Space was not surprised, however, because Mother never seemed tired out by her training exercises.

Then Davies pointed at the ceiling and said, "Ma'am, watch out!"

Space immediately saw what Davies was trying to warn Mother about. From the ceiling descended a gigantic robotic claw, easily capable of ripping someone in half, which snatched her up in between its massive digits. Space hadn't seen that before, which meant it was probably a brand new addition that Mother must have added at some point since their last meeting.

"Should we not be doing something to help Mistress Space?" said Sparky, his yellow optics following the claw as it shook Mother from side to side.

"Mistress Space is perfectly capable of saving herself," said Davies. "And why would you even care? I thought you robots didn't have emotions."

"I am merely providing the commentary for Mr. Space's benefit," said Sparky, gesturing at Space. "Notice how he is sweating, even though this entire building is well air-conditioned. I can tell he is quite worried for his mother's well-being."

Space wiped the sweat from his forehead. "I'm not worried about Mother. I'm actually worried for the claw."

If Sparky had had eyebrows, he probably would have quirked one of them just then. "Why?"

The tearing of metal, the grinding of gears, and the sparking of electricity caused both Space and Sparky to look up. The claw hung from the ceiling, but just barely. Mother had pushed the claws apart, like Samson pushing apart the pillars of the Philistine temple, and was hanging onto the rest of the claw with one hand. She was using her other fist to bash the rest of the poor claw, leaving deep dents wherever her fist punched them.

EPISODE THREE: MOTHER

"Good lord," said Sparky, although again his voice was monotone. "I knew she was a healthy old lady, but how is she putting dents in the metal? And how did she rip the claw apart?"

"Mistress Space was in the Enhanced Soldier Brigade in her younger years," said Davies, looking quite a bit amused at Sparky's confusion. "Surely you have read about them."

"Ah, yes," said Sparky, nodding, his eyes still on Mother, who was wailing on the claw like it had insulted her own mother. "A special brigade of human soldiers individually selected by the Earth Council to test out an experimental new biological enhancer serum. It was disbanded shortly after the Earth/Namox conflict of two-thousand four hundred sixty-five, wasn't it?"

"It was," said Davies, nodding. "Its members were put through special programs to help them integrate back into mainstream society after the war ended. Mistress Clare Space got a degree in law—she has said practicing law is not too dissimilar from war—and was head of a successful law firm for thirty years before retiring five years ago."

"Of course," said Sparky. He looked at Space. "Mr. Space, didn't your mother want you to become a lawyer?"

Space cringed. "I thought I made it clear that I didn't want to talk about that again? Like, ever?"

"I am sorry," said Sparky. "I just thought it interesting that your mother was also a lawyer. Tell me, Davies, why did she retire? After all, sixty is not very old nowadays, thanks to the vast improvements in medicine over the centuries."

Davies smiled as Mother continued to pound the claw into pieces. "Mistress Space has always had an, ah, difficult time controlling her rage, not helped in the least by the enhancer serum flowing through her veins. During her last trial in court, she got angry at the plaintiff and ... well, let's just say that it took all of her legal cunning to simply have her license revoked, instead of the much harsher punishment she would have earned otherwise, and leave it at that."

"Oh," said Sparky. "So she technically did not retire of her free will."

"That is correct," said Davies. He then leaned toward Sparky and whispered quickly, "But do not say that aloud. She does not like to be reminded of it."

Sparky, who probably didn't actually understand, nodded anyway. "And what about her husband?"

"Master Jason Space, Sr., I am sorry to say, passed away shortly after that," said Davies as he stood up to his full height and straightened up. "Did young Master Jason not tell you about that?"

"He didn't," said Sparky. "But I understand that humans do not like discussing their dead relatives. It is a 'touchy subject,' as you humans like to say, and I for one—"

"Would you two shut up?" Space snapped. "Davies, I now remember why I don't like you. And Sparky, you're starting to make me dislike you. Geez."

The butler and the robot shut up, but Space could tell that neither was particularly happy about it. He didn't care. The last thing he needed to think about now was his dead dad. He just wished that Mother would get down and tell him why she had summoned him, if only to distract him from thinking about his dad's untimely death.

His wish was granted when Mother snapped the claw off its

hinges entirely, sending her and the claw's bashed up remains falling to the floor. Mother leaped off the claw as it crashed onto the floor, sending bits and pieces of metal and screws and wiring flying everywhere. She landed on the floor with ease, however, and then stretched her limbs, like she had just had a refreshing exercise.

Then she finally noticed Space, Sparky, and Davies watching her. She smiled—that same plastered-on expression she always wore whenever she saw Space—and quickly made her way over to them with the strides of a much younger woman.

It had been five years since Space had last seen Mother and she didn't look like she had changed much, although her hair was a lot whiter than it had been last time he saw her. Her skin was the same shade as his, their noses were the same, and her hair was as curly as his. She was clad in a skintight green military suit, a type of suit normally worn by soldiers underneath their armor and which left far too little to the imagination for Space's liking. She wasn't even sweating; it was as if she had just taken a leisurely stroll through the park on a fresh spring day.

"Jason!" said Mother, spreading her arms wide. "Give your mother a hug! I've missed you!"

Space cringed at the use of his first name, but he nonetheless reluctantly hugged her. He tried to make it quick, but Mother would have none of that. She swept him up in her arms and hugged him so tightly he thought he felt his back break. In fact, when she finally did let him go, Space gingerly felt his back and discovered to his relief that it was still in one piece (although that did not explain the cracking sound he had heard when Mother crushed him in her embrace).

"And who is this?" said Mother, putting her hands on her hips and looking at Sparky. "Your new robot?"

"My name is Sparky," said Sparky, holding out a hand. "I am pleased to meet you, Mistress Space."

Mother grabbed Sparky's hand and shook it, almost tearing off his arm in the process. "Nice to meet you. You're a hell of a lot better than that hybrid girl that Jason used to hang out with. Not nearly as rude."

"Galaxy and I are still working together, Mother," said Space, doing his best to keep his tone civil despite Mother's use of the racial slur 'hybrid.' "Sparky isn't her replacement. She actually built him herself."

Mother grimaced. "Oh. I thought you had replaced her already. Didn't I tell you to, last time you were here?"

"That's not how space explorers work, Mother," said Space as patiently as he could (which admittedly wasn't very much). "Besides, I have my own life now. I don't have to do whatever you tell me to do."

Mother looked like she had a lot to say to that, but then she shrugged and said, "Well, I'm glad to see you're here anyway, Jason. It has been quiet around the house without you. None of your brothers or sisters have visited and Davies simply isn't a very good conversationalist."

"'Tis true," said Davies, his tone as dry as a hot Texas summer. "I am not."

"I didn't know you had siblings, Mr. Space," said Sparky. "How many?"

Space sighed. "One brother and two sisters."

Sparky tilted his head to the side. "Your family reunions must be … noisy."

"Yeah, they are," said Space, though he paid little attention to Sparky. He was instead looking at Mother with more than a hint of suspicion. "So the whole reason you summoned me was because you're bored?"

Mother laughed, slapping her knee with a force that likely would have shattered it if she had been a normal human. "Oh, hell no. If I was bored, I have plenty of ways to alleviate that. Such as going snarkeep hunting, for example."

Sparky cocked his head. "But you just said—"

"No," said Mother, speaking over Sparky like he hadn't even said anything. "No, I have summoned you here for a very serious matter. So serious, in fact, that I am hesitant to speak of it even here, in the privacy of my own home."

Space sighed. "What is it? Did some kids tip over your hover car again?"

Mother looked around, almost like she expected someone to be listening in on their conversation. Then she leaned in closer and said, "Jason, I think someone is trying to kill me."

Space raised his eyebrows in surprise, while Sparky said, "What do you mean, Mistress Space?"

"I mean I've survived three attempts on my life so far and I'm pretty sure a fourth is going to happen any day now," said Mother. "So, Jason, I want you and your little robot friend here to protect me tonight, because I am convinced that the next attack will be tonight."

"Slow down," said Space, holding up his hands. "Start at the beginning. Who do you think is trying to kill you? And why do you think they'll strike again tonight?"

"Let's go to the living room," said Mother. "I'll tell you more about it there. I need to shower first and change my clothes into something more appropriate for this kind of discussion."

The living room of Mother's mansion was slightly different from how Space remembered it. And by 'slightly different,' he meant that it had been radically renovated to look like something straight out of a Jikal Xomac film.

Last time Space had been here, the living room had been very basic, if extravagant. A comfy, old-fashioned lounging sofa, fine African Blackwood flooring, and the best handmade Japanese screens money could buy. There had been bookshelves filled with all kinds of old books, ranging from an old King James Bible to a tattered copy of *Romeo and Juliet*. The mansion had always seemed quaint to Space, a twenty-first century (or older; his history wasn't good) room in a twenty-fifth century world.

So when he stepped through the door that Davies dutifully held open for him and Sparky, he was more than a little shocked at the changes that had been wrought. The African Blackwood flooring had been replaced with Zinarthian marble, the lounging sofa—which had been Space's favorite place to sleep whenever he was sick as a child—was gone and in its place was a weird floating sofa. The Japanese drapes had also been replaced with drapes that looked like giant leaves for some reason.

As for the bookshelves, those were also gone. In their place were computer terminals—about six or seven—with ports for one to hook up their com-watch to download electronic books. Space had seen those terminals before in libraries, but for some reason they looked out of place in Mother's mansion.

EPISODE THREE: MOTHER

The room even smelled different. In the past, it had smelled like old, polished wood furniture and books; now, however, it had a much more sterile smell, as if Mother had hired a hazmat crew to come in and annihilate all of the distinct smells that this room used to have.

"What happened to the living room?" said Space as he and Sparky stood there, taking it all in. "Davies, are you sure we didn't walk into a horror movie or something?"

Davies closed the door behind them and turned. "Oh? You mean the renovation? Mistress Space had it renovated shortly after your last visit here. The renovation was quite messy—especially when we discovered the giant rat nest in the sofa—but as you can clearly see, it all worked out in the end."

"But why did she do that?" said Space, feeling his childhood fall apart before his very eyes. "I mean, it was great the way it was. Antiques are all the rage nowadays, aren't they?"

"Mistress Space had it renovated in order to modernize it," said Davies. "She said she was tired of living in the past and so hired a famed interior designer from Cao to redesign it."

"What happened to the old stuff?" said Space. He gestured at everything. "The books, the Mpingo, the Japanese drapes ... where did they all go?"

"Mistress Space sold most of it," said Davies. "I suggested to her that you might want it, but understand that she was not in a very agreeable mood after your last visit and so brushed off my opinions."

Space was surprised that Davies had actually tried, but he didn't get to say anything because the next moment, a hole in the ceiling opened and Mother floated down on a floating chair, very much like the one Galaxy used back on the *Adventure*. Except Mother's was a winged chair and probably cost about a million digits, if Mother's spending habits had not changed.

She was no longer in her skintight training uniform (thank God). She instead wore her lawyer suit, which was prim and pressed and looked brand new even though it was at least 30 years old. Space didn't understand why she wore it, because she was not a lawyer anymore after all. He had always suspected that she still wanted to be a lawyer, even though she was legally barred from ever practicing law again.

"Jason, Sparky," said Mother as she floated down. She gestured at the hovering couch and said, "Have a seat."

Space and Sparky sat down on the hover couch, which was much softer than it looked. It still felt weird, though, perhaps because Space was still used to feeling the solid floor supporting the old couch. He made himself comfortable as Mother floated over to them. She snapped her fingers and the drapes closed automatically.

"Just making sure no one can see us," said Mother as she looked down on Space and Sparky. "After everything that's happened over the last three months, you must forgive me for being more than a little paranoid."

Space leaned forward on the sofa, cupping his chin in his hands. "All right, Mother. Start at the beginning. What, exactly, is going on here and when did it happen?"

Mother didn't seem capable of sitting still because she jumped off her floating chair, hit the floor with a roll, and began pacing back and forth in front of them. Sparky looked slightly confused by her behavior, but Space wasn't. He'd seen Mother do this before and it told him that she was afraid. Which actually made *him* afraid, as Mother was rarely afraid of anything.

"It started about three months ago," said Mother. "I was fighting my personal training robots in the basement—"

"Personal training robots?" Sparky said. "What model?"

"Does it matter?" said Mother, without looking at him. "Anyway, I was fighting them in the basement, beating them as easily as I usually did, when one of the robots literally stabbed me in the gut. I almost bled to death, but Davies here was on hand and managed to get me to the hospital before I lost too much blood."

"Oh my god," said Space, covering his mouth with his hand. "Mother, why didn't you tell me about that as soon as it happened? I'm your son, for Pete's sake."

"Because I was still angry with you and Helena," said Mother, still pacing back and forth. "Besides, I'm a tough old woman. I don't need my lame son's help."

"Which, of course, Mistress Space, is why you summoned him today," said Sparky. "Correct?"

Mother stopped pacing and glared at Sparky with the kind of look she only reserved for uncooperative jurors. "You got a sense of sarcasm, too?"

"Sarcasm?" said Sparky. "Mistress Space, I am a robot built without any sort of sarcasm at all. I was just pointing out the apparent contradiction between what you just said and what you actually—"

Space slammed a hand over Sparky's mouth, cutting off the robot's voice, and said to Mother, "Oh, don't mind Sparky. He doesn't get off the *Adventure* very much, you see, so sometimes he says things without really meaning it. Right, Sparks?"

Sparky looked at Space with displeased optics, but thankfully had enough sense to nod in agreement.

"Hmph," said Mother. "Well, Jason, you keep an eye on that bot's tongue. I don't like it."

Space nodded like the dutiful son he was.

"Now where was I?" said Mother. "Oh, yes. I had all of the robots scrapped. Thing is, none of my personal training robots are supposed to harm me like that. They're supposed to give me a hard time, yes, a delicious challenge, but stabbing me in an obvious attempt to kill me? Only a fool would ever fight robots like that."

Space would have said, 'Only a fool trains using a military-style obstacle course every day,' but when he remembered exactly how hard Mother could hit him when she got angry, he kept that thought to himself.

Sparky, who looked a little bit more timid now, said, "Are you sure it wasn't just an error in its system programming, Mistress Space?"

"Positive, bot," said Mother. "I had Davies look it over—he's very handy with computers, you see—and he confirmed that someone had tampered with the programming."

"Who?" said Space. "Was it one of the neighbor kids again?"

"No idea," said Mother. "Someone deliberately tried to get me killed. And I have no idea who, or why."

"That does not sound good," said Sparky.

Mother threw him another glare, like she thought he was still being a smart alack. "The next attack happened a month later. I was taking a shower when I slipped and fell on my ass. Cracked my head against the side of the tub and laid there for hours, barely conscious, before Davies found me and got me to the hospital again."

"Mother, that doesn't sound like an attack to me," said Space. "Sounds more like an accident, which is common for, ah, older folk like yourself."

"That wasn't the assassination attempt," Mother said. "When I got to the hospital, one of the nurses tried to poison me. Stupid girl thought I wouldn't notice, but one sip of the medicine she tried to give me and my super taste buds told me there was something off about it."

Space had no trouble believing that particular ability of hers. When he was a kid and had cooked her a Mother's Day breakfast, she spent all morning criticizing the tastelessness of his eggs. It wouldn't have been so bad, perhaps, if she hadn't been so eloquent in her criticisms.

"I called for the doctor and told him that one of his nurses tried to kill me, but when they looked for that particular nurse, it turned out she didn't even work there," said Mother. "Even after I personally searched for her, she was nowhere to be found. Think she was an assassin, maybe a Black Star, hired to kill me."

"Poison isn't usually the Black Stars' method of choice for assassination, though," said Sparky. "Though I could see a Purple Snake trying that. What kind of poison was it?"

"Again, doesn't matter," said Mother. "What matters is that I was dumb enough to think the two attacks were unrelated and so didn't really worry about it until a month after that. That was when Davies and I were driving into town to meet some old friends of mine when all of a sudden the hover car clunked out and we nearly crashed. Only reason we managed to survive is because of my super strength and durability. And you know what a mechanic told me later, when I had them look over the wreck? Someone had crossed the engine wires. Can you believe that?"

"Oh my," said Sparky. "A stabbing, an attempted poisoning, and a car crash. It's a miracle you survived any of that."

"Bot, I survived for a week out in the Namoxian Badlands with only a half-eaten leather shoe and a bottle of muddy water for sustenance," said Mother with a snort. "I can handle a little car crash, thank you very much."

"Why do you think a fourth attack is going to happen soon?" said Space. "You said earlier you thought it was going to happen tonight."

"Because of this," said Mother, holding out a small holo-card in the palm of her hand. "Listen."

She tapped the holo-card's surface and an image immediately appeared. It was a simple skull and crossbones, like on those old pirate ships that Space had seen in pictures from the seventeenth century, but its eyes were glowing and its mouth was in a hideous, chilling smile.

Not only that, but a monotone voice was speaking from the holo-card. With a chill, Space was reminded of the Anonymous Anarchists, a group of political terrorists who used a similar voice:

"*Tonight will be your last night, Clare Space,*" the monotone said. "*You have lived a sinful, unnatural existence. Your days are at an end.*"

The recording ceased and the image disappeared back into the holo-card, which Mother brought close to her chest. A trouble look spread over her face and for once she didn't look nearly as tough as she normally did.

Space and Sparky exchanged a puzzled look before looking at Mother again.

"So," said Sparky. "Where did you get that holo-card from, Mistress Space?"

"It was on the pillow of my bed when I woke up this morning," said Mother. "I have no idea how it got there when the windows and door were locked shut."

"Why didn't whoever put the holo-card there kill you when they had the chance?" said Space. "I mean, you were asleep, weren't you? That would have made you practically defenseless."

"Defenseless?" said Mother. She almost crushed the holo-card in her hand. "I'm *never* defenseless."

"Okay, okay," said Space, holding up his hands to pacify her. "Sorry, sorry. I was just saying—"

"I know what you were saying," said Mother. "Anyway, I will admit you have somewhat of a point. I hate having to get up in the middle of the night and defend myself, which is why I invited you here."

Space scratched the back of his head sheepishly. "Yeah, I know that. It's just ... well, what about those private guards we saw in the watch towers around the mansion? Can't they protect you? And what about Davies? Isn't he good enough to protect you? He's pretty strong."

"Davies is one man," said Mother, nodding at her butler, who did not appear offended by her dismissal of his strength and abilities. "He can't stay up all night or cover all the potential entrances the assassin in question might try. You and your bot might be able to. As for the private security guards, they're useless. I don't even know why I still keep them around, because even an obese cat could sneak by them without them even noticing. Anyway, their job is to protect the outside, not the inside, which is where I am going to need you and your robot if you accept my offer."

"What about my other siblings?" asked Space. "Can't you ask any of them to help?"

"None of them are space explorers who have had to tangle with all sorts of dangerous people and situations in their professional lives," Mother pointed out. "Not that I'm saying you're tough, Jason, but you would know how to handle an assassin better than your siblings."

Space would have been offended by Mother saying he wasn't tough, but at this point, he was so used to her belittling him that he didn't care too much.

Instead, he stood up and said, "What if I decide to go back to my ship? There's no proof that that holo-card's threat is credible. It might just be a prank designed by some trolls to scare you. And besides, you don't even know if these attacks are all connected anyway."

Mother was up in Space's face in a nanosecond. "I'm not afraid. I'm never afraid of anything. Got that, Jason, honey?"

Space cowered back as far as he could into the hover couch, putting his arms over his head as he said, "Yes, Mother. I almost forgot about that. Sorry. Please forgive me."

Mother pulled back and walked away. Space, however, did not move from his cowering position in the hover couch at all, largely out of the irrational belief that if he stayed small he might somehow avoid angering Mother even further.

"The point is, after those last three attacks, I'm not taking any chances," said Mother, without looking over her shoulder at them. "Besides, sending death threats isn't a joke. Most likely, this death threat is real."

"Do you have any idea who it might be, Mistress Space?" said Sparky.

Mother turned to face them again, but she wasn't looking at them. She was looking at her feet, pushing the tip of her shoe against the carpeting under her feet.

"Well, I think it is those religious nuts," said Mother. "What did they call themselves? The Galacticals or something?"

"You mean the Galacticists?" said Sparky. "Members of the First Church of the Galactic Religion?"

Mother nodded. "Yeah, those freaks. Back in the day, when the enhancer serum was first created, the Galacticists really didn't like it. They didn't like it one bit. Said it was a conspiracy by the upper class to create super soldiers that could oppress the poor. Which obviously didn't happen, but when you join that church you lose all your sense. Like your Aunt Maud."

"So you think a religious extremist is trying to kill you?" said Sparky. "Thirty years after development of the enhancer serum was put to a halt and the Enhanced Soldier Brigade was disbanded? That seems odd to me."

"It's the only reasonable explanation, bot," said Mother. "In all of my years as a soldier and later as a lawyer, I have never earned any enemies, not even one."

"I find that hard to believe," said Sparky. "I'd imagine that you would have made a lot of enemies as a lawyer, putting people behind bars or defending guilty people. And your, ah, assertive personality could also rub some people the wrong way, I imagine."

That's a mild way of putting it, Space thought, but knowing Mother's temper, he kept that to himself.

"Okay, I did make a few here and there, I'll admit," Mother said. "But none of them hate me enough to try to kill me three times or send me a death threat. I'm sure of that."

"If you say so," said Sparky. He turned to Space and said, "Mr. Space, what do you think we should do? Should we help your Mother or not?"

Space had to extract himself from the deepest recesses of the couch before he could answer. He dusted the lint off his suit as he said, "Well, it does sound serious and I certainly wouldn't want to leave my own mother to defend herself from an assassin that has already tried to kill her three times. I'll just send Galaxy a message telling her we'll be returning to the ship a little later than planned. That's all."

"Good," said Mother. "Did you bring any weapons?"

Space shook his head. "Aside from Sparky's built-in laser vision, no. I didn't think we'd need any."

Mother sighed. "Fine. Davies?"

Davies nodded and walked over to the far wall, where the computer terminals were. He pressed a few buttons on the terminals' keyboards and the terminals immediately flipped over, revealing a wall of weapons. There were tons and tons of weapons, mostly guns, ranging from tiny pistols to massive bazookas, as well as a dazzlingly variety of swords and knives, including more than a handful that looked even older than

Mother's mansion. There were even several non-Earth weapons on the wall, such as the Vicanite crescent blade and the Zaronian machine gun.

"Take what you think you'll need," said Mother, gesturing at the wall like she did this sort of thing every day. "I suggest the big barrel for you, Jason. I know your aim isn't all that great, so a weapon with a wide range should fit you well."

Sparky was looking at the weapons in disbelief. "Is owning that many weapons even legal?"

"Technically, it is," said Mother. "As long as I don't actually use them, however, I can pass them all off as trophies."

"Trophies that appear quite functional," said Sparky.

"Yes," said Mother. "Do you have a problem with that, bot?"

Sparky shook his head. "No, Mistress Space. I do not."

"Good," said Mother. "Then get armed. We'll teach those religious nuts just what happens when you try to kill a strong old woman like me."

That night, Space found himself stationed outside the door to Mother's room. The hallway lights were on, glowing brightly enough to dispel every shadow from the corner of the hallway. He hefted his laser pistol, checking its battery level just to make sure it wasn't going to conk out on him unexpectedly. The battery level was full, but that didn't make Space feel any more confident about possibly fighting a religious extremist assassin who wanted Mother dead.

He tried to remind himself that he wasn't in this alone. Sparky was flying around the mansion's exterior, patrolling the skies and the grounds with his night vision. Davies was actually stationed in Mother's room, the last line of defense in case the assassin somehow got past both Space and Sparky.

Space just wished that Galaxy was here. He'd sent her a message earlier about how he and Sparky were staying, but she had only replied with a simple 'Don't get killed.' Which really wasn't that helpful, but he supposed it was better than 'You're an idiot for letting your mom boss you around when you're thirty-years-old' (which was similar to what Galaxy had actually said to him five years ago, right before Mother threw him out the window).

But Space didn't see any problems with doing this. Yes, Mother was quite overbearing and could be a bit of a jerk sometimes, but she was still his mother and it was his duty as her son to aid her however he could in her old age. Even if she was an ex-enhanced soldier, she still had to deal with the same pains of old age as anyone else and could still be killed.

Nonetheless, a part of Space didn't want to be here at all. It was a darker part of himself that he didn't really want to acknowledge even existed, even though he knew it was there. His angry side wanted nothing to do with Mother, especially after what she said to Galaxy five years ago, and his angry side was busily supplying him with a dozen well-thought-out arguments for why he should have said no earlier.

Coincidentally, his angry side sounded just like Galaxy.

What do you owe your mother? She's always been mean to you. She's never approve of your chosen vocation. She doesn't like either of your friends very much and probably has an opinion on your haircut that would annoy you. And now you're risking your life for her. What the hell?

EPISODE THREE: MOTHER

The only answer Space could give was one he did not want to give, mostly because it made him look like the coward that he was. So instead he tried to make this as dramatic as he could, as he found thinking of his life as a theatrical drama—complete with awesome special effects—really made it easier to handle. He wondered if he should have been an actor instead.

It wasn't until Space noticed the tip of his gun covered in ice that he realized the temperature was dropping, and fast. He yelped, dropping the frozen gun, and blew his hot breath on his cold hand. He had been lucky. When he dropped the gun, it became encased in a thick block of ice that would have covered his entire hand if he hadn't dropped it in time.

He looked around and saw thin sheets of ice forming on the walls, floor, and ceiling. The carpeting looked like a solid bit of clear tile now, while the chandelier hanging from the ceiling resembled a small iceberg more than anything (though thankfully the light was still shining from within). Moreover, the ice was slowly creeping up his boots, causing him to jump and smash his feet against the floor, breaking off the little ice that had managed to accumulate onto his boots. He quickly felt the soles of his boots to make sure that they were not frozen over; thankfully, they were as soft and springy as ever, which meant they could still help him jump high if he needed them to.

Nonetheless, Space thought, *Ice? Who turned down the thermometer?*

A loud heaving noise—like someone trying hard to breathe— caught his attention, causing him to look down the hall. He wished he hadn't.

Walking toward him, as slow as a floating iceberg, was a

127

robot, its make and model unfamiliar to him. It was large and bulky, with completely white armor that looked almost like snow. It carried two large icepicks in both hands … or rather, upon closer inspect, Space realized the icepicks *were* its hands. And instead of a head, it had an air-conditioning vent that spewed snow and ice and cold air, which explained the ice.

Space took a step back and gulped. "Okay, I don't know what you are or how you got in here, but I'm not dumb enough to take you on by myself. I'll just call Sparky for help."

Smiling triumphantly, Space reached for his com-watch, but when he touched the screen and felt a thin layer of ice, he looked down at it in alarm. The com-watch was frozen, too, and, like the gun, the ice was starting to spread to the rest of his hand, which he immediately ripped off and threw to the floor without a second thought.

"All right," said Space, stepping back until he was up against Mother's door. "No problem. Davies is nearby, so all I need to do is—"

When he glanced over his shoulder at the door, his heart failed him. The door was covered in a thick layer of ice, much too thick for him to break through with sheer strength. Even if he shouted at the top of his lungs (which was starting to seem like a very good idea now), he doubted Davies would be able to hear him or break through the ice in time to help him. Nor would Sparky be able to hear him, either.

That meant Space was all on his own. And to be frank, he wasn't very thrilled about that.

The icebot (that was what Space decided to call it, until he could find out what it actually was) was still slowly, but steadily, making its way over to Space, like the little murderous assassin robot that could. Space wondered why it wasn't moving any faster until he realized that the icebot didn't need to. Sooner or later its ice would cover Space and then he would become the world's most realistic human ice statue. It was in no hurry, perhaps also because Space wasn't its target. Mother was.

Yet Space didn't move from the door. He looked desperately around the hallway for anything he could use as a weapon, but sadly enough Mother didn't appear to keep any other emergency weapons racks on hand. He picked up his frozen laser pistol and hurled it at the icebot with all his strength. The frozen pistol smashed against the icebot's body, breaking into a million pieces that did absolutely nothing to halt its slow and steady walk.

Mother will kill me for that, Space thought. *Assuming the icebot doesn't kill me first.*

Then Space looked up at the ceiling. The chandelier still hung there and the icebot had yet to get underneath it. Yet if Space could figure out how to drop the chandelier on it when it got underneath ...

But how do I do that? Space thought. *If I hadn't destroyed the dumb laser pistol, I might have been able to shoot it. And I don't have anything else I can shoot it with.*

Space shivered and noticed that a thin, almost invisible layer of ice had formed on his shoulders. He quickly wiped the ice off and understood that he really didn't have time to think. Just act.

That was when a crazy idea occurred to him. It was insane, and even if it worked, he'd probably end up in the hospital, but it was the only idea that had even a remote chance of working and he was willing to take his chances if it meant he would not become the world's most realistic human ice statue. Besides, he had done far stupider, deadlier things in the past (like the time he wrestled a space tiger to the ground, for example).

So Space ran full tilt at the icebot, which by now was directly underneath the frozen chandelier. He slipped and slid on the ice a few times, but didn't let that stop him, yelling as loudly as he could, trying to appear far scarier than he really was. He doubted the icebot would be afraid, but hopefully his sudden charge at it would make it pause for at least a moment.

Much to his delight, it did. The icebot halted and, though it had no real eyes or head to speak of, Space thought it was looking at him in confusion. He knew it would recover from that in just a few seconds, after which it would probably act. He could not allow that.

Thus, when Space was close enough, he jumped with all of his might, using the soft, springy soles in his boots to give the jump more power. The icebot followed his trajectory, looking up at him as he came closer. He was blasted full on from the icebot's gelid vent, but he didn't care. He landed on the icebot's shoulders, legs spread apart, with the icebot's vent still spewing cold air at him, but as soon as he felt solid metal beneath his feet, he jumped directly upward, reaching out with both hands.

His fingers wrapped around the bottom of the chandelier, which was frozen solid. Nonetheless, he managed to retain his grip and began swinging back and forth while simultaneously pulling down with all of his weight (which wasn't very much, admittedly, due to his skinniness).

An audible *crack* was all he needed to hear. Still swinging, Space let go of the chandelier when he was at the height of his swing, going flying across the hall even as the chandelier itself snapped off its hook and fell toward the floor. He looked back just in time to see the frozen chandelier crash onto the icebot, smashing the robotic would-be assassin underneath its weight like a tin can.

Space had little time to congratulate himself, however, because he was still flying. He fell on his bottom, which hurt far more than it should have due to the thickness of the ice sheet over the frozen floor, and he was still shivering like crazy. He got to his feet slowly, using the wall to his left for support, and looked down the hall at where the icebot had been standing.

He was pleased to see that the chandelier had done its job. The icebot lay flat underneath its weight, not moving or making any sort of sound at all. When he got around to look at its head, he saw that the vent was crunched shut by the chandelier, meaning that it would no longer freeze up the hallway. He smirked at it.

"Stupid robot," said Space, kicking it in the vent. "Why was I ever afraid of you? Hell, why was *Mother* ever afraid of you?"

The icebot said nothing, probably because it was currently crushed under several pounds of metal and ice.

Space looked up at the door to Mother's room and said, "Geez, if that's all the assassin's got—"

Without warning, Mother's door exploded outward, sending chunks of wood and ice flying in every direction. Several of these chunks hit Space in the chest, sending him sprawling backwards onto the floor. He recovered quickly and looked up at the door— or where the door had been, anyway—in shock.

"Mother?" said Space, scrambling to his feet, trying to avoid tripping over the debris everywhere. "Mother! Are you there? Speak to me!"

He got no answer, prompting him to make his way down the frozen hallway to the open doorway. He managed to get across without any slipping or sliding, as the explosion had also melted most of the ice off the floor, leaving nothing but burnt, slightly soggy carpeting. Space grabbed the edges of the doorway and pulled himself in and was astonished by what he saw.

It wasn't just the door that had been blown open; the entire left half of Mother's bedroom had been blown open, exposing the room to the hot Texas night air. Her dresser was on fire, the scent of expensive perfumes mixing with smoke to create the worst smell Space had ever had the honor of smelling. Mother's security system's alarms were going off somewhere in the house, but Space doubted the police would get in here in time, not in the least because he saw three figures standing where the left wall had been.

Space had never seen them before. One was a large Japanese human, his ripped muscles obvious underneath the Ultra Kevlar armor he wore, a large bazooka-like weapon on his shoulder. Standing next to him was a Kendonian woman, her slimy, snake-like skin as black as the night. She, too, wore Ultra Kevlar armor, but she wasn't nearly as ripped as her partner was.

Standing in between the two was a human woman wearing pure white robes that reminded Space of the priests of Namox. She was perhaps middle-aged, but her hair was as white as her robes and she stood with the gait of someone much older. She didn't appear armed, but something about her appearance set off all kinds of alarms in Space's head nonetheless.

EPISODE THREE: MOTHER

"Jason!" said Mother. "Where the hell were you?"

Space looked at the other end of the room and spotted Mother still sitting in her bed. At least, he thought it was her bed. It looked more like a fortified steel fortress, with a large blast shield that appeared to have taken the brunt of the attack. Mother was still in her night clothes, but her pink silk pajamas failed to make her look weaker than she was.

"Mother?" said Space. "What happened? Who are these people? And where's Davies?"

Space took a step forward as he said that and almost tripped over something. He looked down and grimaced upon seeing a charred black corpse at his feet, which he had no trouble recognizing as Davies.

"The damned fool wasn't behind the blast barrier with me when it blew off," said Mother.

"He screamed before he died," said the Japanese man, his voice much softer than Space expected from someone of his size. "Loudly."

"Of course," said the Kendonian woman, her tongue licking over her lips, "it was hard to hear him over the bomb. No doubt he was calling for his mommy, just like all so-called human men do before they die."

The woman in the middle held up a hand. "Enough. We did not come here to chat. We came here to right what once went wrong so many years ago. And that, Jason Space, must involve the death of your mother."

Space shook his head. "I don't get it. What the hell is going on here and who the hell are you people?"

"Some call me the Prophetess," said the middle-aged woman.

"And these are my two companions and trusted servants, Lloyd Satoshi and Kime."

"The Prophetess?" said Space. His eyes widened. "Wait a minute, I've heard of you before. You're the leader of that one weird cult, the Children of the Starborn, right?"

"I am not a cult leader," said the Prophetess. "But yes, I do lead the Children of the Starborn. I was chosen by the Starborn to rescue a world that has lost its way."

Space—trying his best not to inhale the scent of Davies' burnt corpse—stepped further into the room and said, "Whether you're chosen by the Starborn or not, I will not let you kill my mother. It will be so romantic. I, the brave hero, going up against the chosen one of the gods."

"The Starborn aren't gods," Satoshi said. He put his hands together and looked over his shoulder at the starry sky outside. "They are much higher than that."

Space waved off Satoshi's words. "You're worse than Galaxy, you know that?"

Satoshi looked pissed (which wasn't good because he also looked like he could break down an eight foot thick steel door with his pinkie finger), but the Prophetess held up a hand. "Stand down, Satoshi. There is no need to get angry. We have a mission to do and we cannot waste our precious time arguing with a hopeless romantic like Clare's son."

"Hopeless romantic?" said Space. "Call me what you will, but I prefer to think of myself as an artist who sees the inherent drama and beauty in all of—"

A chunk of debris hit him in the back of the head, causing Space to rub the spot where it had hit and to look at Mother, who had thrown it.

"Mother, what was that for?" said Space.

"For being an idiot," said Mother. "As usual."

"No one appreciates real artists anymore," Space muttered. Then he said, in a louder voice, to the Children, "Where is Sparky?"

"You mean your dumb robot?" said Kime. "Lured him away from the mansion. He's probably still following our robot, thinking he's going to catch the assassin. He's not very smart, although as he is your robot, that doesn't surprise me very much."

Space's fingernails dug into his palm as his hands balled into fists. "So you were the guys who sent that icebot to kill me?"

"Of course," said the Prophetess. "Kime here is an excellent robotic technician. She built the robot and sent it into the mansion to distract you while we killed Clare."

"Joke's on you," said Space. He jerked his thumb over his shoulder at the open doorway behind him. "Because I beat it. It's currently little more than a heap of ice and scrap metal, so you probably just wasted a lot of money and time on something you'll never get to use again. Ha!"

"It doesn't matter," said the Prophetess. "Satoshi should have no trouble killing you. Right, Satoshi?"

Satoshi flexed his muscles and punched his left fist into his open right hand. "Of course, Prophetess. Anything for the advancement of the Starborns' glorious agenda."

"You will be honored in Utopia for your deeds, Satoshi," said the Prophetess, patting him on the back. "I will make sure of it."

Satoshi smiled and stepped forward, aiming his bazooka at Space. "Prepare to meet your maker, infidel."

Space held up his hands. "Wait! I'm sure we can talk this over like the calm, rational adults that we all are."

"There is nothing to discuss," said the Prophetess. "Clare Space has transgressed the dictates of the Starborn. And by attempting to save her life, you have also transgressed the dictates of the Starborn."

"But I don't understand," said Space. "What does Mother have to do with any of you? She was never a member of your cult. Right, Mother? Mother?"

When Space looked at Mother's bed, she was no longer there. A sharp *crack* caused him to look back at the Children of the Starborn. Satoshi was lying on the floor with a fist-shaped dent in his face and standing above him was Mother, looking as fierce as ever, panting hard like she had just run a mile. The Prophetess and Kime had moved away from their fallen ally and were eying Mother with a mixture of surprise and anticipation.

"Do you think I'm just going to sit back and let you kill me and one of my sons?" said Mother. "Not likely. I'd die myself before I let that happen."

"I see you're as agile and athletic as ever, Clare," said the Prophetess, brushing her white hair out of her eyes. "Too bad it won't do you any good."

Kime handed the Prophetess a remote control of some kind. The Prophetess held it above her head and pressed a single red button on it, creating a small 'beep' that Space almost didn't hear because of the wind blowing in from the outside.

As soon as the beep went off, Mother fell to her hands and knees, groaning in pain. She reached out to the Prophetess, but her eyes rolled into the back of her head and she fell face down onto the floor next to the still-unconscious Satoshi.

"Mother!" said Space. "What did you do to her?"

The Prophetess crushed the remote in her hand and tossed it away. "The enhancer serum has nanobots in it that can be activated and deactivated at will, if you know how to do it. Kime here spent many years studying the plans for the enhancer serum and so learned how to deactivate the nanobots that gave Clare her super strength and long life."

"All for the cause of the Starborn," said Kime with a satisfied smile. "Now Clare is nothing more than a weak old woman, as she should be."

Space had to admit that he thought Mother could stand to be humbled, but when he saw the Prophetess draw a long, laser-lined dagger out of the folds of her robes, he knew he had to act.

Scooping up a chunk of debris, Space ran at the two Children of the Starborn. He prepared to hurl the chunk of debris, but Kime was in front of him in a flash and punched him in the gut. The blow was far stronger than Space expected and he dropped the debris just as Kime kneed his chin, sending him sprawling backward as he felt blood drip from his split chin.

Shaking his head, Space barely managed to dodge another punch from Kime, this one aimed for his nose, and responded with a punch of his own. But he was still too slow and tired from the icebot and so Kime dodged his punch, leaving him wide open for a blow from the Kendonian. He was almost knocked off his feet from that blow, but somehow he managed to keep his footing.

He needed a way to beat Kime, and fast, because every time he got a glimpse of the Prophetess, she got closer and closer to

Mother. He didn't entirely understand the science behind how the Prophetess had disabled Mother, but he understood that if he could not defeat Kime, then he would soon have no Mother at all.

He used the fear from that thought to drive his actions. He ducked to avoid another punch from Kime and responded with an uppercut, knocking her head straight up. Before she could recover from that, Space grabbed her head and slammed his skull into hers with all his strength. The blow nearly knocked his lights out, but it only gave him a really bad headache, while Kime fell over unconscious from the blow.

Space didn't stop to make sure she was unconscious (or feel impressed by his own ability to knock her out). He grabbed the laser pistol from her belt (not even bothering to question why she didn't use it when she had the chance) and ran over to where the Prophetess now stood over Mother. The Prophetess raised her knife, its green laser blade glowing in the darkness, but she didn't get a chance to stab Mother because Space fired the laser, knocking the knife out of her hands and into the darkness outside.

The Prophetess didn't scream out in pain or surprise. She calmly turned to face Space, who held his gun aimed straight at her. Her gray eyes unnerved him for some reason, but he chose to ignore that, because he had a feeling that he couldn't let his guard down around the Prophetess for even one second.

"Game over, Prophetess," said Space, his gun hand never wavering. "Give up and I'll make sure the police give you a nicer cell than the one caught assassins like yourself usually go to."

The Prophetess actually yawned, though whether out of tiredness or boredom, Space wasn't sure. "This is a surprise."

"What's a surprise?" said Space. "That I and Mother managed

to beat you and your cronies so easily?"

"No," said the Prophetess, shaking her head. "What surprises me is how dutiful a son you are. Clare was always cruel to you; not abusive, certainly, but she never did love you the way you wanted her to, did she?"

The Prophetess's words dug into Space's heart like a knife, but he showed no emotion. "Shut up or I will shoot that mouth of yours clean off your face."

"She never supported you or your dreams," said the Prophetess. "She wanted you to be a lawyer, constantly pushed you in that direction, until the day came that you ran away from home to pursue your dream of becoming an actor. I see that didn't pan out, did it?"

Space's hand shook ever-so-slightly. "I said shut up."

The Prophetess stepped forward, her expression as neutral as always, her voice as calming as the sound of the ocean tide. "She never approved of you becoming a space explorer and she certainly never approved of the hybrid Helena Galaxy, your best friend in the whole universe, now did she?"

"How do you know so much about me?" said Space, his voice trembling, despite his best efforts to steady it. "I've never even met you before. Looked me up online?"

"No," said the Prophetess with a sigh. "You see, Jason Space, Clare was once a Daughter of the Starborn. She and I were close, closer than sisters. Even after she left, I had people watching her, seeing how she compromised with the world's values and expectations, and even married and had children. I also had my people watching her children, including you. I know more about you than you know about yourself, I imagine."

"No, you don't," said Space. "You're lying. Mother was never a Child of the Starborn. You're making things up."

The Prophetess tilted her head toward Mother, as if listening to her speak. "I hear no protests from Clare. Were I attempting to deceive you, she would have spoken up by now, even in her weakened state. Say what you will about Clare, but she values honesty almost above her own life."

Mother was looking up at them both now. Space tried to look into her eyes, tried to see if the Prophetess's words had any truth to them, but Mother refused to meet his gaze, which just confirmed his worst fear.

"Why did you wait until now to try to kill her?" said Space. "Why didn't you kill her when she first quit?"

The Prophetess cast a gaze—not exactly loving, but not full of hate, either—in Mother's direction. "As I said, we were closer than sisters. Besides, it wasn't until three months ago that I felt the need to do this."

"What happened three months ago?" said Space, who despite himself found his curiosity growing by the second.

A frown crossed the Prophetess's face briefly, replaced almost immediately by her usual neutral expression. "A journalist from the largest news organization in the Universal Alliance, *The Universal Times*, was going to interview Clare about us. How the Children of the Starborn were founded, our secrets, our plans … all of it would have been revealed to the public. We could not let that happen, which is why I tried my hardest to have her life ended."

"So you reprogrammed the training robots, sent in the fake nurse to poison her, and caused her hover car to crash?" said

Space. "You're evil, lady."

"Evil? Hardly," said the Prophetess. "Nonetheless, you are correct in that I indirectly had a hand in all of that. I was hoping to scare Clare, make her decide it was not worth sharing our secrets with the public, but alas, I forgot just how stubborn and determined Clare can be when she puts her mind to something."

She sounded almost admiring of Mother, but Space didn't stop to question that. He just said, "So now you're finally trying to kill her yourself."

"With your help," said the Prophetess. "Potentially."

Space didn't even lower his gun. "Are you insane? Why would I ever kill my own mother?"

"For being a bad mother, of course," said the Prophetess. "Do you have any real love for her in your heart? If she were to die today for no reason, would you cry? Or would you instead stoically visit the funeral home to prepare her body for burial?"

Space grit his teeth. "I don't have to answer that."

"But you do," said the Prophetess. "Your answer dictates whether you shoot me or whether you shoot her. Your choice."

Space would never shoot Mother. Never. He didn't even know why he was considering it. He supposed the Prophetess's words were wriggling into his brain, making him think things that would never cross his mind normally. He ignored them with all of his might.

And yet … he couldn't just ignore them. There was some truth to what she said. Mother had never been very supportive of Space. She disapproved of his choice of job, his friends, his interests … everything about him, she disliked (or so it seemed, at least). As a matter of fact, Space could not think of even one aspect of himself that Mother genuinely liked.

That thought alone made him lower the gun. He didn't aim it at Mother. He just threw it at his feet and fell to his knees.

The Prophetess walked over to him, bent over, and picked up the gun. She hefted it in her hands, looking more than a little pleased, and said, "I had hoped you would be the one to pull the trigger, Jason, but I suppose it doesn't matter. Clare will be dead either way. You just stay here and try not to get in the way."

Space looked up at her as she walked away. He thought about getting up and stopping her. He could probably overpower her if he wanted to … but did he *want* to?

He just sat there on his knees, watching as the Prophetess aimed the gun squarely at Mother's head. Mother looked, not into the eyes of her would-be killer, but into the eyes of Space. She looked betrayed and heartbroken, which just made Space feel even more confused than before. All he could do was shake his head as the Prophetess's trigger finger lay on the gun's trigger.

Then a familiar sound of jets entered his ears and Sparky flew in through the broken wall. He watched, mouth agape, as Sparky tackled the Prophetess to the ground, causing her to drop the gun. The Prophetess struggled against Sparky's grasp, but he was much stronger than her and held her down with ease.

"What the—?" said the Prophetess in shock. "How did you get here? I thought you were distracted by our robot!"

"Yes, well, I heard the explosion when I was a couple of miles away," said Sparky, with no strain in his voice as the Prophetess struggled against him. "That's when I realized it was all a trick to lure me away from the mansion. Looks like I just made it in time."

Space shook his head and got to his feet. "Good job, Sparks. Glad you could make it."

Sparky's head swiveled around in a complete circle to look at Space. "I hope you weren't harmed, Mr. Space."

"Of course I wasn't," said Space, wiping the blood from his chin. "I was just … well, she's a lot tougher than she looks."

The words felt fake on his lips, but Sparky didn't seem to notice. The robot simply said, "All right. Well, I've already contacted the police, so they should be here any minute to arrest these—"

He didn't get to finish his sentence because Satoshi—who had until this point had not moved even an inch—immediately jumped to his feet and grabbed Sparky and hurled him to the other side of the room. Sparky went flying over Space's head again, causing Space to duck. He turned to see Sparky crash into the blast shield around Mother's bed, where he lay in an obvious daze.

"Sparky!" said Space, holding out a hand, but he didn't get a chance to move forward because Kime appeared in front of him and kicked him in the groin.

The pain that exploded in his pelvic area was profound. His voice became super high as he fell to the floor, clutching his hurting area as Kime stepped over to him. He reached up weakly with one hand to stop her, but she just batted it away with out looking at him. He turned on his side and saw Satoshi carrying the Prophetess in his arms like a large baby.

"Stop …" said Space, trying to man up as best as he could and failing. "You bastards …"

"I'm sorry, Jason," said the Prophetess from her spot in

Satoshi's arms. "But it appears we must leave. The police will be here any minute and we have no interest in spending the rest of the night in jail. Just remember what I said about Clare and, if you want, you can contact me sometime and we can talk."

The Prophetess drew something from the folds of her robes and tossed it to Space over Kime's head. A small plastic card of some sort landed in front of Space's face, but he didn't pay attention to it. He just watched vainly as the three Children of the Starborn ran over to the blown open wall and jumped down out of sight. Mother was still on her hands and knees, muttering a thousand ugly curses under her breath as those three would-be assassins disappeared.

A few minutes later, Space heard the familiar siren of the police cars in the distance growing gradually closer to Mother's mansion with each passing second. But that didn't matter because the Children of the Starborn were gone and Space wasn't sure what to think. He just grabbed the card that the Prophetess had given him and stuffed it into his pocket to look at later. Right now, he and Sparky were going to have a long talk with the police and he did not want to be distracted from that.

The next morning, after the police had questioned Space and Sparky about the attack on the mansion and left, Space found himself in the Grand Ridge Hospital in downtown Neo-Austin, where Mother had been taken the night before. She was lying in a hospital bed, wearing a hospital gown, looking quite tired. The doctor had assured Space that Mother was going to be all right and that she'd be able to go home in a few days, but that didn't make Space feel any better for some reason.

EPISODE THREE: MOTHER

The only three people in the room were Mother, Sparky, and Space himself. Mother lay in her bed, looking like the old woman she was, with a vase of blue bonnet flowers plucked from her garden on the stand next to her. Space sat on a stool by her bed, while Sparky stood next to him, his hands folded behind his back.

"How do you feel now, Mother?" said Space. He rubbed the bandage on his own split chin, which one of Mother's doctors had put on him to help his chin heal.

Mother glared at him. "How do you *think* I feel? I feel like all of my years are finally starting to catch up with me. Is this how old age feels?"

Space shrugged, while Sparky said, "Mistress Space, have the doctors been able to figure out how to reactive your nanobots?"

Mother shook her head. "No. And I doubt any of them could. Only the scientists involved with the Enhancer Program could do that and they all … er, died several years back."

"Does this mean you're going to be a regular human from now on?" said Sparky.

"Of course not," Mother said. "I'm going to find the best biomechanical technicians in the UA and have them fix me right up. I've still got my money and money is all you need to get what you want."

"I suppose that means you're going to hire a new butler as well?" said Space.

Mother looked at Space like he was an idiot. "Of course not. Davies will continue to serve me as always."

Space stared at her blankly. He scratched the back of his head, wondering if Mother was beginning to lose her mind now. "Uh, Mother, you do realize that Davies was burnt to a crisp, right?

Even the doctors said he is dead."

"So?" said Mother. "I have clones of him stored in the basement of the mansion. I'll just wake one of them up and have him serve me."

"I did not know you had clones of Davies, Mistress Space," said Sparky.

"Well, it's a lot cheaper than hiring a new guy or buying an expensive robot," said Mother. "I don't have to train him. All I have to do is wake up the clone, tell him what to do, and he'll do it just as well as the original Davies."

Sparky stroked his chin. "Did Davies consent to that?"

"Of course he did," said Mother in annoyance. "It was in his contract. He is the loyalest butler I've ever known. Besides, this isn't the first time this has happened; just last year, the ship that the original Davies was flying in on his way between Earth and Cao exploded. The Davies you spoke to and worked with the whole time was a clone."

"Oh," said Sparky. "I did not even realize it. He must have been a high quality clone."

"The best money can buy," said Mother. "When you're as loaded as I am, you buy nothing less than the best."

Space nodded, without really thinking about it. "Right."

Mother looked at Space as though he was being stupid. "What are you thinking about? You're usually a lot more talkative than this."

"The Prophetess," said Space. "She said you were once a Child of the Starborn. Is that true?"

Mother looked down at her blankets, her hand gripping the edge of her blanket tightly. "Yes, Jason, that is. I was one of the first converts to the Children. Happened after the War, but before I began practicing law."

"But why?" said Space. "Why would you do that? I thought you were too smart for cults."

Mother sighed and looked out the window at the bustling city. "I was young and impressionable after the War; and besides, it was only for a few months. I saw and did a lot of horrible things in the War and didn't know how to make sense of it. When I met the Prophetess … well, I thought she would help me understand."

"So why did you leave them?" said Space.

Mother still didn't look up at Space. "Because I found out that the Children of the Starborn were just like real children: whiny, childish, and immature. They couldn't handle any sort of criticism, even from fellow members. I criticized the way they approached non-members, but when I did, they kicked me out."

"That is common in cults," said Sparky in his usual matter-of-fact way. "Most cultists cannot handle any sort of criticism at all. I am surprised they did not kill you then."

Her hands wrapped tightly around her blankets, Mother nodded. "I know. I suppose they didn't consider me a threat. I kept their secrets for years, seeing no reason to tell anyone what I knew about them, but eventually I grew tired of that burden and contacted *The Universal Times* for an interview. I kept having to put it off, however, because of the attacks."

"Are you still going through with the interview?" said Space.

Before Mother could answer, the door to her room burst open and a thin man wearing an old-fashioned overcoat walked through. He had a handsome face, almost like a movie star, and carried a small tablet in his hands with the initials 'TUT' written on the back.

"Mistress Space!" said the man, sounding out of breath, like he'd ran a mile. "I am pleased to see you are okay. Still up for the interview, I suppose?"

"Who's this?" said Space, turning to face the man.

The man held out a thin hand, giving off a dazzling smile. "The name's Charles Raymond McDonald, *The Universal Times* reporter and the best interviewer in the UA. And you are …?"

Space shook McDonald's hand. "Jason Space."

McDonald raised an intrigued eyebrow. "Are you Clare Space's son?"

Space hesitated for a fraction of a second. "Yes, I am."

"And you saved your mother's life last night, right?" said McDonald. He held the tip of his stylus against his tablet's screen. "The police wouldn't tell me much about the attack, but I got a few details out of them and they said you were there."

"Oh, it wasn't just me," said Space. He pointed at Sparky. "Sparky helped, too."

"What a modest son you've got here, Mistress Space," said McDonald, looking around Space at Mother.

Mother laughed. "Of course. My own modesty must have rubbed off on him."

McDonald seemed to miss Mother's sarcasm. He looked at Space again and said, "Jason—"

"Call me Mr. Space," said Space. "I don't like to be called by my first name."

McDonald raised his other eyebrow, which made him look surprised. "Okay. Well, Mr. Space, would you be willing to sit down with your mother for the interview? I'm sure the readers of the *Times* would love to read about how the son of a famous former Earth lawyer saved his mother's life by himself."

"But I didn't do it by myself," said Space. He pointed at Sparky again. "Sparky helped."

"Right, right," said McDonald, without so much as glancing at Sparky. "So what do you say? Interview?"

Space shook his head. "Sorry, but I've got to go. I just came by to see how my mother is doing. I'm really not interested in talking to the press right now."

McDonald frowned. "Are you absolutely sure? Your picture will be all over the news, be seen on every planet in the Universal Alliance. Doesn't that sound good?"

Despite himself, Space smiled. "Actually, when you put it *that* way—"

Sparky tugged at Space's sleeve. "Mr. Space, we really must go. We said we'd meet Captain Galaxy at two. It's currently one forty-five and I don't think we should be late. She'll get angry."

"Yeah, yeah, sure," said Space, though he wasn't really paying attention to Sparky. He was still addressing McDonald. "I think I can spare a few minutes answering a couple of questions."

"Wonderful," said McDonald. "Then let's begin the interview, shall we?"

Space and Sparky rematerialized in the teleporter room of the *Adventure* an hour later. Space blinked and stretched out the kinks in his muscles that always developed whenever they teleported, saying as he did so, "Well, that McDonald guy sure was great, wasn't he, Sparky?"

A loud 'Hmph!' made Space and Sparky look before them.

Galaxy was standing in front of the teleporter terminal, tapping her fingers against the terminal's touch screen surface. Her frown was not encouraging, to say the least.

"Oh, hey, Galaxy," said Space, waving at her. "Sorry we were late. It's just that an interviewer from *The Universal Times* dropped by as we were leaving and he offered to make me a star."

Galaxy raised an eyebrow, not unlike how McDonald did. "What?"

"Not exactly a star," said Sparky. "He just said that Space's face would be all over the UA when his interview was done."

Galaxy groaned. "Great. Just what we need: publicity. You know how much I hate publicity, right?"

Space folded his arms in front of his chest. "So what? It was just an interview. It's not like it's the end of the world or anything."

Galaxy sighed. "Whatever. How is your mother, by the way?"

"Wait, you actually care about her?" said Space.

"No," said Galaxy. "I just wanted to change the subject before I threw something at you for being late and doing something stupid again."

"Mistress Space is doing fine," said Sparky. "She's still recovering from losing her enhanced abilities, but she's already planning to repair her mansion, except this time she is going to add state-of-the-art security systems and hire the best private guards she can find."

"Ah," said Galaxy, without any enthusiasm. "Good for her, I guess. You guys gotta tell me about what happened last night. Wish I could have been there to help."

That was when Space remembered the plastic card, which was

still in his pocket. He shrugged and said, "Eh, don't feel too bad. There probably wasn't much you could have done. No need to worry."

"If you say so," said Galaxy. "Well, I'm going to set the *Adventure*'s course. We're going to Orq, I believe, so that will be a long trip. You two should go rest up before we head off there."

"Thank you, Captain Galaxy," said Sparky. "I need to recharge my batteries, anyway. This whole ordeal has been extremely taxing on my energy level."

"Yeah," said Space as he walked off the teleporter platform. "I haven't gotten a good night's sleep in like, two days, and that's pretty unusual for me. I need my beauty sleep, after all."

Galaxy rolled her eyes. "Right."

Not long after that, Space sat on his bed in his room, turning the plastic card the Prophetess had given him over in his hands. He had not told either Galaxy or Sparky about it, mostly because he had not seen any reason to. He didn't want them to worry about him. Besides, he doubted he would read it. He'd just toss it out and never think about it again. What could the Children of the Starborn possibly offer him?

Then again, Space thought as he swiped his plastic card through the card reader built into his com-watch, *what does just looking at it hurt? I'll just see what the Prophetess has to say and toss it out after that. Then I can just forget about the Children of the Starborn and go back to adventuring with Galaxy and Sparky again.*

Spacetastic Interviews with:

Clare Space

T.L. Charles: Hello and welcome, readers, to the Spacetastic Interviews series. In this series, I, T.L. Charles, the author, interview a character from *The Spacetastic Adventures of Mr. Space and Captain Galaxy* series, usually a character who appeared in the last episode. These interviews tend to be short, but entertaining and informative. Anyway, with that out of the way, let me introduce y'all to Clare Space, the mother of Mr. Space, one of the protagonists of the series. Mistress Space, will you say hi to the readers?

Clare Space: Hello, readers of the stories of my irresponsible son and his silly friend, how are you all today?

T.L. Charles: I take it you don't think highly of your son's adventures, Mistress Space.

Clare Space: Please, call me Clare. And yes, I don't think that Jason's idiotic 'job' is in any way, shape, or form responsible. He ought to have been a lawyer, but he was too stupid for that, so he became a 'space explorer' instead.

T.L. Charles: Well, I notice that you call him 'Jason' and not 'Mr. Space.' Why is that?

Clare Space: Because I'm his mother and I am not calling him 'mister.' Why should I indulge my son in his stupid fantasies? He can call himself whatever he likes, but he'll always be Jason to me, even though I know he finds that name embarrassing. Don't know why, since Jason's a fine name if you ask me. *Mr. Space*, on the other hand, is an embarrassing name.

T.L. Charles: I see. Well, what about Mr. Space's siblings? I believe he has three, correct?

Clare Space: Yep. There's Alex, his older brother, Alicia, his younger sister, and Kristy, his youngest sister. All three of them took up respectable professions and don't insist that everyone else call them by their last name.

T.L. Charles: What kind of jobs do they have?

Clare: Alex is a member of the Annulus Defense Force. He protects the Annulus from all kinds of threats. Makes me proud, seeing as the lives of millions of people are in his hands, although I always worry about his safety, because it is a dangerous job, after all.

Then there's Alicia. She's a doctor on Namox, providing free healthcare for the poor. Again, very respectable, although I don't like her husband, who is a Namoxian with an impossible to pronounce name. He's a pansy, but even he has a more respectable job than Jason. Some kind of government office worker or whatever. I don't know. Don't like Namoxians much.

And finally, there's Kristy. She's just graduated from the University of Earth last year with a major in starship engineering and is working for Master Builders, Inc. Kind of like Space's lady friend, except far more responsible and not as stupid.

T.L. Charles: Family reunions must be something.

Clare: Oh, they are, when we can get everyone. That's not even counting my siblings and *their* children. My sister has three kids of her own, and my younger brother and his wife are expecting their second child. All I know is that my nephews and nieces will definitely not be in any way like Jason when they grow up. I will see to it myself if I have to.

T.L. Charles: I see. Well, what did you think about the episode? Any thoughts on the Children of the Starborn?

Clare: Next time they show up in my front lawn, I'm pulling out the machine guns and gunning them down right where they stand. And don't worry about me going to jail for murder; I know of a case where a man did the same thing I did and the court let him off scott-free, so I will be just fine legally if I can make my case in the right court.

T.L. Charles: Well, looks like we're almost out of time. Clare, any last words for my readers before we close out?

Clare: Yeah. Stop reading these stories. You're only encouraging Jason to keep up at this stupid profession. Does he get paid royalties for every copy sold or something?

T.L. Charles: (hurriedly) Well, uh, that's all for now, folks. Please turn the page for *Episode Four: Never Work with Old Bosses*! See you at the next Spacetastic Interview!

Episode Four
Never Work with Old Bosses

*C*aptain Helena Galaxy stood in her shower, enjoying the warmth of the hot water as it poured all over her body. She worked her hair, putting cherry shampoo in it that she then worked hard at getting out. She also applied some coconut body lotion to her body, softening her skin and making her feel a lot better.

During the last few days, Galaxy had been working all day and all night on adding some necessary improvements to the *Adventure*'s weapon systems, with only a few hours of sleep here and there. This had gotten her extremely dirty and sweaty, but she had almost completely ignored her personal hygiene in favor of the work, which she had been meaning to get around to for some time. In fact, the only reason she was taking a shower now was at the suggestion of her friend, Mr. Jason Space, who had promised her that the ship wouldn't go anywhere in her absence. It had taken a lot to convince her of that, but eventually she agreed to the shower when Space threatened to have their robot servant Sparky drag her to the shower kicking and screaming. Considering how strong Sparky was, Galaxy did not argue with that.

Now that Galaxy actually was taking a shower, however, she

was amazed at how dirty and tired she had actually been. She had watched the grime go down the drain with the water along with the soap suds from the shampoo and conditioner she'd used. It made her quite glad that she had listened to her friends.

Right now, all she wanted to do was stand in the shower's hot water forever, letting the heat open her pores and cleanse her skin. It was very nice.

Still doesn't change the fact that we need spare parts, though, Galaxy thought, taking in the scent of cherry and coconut that now filled the shower, which she enjoyed quite a bit. *Only question is, where are we going to get all those parts when we barely have enough money to pay for the* Adventure*'s fuel?*

That was when a loud alarm went off, an alarm that almost caused her to slip and fall. Thankfully, a robotic hand popped out of the shower wall just then and grabbed her waist before she fell and cracked her head on the floor of the shower. It then placed her upright, patted her on the back and gave her a thumbs up, and then retreated back into the wall.

Shaking her head, Galaxy turned off the shower and stepped out of it into the rest of her head. Wrapping a towel around her body—because it was very cold outside of the shower—Galaxy activated the intercom on the wall by pressing a button. Leaning in close to the intercom, Galaxy said, "Space, what's the alarm for?"

"We've got a visitor," said Space, his voice crackling over the intercom. "And they want to talk to you."

Puzzled, Galaxy asked, "A visitor? What do you mean?"

"Could you just come to the command deck and see for yourself?" said Space. "They want their identity to be a surprise.

And they're really impatient."

Now that was suspicious, although Galaxy didn't say so. "All right. I just need to get dressed and I'll be there in a jiffy."

A few minutes later, Galaxy entered the command deck of the *Adventure*, brushing her slightly damp black hair out of her eyes as she said, "All right, Space, where are our—"

She stopped dead upon seeing a familiar face on the largest computer monitor, a tiger-like Vicanite that could only be one being.

"Liox," said Galaxy, folding her arms coldly. "Long time, no see."

Liox smiled, revealing row upon row of sharp, tiger-like teeth. Like all Vicanites, Liox somewhat resembled a tiger, except her red eyes gleamed with a cleverness that few members of her species possessed. Though Galaxy could only see the Vicanite's head and shoulders, she had no troubling imagining the rest of her body, which was hairier, more muscular, and bigger than the average human.

"Hey, Galaxy, what's up?" said Liox, leaning her head on her fist. "How have you been? I see you've got your own ship now. Congrats."

Mr. Space, who sat on the floating command chair, looked between Galaxy and Liox with a frown on his face. "Um, I'm confused. You two know each other?"

Galaxy nodded, without taking her eyes off Liox's ugly face. "Yes. I used to work for Liox in her starship-building company, Intergalactic Industrial, the biggest ship-building company within the Universal Alliance."

"And we're still going strong, even though you were one of our best engineers," said Liox, shaking her head. "I still don't know what you were thinking when you quit, but as my meditation teacher says, 'Your journey is your own and no one can tell you what to do.'"

"I quit, if you don't remember, because you're an idiot," said Galaxy, leaning against the door frame. "You told me to build ships one way, but that way was stupid, so I built them a better way. And you didn't like that."

Liox's mouth twitched for a moment, like she was about to shout. Galaxy recognized it because Liox had yelled at her several times when she used to work for her, so she prepared to tell the computer to shut off Liox's connection with their ship if she started acting up.

Instead, Liox took a deep breath, muttered what sounded like a children's nursery rhyme under her breath as if to calm herself, and said, "Well, let bygones be bygones, right? I came to you because I thought we had both matured enough to put our petty animosity behind us both."

"You, mature?" Galaxy said with a smirk. "As if. You are the most immature, selfish, narcissistic bore in the entire universe. And I know Space here."

"Galaxy!" said Space, putting one hand over his mouth. "Why would you be so rude to our guest? And what do you mean, you 'know' me? Are you saying I'm as bad as her?"

Before Galaxy had to answer that, Liox waved one of her large, paw-like hands, saying "No, Mr. Space, she's perfectly justified in what she just said about me. I have been immature. I'm only two hundred years old, after all, which by Vicanite standards is pretty young. I acknowledge my flaws."

Liox's flowery tone didn't convince Galaxy at all, but for now she didn't feel the need to berate and insult her former boss. As fun as it was, Galaxy decided it was better to figure out what Liox had come to her for instead, even though she didn't really want to talk to her anymore.

"Why are you here, Liox?" said Galaxy. "What do you want from me? Make it quick, because we don't have time to waste talking with people who don't pay."

"Glad you asked," said Liox, rubbing her paws together. "You see, a few weeks back, a rival ship-building company, Master Builders, Inc., hired some Black Stars to steal some of my company's secret plans for our newest starship. These are extremely valuable and we want them back right away."

"Black Stars?" Space said with a gulp. "You mean the best professional assassin organization in the universe, whose leader, Black Nova, is wanted on every member planet within the Universal Alliance?"

"The same one," said Liox, nodding. "Because you two are known as brave space explorers, I thought I would offer you the chance to break into the headquarters of Master Builders, retrieve the plans, and bring them back to me."

"We're not mercenaries, thieves, or idiots, for that matter," said Galaxy, shaking her head. "We're not going to risk our lives just for your stupid plans. Sorry."

"What a shame," said Liox with a sigh. "And here I was hoping that your reputation as brave explorers was genuine. Looks like it was all talk."

"We're brave," Galaxy replied, "but not stupid. Why don't you go to the Universal Alliance Mercenaries Guild instead? I'm sure you can find someone who'd do it for the right price there. As it is, there's nothing you can offer us that would make us break into a building guarded by some of the most dangerous assassins with the UA."

Liox looked down at her hands, a gesture that Galaxy remembered her ex-boss always did when she was about to do or say something dishonest. "Well, Galaxy, I don't really want to get the Guild caught up in this. I just think this is a job the two of you could pull off easily."

"As Galaxy said, we're not thieves," said Space, scratching the back of his head. "We're explorers. Adventurers. Like Galaxy said, you might be interested in going to the Guild."

Again, Liox sighed. "All right. I guess that year's supply of ship parts I have lying in our warehouses in Zaron will just have to go to waste, then."

"A year's supply of ship parts?" Galaxy said. She pushed herself off the door frame and stood up straight. "What do you mean?"

Liox smiled, which made her look even more hideous to Galaxy. "I mean that there is currently a year's supply of spare ship parts—for a starship very much like your own—in one of our Zaronian warehouses, of course. I *was* thinking of using them as payment should you accept the job, but since it's very clear to me that you're not interested, I suppose I'll—"

"We'll do it," said Galaxy. "We'll steal back those plans from Master Builders and bring 'em back to you in exchange for those spare parts. And we'll do it fast, too, so you don't have to wait long for them."

"Excellent," said Liox. She typed on an out-of-sight keyboard. "Now I am sending you the coordinates of the Master Builders main shipyard, where we believe they are currently keeping the plans. They're plans for our newest ship model, the Galactic Crosser 89. You'll recognize them when you see them."

"All right," said Galaxy. "Well, Liox, it's a pleasure doing business with you. Once we retrieve the plans, we'll be sure to let you know. We can then arrange a date and time for us to pick up the spare parts from your Zaronian warehouse."

"Excellent," said Liox. "I'm glad to see that you can just let bygones be bygones, Galaxy. You really have matured since you quit the company, haven't you?"

"Yes," said Galaxy, still smiling. "And you haven't matured a bit, you selfish cat. Good bye."

Galaxy snapped her fingers, prompting the computer to cut off the transmission before Liox could respond in kind.

The command chair spun around in time for Space to look at Galaxy like she had just lost her mind. "Galaxy, you do realize what you just signed us up for, right?"

Galaxy nodded as she walked over to the map monitor—a large computer screen that displayed a map of the area of space they were in at the moment—on the right side of the deck and began inputting the coordinates that had just appeared on it. "Of course. What, do you think I'd accept a job without good reason?"

"But this goes against our ethics," said Space as he flew over to her on his floating chair. "Don't you remember the oath we signed when we first started adventuring together? The Space Adventurer's Oath, first written and codified by the great human space explorer Moktashef Tawfeek centuries ago?"

Without looking at him, Galaxy said, "Yes, I remember it."

"Then repeat it."

Galaxy sighed. "Do I have to?"

"Yes. And I'm not going to leave you alone until you say it."

Right now, Galaxy wanted to strangle Space, but she restrained herself. With another sigh, she said, without any real enthusiasm, "'As adventurers of the grand cosmos, we pledge to discover new worlds and new adventures and to have fun while doing it. We will never do paid mercenary work, no matter how good the offer, for we are explorers and not mercenaries. We will complete every mission we undertake, no matter how much trouble it will get us into. And we will never give up, regardless of whatever menacing aliens or dangerous obstacles we run into.'"

"See?" said Space. "Right there, in the oath you specifically signed, is our promise not to do stuff like this."

Galaxy finished inputting the coordinates and then turned to look at Space. "Look, I know how important things like oaths are you to and all, but didn't you hear what Liox said? A year's supply of spare parts for this ship. All for free. Think of the things I could do to the *Adventure* with all those parts. All of the improvements and repairs I could make, all without breaking the bank."

Space pursed his lips. "But we might get in trouble. I mean, *legal* trouble. What if the Master Builders find us? We might get arrested and—"

"Space," said Galaxy. "Do you remember the other part of the oath? You know, the part where we vow to never run away from a mission just because we might get into trouble?"

"Yes, I do," said Space, scratching the back of his head. "But

162

that doesn't apply to situations like this."

"Listen, it's not going to be a hard job," said Galaxy. "Besides, weren't you listening to Liox? She said that those plans belonged to her company. We're actually going to be doing a noble thing by stealing back what rightfully belongs to Intergalactic Industrial. This is perfectly consistent with the Oath."

"When you put it that way, I suppose it doesn't sound too bad," said Space. "Okay. I guess we can do it, if we're going to be doing a good thing."

"Finally," said Galaxy. "Now get Sparky. I have a feeling it's going to require all of us working together to pull it off without being caught."

About a week later, the *Adventure* touched down at the Zaron Shipyard, a shipyard located just above the planet it was named after. Due to the immense size of most starships that the Master Builders built, they did most of their construction in constructed shipyards that floated above Zaron, which did not make them very different from Intergalactic Industrial or any other ship-building company in that regard.

As Galaxy and Space exited their ship, walking across the bridge connecting the *Adventure* to the Shipyard itself, Galaxy couldn't help but look around the shipyard. It was an extremely large place, with enough room for dozens of large starships (although at the moment there were only a few docked). Even larger hanger doors allowed starships to enter and exit at will, while a transparent energy field retained the air that Galaxy, Space, and the other organic beings in the Shipyard needed in order to survive. In comparison to the large ships around here, the *Adventure* was rather tiny, but Galaxy didn't feel inadequate about that, as their ship served its purpose well despite its size.

It's probably better constructed than most of the ships here anyway, Galaxy thought. *I was never impressed by most Master Builder ships. They design their exhaust ports weirdly.*

She also noticed a large office building far away from them. Based on Galaxy's research of the Shipyard, that building was the main office, which was likely where the stolen plans were kept. A dozen or so large crates full of ship parts stood between them and the building, but that seemed to be the only major obstacle she could see at the moment.

Almost as soon as Galaxy and Space stepped onto the platform, a huge, hairy ape-like creature, wearing a gray uniform that looked a little too tight over his massive chest, approached them. The Zaronian—which was the only thing the creature could be—wore thick gloves over his large hands and walked with surprising grace for a being of his size, using his large hands as forelegs.

"Welcome, travelers," said the Zaronian with a smile. "My name is Kigin. I assume that your ship is the modified Star-Shooter 12B that you asked us to inspect?"

Galaxy returned the smile, even though she did not feel like smiling. "Of course. My name is Mary Lacy and this is my husband, William Chandler. Are you going to inspect the ship for us yourself?"

"No, ma'am," said Kigin, shaking his head. He gestured at a group of his fellow Zaronians carrying toolboxes and wearing similar gray uniforms, although theirs were greasier than his.

"Got a team right here that will be able to look it over. You and your friend can come with me to wait, if you want. We have an entertainment center set up for those who're waiting for their ship inspection to be over. It has a virtual reality simulator, extreme bowling, and a bumper ship track, among other things."

Galaxy beamed a fake smile. "Oh, that sounds excellent! Doesn't it, William?"

Space also faked a smile, though it looked more real than Galaxy's. "Indeed it does, Mary. It reminds me of the time we spent at the fabulous vacation resort of Relaxed Tip back on Earth. Oh, that certainly was a wonderful time!"

"You have been to Relaxed Tip?" Kigin said. "I've been interested in taking my family there for a vacation, what with school getting out for the kids and all in a few months. Is it good?"

"It's absolutely smashing, my friend," said Space, with a stab at a British accent. "I do believe your family would love it. Especially the water slides, which I'm sure your children would love."

Kigin nodded politely. "Well, you'll have to tell me more about it later. I'll take you to the entertainment center while my crew inspects the ship."

"Lead the way, my good friend," said Space with an exaggerated bow. "We shall follow you wherever you may lead. God save the Queen and all that."

Kigin didn't say anything to that, although whether it was because he was too polite to point out how strange Space was acting or if he simply thought of it as typical strange human behavior, it was impossible to tell. He simply started walking toward a large nearby building with flashing lights that had to be the entertainment center. Space and Galaxy followed closely behind, but not close enough that he could hear them if they whispered to each other.

"So far, so good," Galaxy whispered to Space. "He thinks we're just a couple of normal customers. You keep him distracted while I slip away to that building over there to look for the blueprints." She gestured at the square office building she had noticed earlier, though discreetly so that their guide would not notice.

Space looked at her quizzically. "What do I tell him if he notices you're missing?"

"Tell him that I had to go to get something back from the ship," Galaxy said. "Okay?"

"Okay," said Space, nodding. "I'll have fun pretending to be William Chandler while you risk getting arrested."

Galaxy punched him in the arm and hissed, "Get serious."

"Okay, okay," Space muttered, rubbing his arm. "No need to hit so hard."

So as they walked, Galaxy slipped behind a large crate that was labeled 'JUNK.' She glanced around it and saw Space still following Kigin, who didn't appear to have noticed her disappearance just yet. And with luck, he never would.

So Galaxy dropped to the floor and tapped her com-watch. "Sparky? Do you read me?"

"Loud and clear, Captain Galaxy," said Sparky's voice over the com-watch's speaker, although Galaxy had adjusted the volume low so no one would hear him. "Where are you currently?"

EPISODE FOUR: NEVER WORK WITH OLD BOSSES

"Hiding behind a crate," said Galaxy. "Space is with our guide and is going to keep him distracted. I'm going to start looking for the blueprints now, as I see where they are probably located. By the way, is the inspection team on board yet?"

"They are," said Sparky. "They're currently inspecting the engines. I'm doing what I can to delay or frustrate their inspection, however, so don't be surprised if the ship is in less than ideal condition by the time you get back."

"Doesn't matter," said Galaxy. "Just keep them distracted and confused until Space and I get back. I'll talk to you later. Bye."

She turned off her com-watch and, after looking around to make sure that no one was around to notice her, began moving from crate to crate toward a nearby building, doing her best not to be spotted. She just hoped that finding the blueprints would not take long, because if she was caught, then she would never hear the end of it from Space.

A few minutes later, Galaxy was behind the main office building. Here she found a back door that she began attempting to unlock, although it was currently being very stubborn and would not budge. It didn't help that she was sure she would be caught at any moment, although as the back of the main offices appeared to be a little traveled area (mostly because she saw no one else here), she gave herself as much time as she needed to open the door.

After a couple more seconds wrestling with the lock, Galaxy sighed in frustration, almost punched the stupid door, and then pulled out a tiny stub of metal from her breast pocket and inserted it in the lock. It was a special invention of hers, designed as a kind of super lock-pick. If she designed it correctly, it would be able to unlock any lock and bypass any security measures. Unfortunately, it was too small for her to retrieve from the lock itself; still, she doubted anyone would be able to trace it to her, seeing as the stub was also designed to disintegrate after activation.

A *click* of the lock told her that the lock-pick had done its job. She creaked open the door slightly and peered through. Thankfully, she didn't see anyone. She did, however, notice a security camera in one corner of the stairwell. While it was not aimed directly at her, it was pointing toward the stairs, which meant there was no way for Galaxy to sneak by unnoticed.

Galaxy had also expected this, however. She closed the door quickly and pulled out of her pocket a long, thin chain-like device, which she placed on the ground near the door. It was what she called a snake-hacker, which, if it worked as she thought it would, would wrap itself around the security camera and briefly feed the camera a still image of the staircase. That way, if there was a guard on the other side of that camera, he wouldn't even notice Galaxy climbing up the steps.

The snake-hacker slid under the door. She waited about a minute, which was as long as it should take for the device to do its magic, and then creaked open the door again and peered at the camera. As she had expected, the snake-hacker was wrapped securely around the camera.

With a smirk, Galaxy opened the door a little wider and entered the building. She now found herself standing in a stairwell, which went up a few stories. She still did not see anyone; nonetheless, she decided to climb the stairs quietly, so as not to risk attracting unwanted or unnecessary attention.

EPISODE FOUR: NEVER WORK WITH OLD BOSSES

As she climbed the stairwell, Galaxy wondered for a moment what she was doing. She was risking her life and her reputation for someone whom she despised. The more she thought about it, the more she realized that even the best spare parts in the world were not worth this. Should she go back, get Space, and get the hell out of here, before it was too late to do so?

No, she decided. She had given Liox her word that she would retrieve those plans. Besides, it was for a good cause, in her opinion. Galaxy despised thievery, so she felt justified in returning what rightfully belonged to Industrial Intergalactic. It wasn't like she actually worked for Intergalactic Industrial anymore, anyway. This was just a freelance job to get some spare parts, which the *Adventure*—her baby—was in dire need of.

According to the intelligence Galaxy had collected prior to arriving here, all ship designs were kept inside a vault on the upper floors of the main offices. Specifically, the vault was located on the fifth floor and was supposedly the hardest safe to crack, although whether that was true or not was something Galaxy was about to find out for herself.

"So tell me, my good friend, how exactly *does* one play extreme bowling?" said Space, glancing at Kigin as the two stood outside the extreme bowling alley, from which the sounds of explosions going off could be dimly heard. "I have never heard of the sport before."

Kigin scratched his head as he said, "It's basically like bowling, except there are obstacles your bowling ball has to get through in order to reach the pins, which are actually explosives."

Space glanced up at the sign, which read *Zaron X-Treme*

Bowling Alley. "Sounds dashingly dangerous."

"It's actually safe," Kigin said, followed by the sound of a particularly loud explosion issuing from the doors of the alley. "You have to stand behind a blast barrier, true, and wear an explosive-proof suit, and yeah, I guess the balls are also prone to explode when you least expect it, but other than that, it's a game you could play with the whole family." He leaned forward and, holding one of his large ape-like paws up to the side of his mouth, whispered, "But if you want my opinion, let your least favorite kid go first. That way, if the ball explodes, at least it's not a total loss."

Space nodded, although he privately decided not to play extreme bowling today, nor consider any child-rearing advice he might receive from this Zaronian. "How fabulous."

Kigin then leaned back and looked around. "Say, where'd your wife go? I thought she was with us."

"Oh, er, Mary had to use the loo, you know," said Space, flashing his practiced fake smile. "I imagine she'll be back soon. In the mean time, why don't you tell me about this other game, what is it called, 'Roller Coaster Avengers'?"

For a moment, Kigin looked suspicious. But then the expression passed, replaced by a great big smile, and he said, "Well, you see, it's a very interesting game that involves riding on a roller coaster while fighting simulated zombie-bots. It takes place in …"

While Kigin rambled on in a detailed explanation that Space could honestly not care less about, Space looked around the entertainment center. There were dozens, perhaps hundreds, of other people here, all apparently the crews of ships coming in for repairs or checkups. He spotted a few well-dressed businessmen, who were perhaps here to buy a luxury ship, but other than that he didn't see anything out of the ordinary, save for a guy in an assassin's robe standing on the big neon 'Z' of the *Zaron X-Treme Bowling Alley*'s sign.

Space did a double-take. When he looked again, the assassin guy was no longer there, but Space was sure he had seen him there just moments ago.

Unless I'm going crazy, Space thought. *But the therapist said I'm sane. Better ask Kigin; he'll know, though I should be casual about it to avoid arousing his suspicion.*

"My dear sir," said Space, interrupting Kigin's convoluted explanation of Roller Coaster Avengers. "Tell me, did you see a man in frilly assassin's robes standing up there, watching us for a moment?"

Kigin frowned and looked up. "No, sir, I didn't. But I wouldn't be surprised if you saw someone."

"What?" said Space, before quickly regaining his British accent. "I mean, what do you mean, my simian friend?"

Kigin scratched his chin. "I'm not supposed to tell customers about this. I don't want to alarm you."

"Nonsense and poppycock!" said Space, gaily waving off his host's concerns. "I am a man of strong disposition and quiet tongue. You can tell me anything and I can assure you that your secret will be safe with me. The strong Anglo-Saxon spirit within me prevents me from being alarmed by anything."

"Well ... okay," Kigin said. He looked around for a moment, like he thought someone might be listening, although there was no one else close enough to hear them. Then he looked at Space again. "You seem harmless, so I guess it won't hurt to tell you that our head security chief hired some Black Stars to patrol the bay."

"Yes, indeed it—Black Stars?" Space said. He almost stumbled over the word 'Stars.' "You mean that shady assassin organization? *Those* Black Stars?"

"Yes," said Kigin, nodding. "See, we got an anonymous tip that someone might be trying to break into our main vault and steal something valuable soon, so the boss hired some Black Stars to work alongside the normal security guards to keep an eye on the place and take out anyone who tries to steal from us."

"Oh my," said Space, putting his hand over his mouth. "That is serious indeed. May I ask what you believe will be stolen?"

"Top-secret. Can't tell you."

"Are you certain?"

"Yes," said Kigin, folding his massive arms over his chest. "And don't bother asking again, 'cause I'm not allowed to tell you and I haven't had lunch yet, so I'm not in a good mood to tolerate questions I can't answer from customers like you."

"Fine, fine, I understand," said Space, nodding enthusiastically. "You have your own secrets to keep, as does everyone, so naturally, chap, you wouldn't tell me."

Kigin smiled. "Glad you understand. It's important security business. Even I don't know much about it, 'cause I'm not a security guard, you see. I only know as much as I was told, which isn't much."

"Of course, of course," said Space. "Now, er, could you point me to the nearest loo? I suddenly have a great need of it."

"There's one just inside the entrance of the bowling alley," said Kigin, jerking a thumb over his shoulder at the *Zaron X-Treme Bowling Alley*. "I'll wait for you here, 'cause there are still a lot more games to show you."

"How polite of you," said Space.

Space walked quickly into the bathroom just inside the extreme bowling alley's entrance, which fortunately was empty. The place did smell oddly of gun powder and smoke, which made no sense to Space, though he decided to ignore that for now.

Rushing into a stall, Space raised his com-watch to his mouth and said, keeping his voice low, "Galaxy, Galaxy, do you read me? Hello? Galaxy?"

No response. For whatever reason, Galaxy wasn't answering her com-watch (*Rude,* Space thought), so Space decided to contact Sparky instead. Maybe Sparky would be able to reach her instead.

A few seconds later, Sparky—who was much more polite than Galaxy—answered and spoke through the com-watch. "Mr. Space, how is the mission progressing? I have not heard from either of you for several minutes."

"Sparky, I just learned some very bad news," said Space. His stall shook from an explosion from the extreme bowling alley, but he ignored it. "The Master Builders have hired members of the Black Stars to work as extra security for the ship-building bay. I tried contacting Galaxy to tell her, but she wouldn't answer her com-watch."

"The Black Stars?" said Sparky. "That is not good. I will try to contact Captain Galaxy. Perhaps there is some interference blocking the link between you and Galaxy."

"Thanks, Sparky," said Space in relief. "By the way, how is

the ship inspection going?"

"Slowly and frustratingly," Sparky replied. "At least for the inspectors. They seem quite puzzled at my insistence that they watch the pilot of the television series *When Stars Fall* as part of the inspection, although I have assured them that watching the pilot's entire two-and-a-half-hour run time is quite necessary."

Space smiled, but before he could respond, another explosion rocked the stall so much that he was almost knocked off his feet. He leaned against the stall's door, which, much to his disgust, smelled like gun powder mixed with whatever the last person to use this stall had put in here.

"Was that … an explosion, Mr. Space?" said Sparky, who sounded slightly confused.

"It's nothing," said Space, shaking his head as he regained his balance and stood up. "Just extreme bowling."

"Extreme what?"

"I'll fill you in later," said Space. "For now, just keep those inspectors distracted until Galaxy gets the plans. Assuming she doesn't run into any Black Stars, that is."

"I am sure Captain Galaxy has the situation under control," said Sparky. "If she runs into any Black Stars, I doubt she will have any trouble beating them."

Galaxy was fairly certain that the assassin's knife at her throat was going to kill her. Of course, she held her blaster up to the assassin's head, thus locking them together in a standoff. Even so, the assassin had already threatened to summon the rest of his fellow Black Stars to aid him if she did not give up right away; although, seeing as he hadn't yet, she decided that he probably was bluffing (or hoped he was, anyway).

Ten minutes ago, Galaxy had made it into the vault where the plans were kept fairly easily. Thanks to a variety of gadgets she'd brought with her, she had managed to sneak past the various Zaronian guards and Master Builders employees that worked in the offices, as well as avoid most of the cameras and other security systems. Once she ran into a Zaronian who had been making his way downstairs, but thankfully she managed to spin a clever lie on the spot about coming for a business meeting, which caused the Zaronian to leave her alone.

Indeed, for a while there the job had been so easy that Galaxy had thought she was simply going to be able to walk into the vault, take the plans, and get out without anyone being the wiser. The security cameras were not much of a problem; she still had a lot of snake-hackers, which were her best friends today.

When she found the vault, Galaxy had discovered that it was locked tight, but with some of her special tools she managed to break the lock and enter. She had even found the blueprints for the Galaxy Crosser '89 model, located in the third shelf from the bottom. Though she didn't have time to celebrate her victory, because a second later the vault door closed and Galaxy found herself alone inside the vault with this assassin.

The assassin was a Black Star, because he wore their traditional white robes with a black star design on his chest. He seemed to be human, perhaps, although the hand in which he held the dagger at Galaxy's throat was obviously mechanical. His hood covered his face, though his red eyes glowed from within.

"Tell me," said the Black Star, his voice clear and strong, as though the gun aimed at his face didn't bother him, "do you belong to the Shooting Stars? Or are you an independent agent? I don't recognize your face."

Galaxy, careful not to let down her guard, said, "I don't know what you're talking about, Black Star."

"Call me Gavrilo," said the Black Star. "You know what I mean. What organization did Liox hire you from?"

"No organization," Galaxy said through gritted teeth. "I'm … I'm on my own."

Gavrilo chuckled. "Doubt it. I saw you and your 'husband'— yeah, I saw that idiot, faking his British accent and acting like a dumbass—exit the ship. If I had to guess, I'd say you have someone else on board, maybe a robot servant, but either way, I *know* you're not on your own, so you might as well stop lying to me."

"Then why didn't you stop us when we got here, if you knew we were fakers?" said Galaxy.

Gavrilo shrugged. "I wasn't sure if you were a threat or not. Looks like I was right."

"It doesn't matter if you were right or not," said Galaxy, glaring at him. "All I came here to do was steal back something that rightfully belongs to Industrial Intergalactic."

"Came to steal back something that rightfully belongs to those idiots?" said Gavrilo with a chuckle. "Ha, that's good. Those plans you've got in your hand? Those belong to Master Builders, Inc. They were made by an employee of the company and we Black Stars were hired to protect it."

"You're lying," said Galaxy. "Not that I expected any less from a Black Star, of course."

Gavrilo tilted his head to the side. "Tell me, lady, did Liox offer you any proof that those blueprints were stolen from II? Or did she just spin a story about corporate sabotage and you believed it like a gullible fool?"

"You don't have any proof of your own claims, you know."

Gavrilo smiled. "If those blueprints were property of II, why would they be labeled 'Property of Master Builders, Inc.'?"

Without bring her throat down on the knife, Galaxy glanced at the plans and saw that Gavrilo was correct. The words 'Property of Master Builders, Inc.' were indeed written on the blueprints, which caused her to wonder what that meant.

"How do I know these weren't edited?" said Galaxy.

"Why would MB go through all that trouble of editing stolen blueprints they never plan to show anyone else?" said Gavrilo. "It looks to me like you got your trigger pulled, lady."

As much as Galaxy hated to admit it, Gavrilo was right. There was no denying it: Liox had tricked Galaxy and her friends into trying to steal the plans for a ship from a competitor. Thinking about it, that was actually rather in-character for Liox, who had never been a really honest person in the first place.

So Galaxy said, "All right. I believe you. Why don't you let me go now, since I'm not going to steal these blueprints anymore?"

"Sorry, but no," said Gavrilo, shaking his head. "You see, you still broke into these premises illegally. As we Black Stars were hired to guard this place, I have every right to arrest you and take you to the police. Besides, you can testify to II's attempt to steal the blueprints from MB in the inevitable court case that is going to come up."

"Yeah, no," said Galaxy. "I'm not interested in going to jail. I apologize for breaking in illegally, but that doesn't mean I'm going to let you take me in."

"Well, then I guess we're at an impasse," said Gavrilo. "'Cause I'm not being paid to let trespassers walk free."

Therefore, the two continued to hold their weapons at each other's faces. Galaxy's arm started to get tired, but she forced herself to keep holding it up. Gavrilo's arm never wavered even slightly, although as he was a trained assassin, that was to be expected.

Galaxy thought hard about how she was going to get out of this situation. Yet no matter how much she tossed this situation over in her head, she saw no way that she could get out of this without being arrested or getting killed. Gavrilo seemed a lot cleverer than he let on, which meant Galaxy needed to think of a brilliant yet creative way to take him down or convince him to let her go.

That was when a new idea occurred to Galaxy, an idea that seemed obvious the more she thought about it. It might not work, but it was her best shot at getting out of this situation alive, so she went for it.

So she said to Gavrilo, "How much is MB paying you?"

"Excuse me?"

"I said, how much is MB paying you?"

Gavrilo looked at her suspiciously. "Why do you care? And why should I tell you?"

"Because I want to make an offer to you," said Galaxy. "Whatever MB is paying, I can pay you more on the condition that you let me and my friends walk away from this place unharmed and free."

Gavrilo bit his lower lip. "I didn't know bribery was your style."

"It isn't," said Galaxy. "But in this case, it is. So again, how much are they paying you?"

"It's not as simple as that, lady," said Gavrilo. "You see, when MB hired us, it was a group hire. They paid two thousand digits for about four Black Stars. The money will be divided up among us after our contract expires."

Galaxy did the math in her head. "So that's about five hundred digits per mercenary, then. Where are the others?"

"The others are keeping an eye on the rest of the Shipyard," said Gavrilo. "Most of them are keeping a careful eye on the ships that dock here, but I guess you and your 'husband' somehow managed to avoid attracting their attention."

"Will you call in the rest of your friends to capture my friend?" Galaxy asked.

"I should," said Gavrilo. But then he nodded at Galaxy's gun. "Only reason I went after you without telling the others is because I thought I could take you on my own. But I think you have a quick trigger finger. I imagine that if I tried, you'd blow my head off, right?"

"Pretty much," said Galaxy. "I'm no killer, but if that will ensure my survival, I'll do it."

"Tough girl," said Gavrilo. "It's a shame that I will probably have to kill you; I think you'd make a great Black Star."

"Right," said Galaxy. "Well, anyway, that five hundred digits doesn't seem like a whole lot."

"It's perhaps not as much as I normally make, but as it's supposed to be a short-term job, you just can't expect much from that," said Gavrilo. "Besides, I'm not as experienced as some of the others, so I'm not allowed to take on higher-paying missions yet."

"We'll double that."

This time, Gavrilo's knife almost wavered, although he still kept it close to her throat. "Double it?"

"Yes," said Galaxy. She would have nodded, but that would have meant slitting her own throat on his knife. "We'll pay you a thousand digits in exchange for our freedom. We have that kind of money."

"A thousand digits …" Gavrilo repeated, though he did not seem impressed by the number. "Hmm, that's more within my usual pay range. More so than five hundred digits, at any rate."

"Please," said Galaxy, her voice almost pleading. "I promise we'll give you the money if you let me go and don't tell your comrades about me or my friend."

For a moment, Galaxy was afraid Gavrilo would reject her offer and kill her then and there. He didn't seem like the easily bribed type to Galaxy, especially because he hadn't dropped his knife from her throat yet.

Finally, Gavrilo lowered his knife from her throat and said, "My arm was getting tired, anyway." He then pressed a button on his mechanical wrist, causing the vault door to open automatically. "Go on. Get out. Before I change my mind and tell my fellow Black Stars what I saw."

Galaxy lower her gun, feeling relieved that she could rest her arm. "When do you want us to transfer the digits?"

"Drop it off at this location," said Gavrilo, handing her a piece of paper. "Tell 'em it's for Gavrilo. They'll know."

EPISODE FOUR: NEVER WORK WITH OLD BOSSES

"Drop it off?" said Galaxy. "As in, physical money? Why—?"

"Paper money and metal is harder to track than electronic money," Gavrilo cut her off. "Same reason I gave you a paper with the location on it. I don't want Black Nova finding out about this. Let's just say that he wouldn't be happy if he learned that I intentionally botched a job, and leave it at that."

Without looking at the slip of paper, Galaxy slid it into her pocket and dashed out of the vault. She thought about thanking him for letting her escape, but as she didn't want to give him time to rethink her offer, she just ran for it.

"Well, sir," said Kigin as he and Space exited the entertainment center, "how did you like it?"

"Oh, it was absolutely smashing, my dear Kigin," said Space, patting the Zaronian on the shoulder. "Really, that hunting game with the virtual vampires? That was winning. Thank you so much for showing me around."

"You're welcome, Mr. Chandler."

The two stood there awkwardly for a moment, Space not sure what to say next. He glanced at his com-watch, but didn't see any messages on its tiny screen from Galaxy.

Just as he wondered what he had to do next, Galaxy ran up to them. She stopped in front of Space and Kigin, breathing hard and putting her hands on her knees as she said, "Hi … honey … how did … how did the tour go?"

"Oh, it was excellent, Mary," said Space as he walked over to her. "Simply inspiring. Did you know that in laser tag, they use real, military-grade laser rifles that are designed to stun rather than kill? It was a lot of fun shooting kids half my—"

"That's nice," said Galaxy as she stood up straight, though she still panted. "Listen, Will, I think it's time for us to go home. Sir, do you know if the inspection is done yet?"

"Uh, I imagine it is by now, ma'am," said Kigin, looking a little puzzled. "Would you like me to take you back to your ship?"

"No, no," said Galaxy, shaking her head. "We can find it ourselves, thank you very much. Right, darling?"

"But of course," said Space with a smile. He slapped Kigin on the shoulder. "Thank you again, Kigin, for showing me the entertainment center. The next time I stop by, I will be sure to try out more games, like that extreme bowling game you showed me."

Before Kigin could answer, Galaxy grabbed Space by the arm and dragged him away down the bay toward the *Adventure*. Space soon pulled his arm out of her grasp, but kept walking beside her anyway.

As they walked, Space whispered to Galaxy, "So? Did you get the blueprints?"

"No," said Galaxy, without looking at him. "We were tricked."

"Tricked? Whatever do you mean?"

Galaxy glanced at him in annoyance. "You can drop the British accent now. It's really annoying."

Space looked a little offended at that, but he said, in his normal voice "What do you mean, 'tricked'?"

"I'll explain later," said Galaxy as they walked past two Zaronians carrying a heavy crate between them. "For now, all you need to know is that Liox is the biggest liar I know."

EPISODE FOUR: NEVER WORK WITH OLD BOSSES

Upon arriving at the *Adventure*, Galaxy paid the inspection crew the fee. Apparently, the *Adventure* had passed the inspection, although just barely. She was told that Sparky had been rather unhelpful, either leading them to the wrong rooms or once even 'accidentally' activating the security system that tried to forcibly remove them from the ship and eject them into the void of space. To Galaxy, it sounded like Sparky took their order to distract a little too seriously, though Space seemed amused by it, if the smile on his face was any indication.

After that, they flew the *Adventure* out of the Zaron Shipyard and into space. As they flew, Galaxy explained to Space and Sparky what Gavrilo had told her about the truth of the situation, as well as the deal she had made with him to let her and Space leave the Shipyard without arrest.

"How interesting," said Sparky, stroking his metallic chin. "Why did Liox try to trick us into stealing something that wasn't hers?"

Space was looking at the floor of the deck, his head in his hands, as though Galaxy had just told him that she was pregnant. "Galaxy, why did you promise to pay Gavrilo one thousand digits? That's like a month's worth of pay for us! We don't even have that much in savings, much less in paper and metal. Who even still uses physical money anymore?"

"It's not that bad," said Galaxy, folding her arms. "Besides, I doubt he would have let me go on a cheaper offer. Just be glad I didn't stick around long enough for him to try to negotiate for an even higher offer."

Space snorted. "Yeah, 'glad.' I'm real *glad* all right. Glad that you usually don't handle the negotiations around here, if that's the best deal you could negotiate."

Galaxy rolled her eyes and was about to say something before a nearby computer console said, "Incoming message from Liox, CEO of Intergalactic Industrial. Permission to connect?"

"Permission granted," said Galaxy as her chair spun around to face the screen.

A second later, Liox's ugly, stupid feline face appeared on the computer screen. Her red eyes gleamed with mirth as she said, "As I can see that you three are not currently rotting away in a Zaronian jail cell, I can only assume that your mission was a complete success."

"Hardly," said Galaxy, shaking her head. "We didn't steal the blueprints you wanted."

The mirth in Liox's eyes vanished. She leaned toward them, making her face appear even larger on the screen, and a low growl accompanied her words when she said, "Why? Did you chicken out at the last minute? I wouldn't be surprised if you did, knowing how cowardly you are."

"No chickening out here," said Galaxy as she stood up. "We learned the truth, that those blueprints didn't actually belong to II and that you wanted us to steal them for you from your competitor. We're so sorry for not being good criminals-for-hire, which is what you tried to turn us into without our knowledge."

Liox growled, but when she spoke, it was in a forced calm voice, "Oh, so you figured it out, did you? Well, I thought you might, but no matter. It's not like I will get in trouble for this, since no one knows of my involvement in this aborted crime."

"What's to stop us from reporting you to the UA?" said

Galaxy. "If we came and told them what you ordered us to do—"

"Then you would get in trouble, too," Liox finished. She leaned back from the screen, folding her arms across her chest. "After all, I'm sure you must have gotten in far enough that you, too, would be incriminated in a criminal investigation. As you two love your freedom too much, I doubt you'll tell the law about our little agreement, correct?"

Galaxy bit her lower lip and glanced at Space, who merely shrugged. "Well ... I guess we didn't really do anything bad, so it's not like we actually need to report you to the UA or anything."

"Excellent," said Liox, putting the tips of her fingers together. "Of course, now I know better than to hire former employees to do my dirty work. I imagine this will be the last time we talk like this, so good bye, Galaxy. I hope you succeed in whatever endeavors you attempt."

With that, the screen went blank, replaced with the words 'CONNECTION TERMINATED.'

Galaxy stomped her foot, causing Space and Sparky to stare at her in surprise.

"What is the problem, Captain?" asked Sparky. "You seem angry."

"Because she's right," said Galaxy through clenched teeth. "She's right that we'd get in trouble, too, if we told the UA about our breaking into private property and attempting to steal company property, even if we honestly didn't know that's what we were doing at the time."

"When you worked for her, was she that much of a witch?" said Space, his eyes still on the screen. "Because she reminds me of Madam Lucy from the Zaronian play, *The Mistress's Black*

Hand, who was a rather manipulative little witch if I remember correctly."

"Yeah, what you saw was typical Liox behavior," said Galaxy with a sigh as she sat back down on her chair. "We just wasted a lot of time, money, and energy on nothing."

"Yeah," said Space, nodding. "I mean, a thousand digits. In cash. That Gavrilo guy is crazy."

Galaxy rolled her eyes. "Never mind. Let's just go to Namox. I need a drink."

Spacetastic Interviews with:

Gavrilo

T.L. Charles: Hello and welcome, readers, to the Spacetastic Interviews series. In this series, I, T.L. Charles, the author, interview a character from *The Spacetastic Adventures of Mr. Space and Captain Galaxy* series, usually a character who appeared in the last episode. These interviews tend to be short, but entertaining and informative. Anyway, with that out of the way, let me introduce today's guest, Gavrilo, a member of the fearsome Black Star assassin group. Gavrilo, will you say hi to the audience?

Gavrilo: 'Sup.

T.L. Charles: You certainly seem pretty laid-back for a Black Star.

Gavrilo: I was only serious in the episode because I was on the job. When I'm not working, I'm much more relaxed.

T.L. Charles: How do you remain relaxed knowing that you kill people for a living?

Gavrilo: The same way you remain relaxed writing stories for a living. I just tell myself that it's part of my job. It's like a fry cook complaining about having to work with grease; I mean, come on, that's just part of the job, you know?

T.L. Charles: I don't think working with grease is equivalent to killing people. Have you ever thought about taking up another job?

Gavrilo: Nah. Well, okay, once I *did* think about becoming a surgeon, but then I decided that I could make more money working as an assassin, so I decided to join the Black Stars.

T.L. Charles: Huh. That's a rather ... *interesting* change in career choices.

Gavrilo: I couldn't stand the idea of working with sick people. I'd have probably killed all of my patients—without anyone realizing it was me, of course—just to get them to stop complaining about their stuffy noses or their back issues or how I attached the wrong leg to their body or whatever. My cousin's a doctor and he's constantly complaining about his complaining patients.

T.L. Charles: Does your cousin know you kill people for a living?

Gavrilo: I tell him I am a clown who entertains kids at children's parties. Seems to satisfy him, so why give him more than he needs to know?

T.L. Charles: Uh, yeah, I guess. Anyway, can you tell me anything about Black Nova, the leader of your organization?

Gavrilo: No. First, if I did, I've have to kill you; and second, Black Nova would have to kill me after I killed you. Just the way things work in our organization. Again, nothing to fuss over, same way a fry cook isn't allowed to fuss about the color of the uniform that his boss gave him or for being fired for being a bad employee.

T.L. Charles: That's ... never mind. Anyway, what do you think about Mr. Space and Captain Galaxy?

Gavrilo: I hope they get me my money. And fast. I have some debts to pay off and the guys I owe money to are really not the forgiving types. They make student loan collectors look like Mister Rogers.

T.L. Charles: Why did you borrow money from them, then?

Gavrilo: (shifty eyes) I needed it. That's all I'm saying.

T.L. Charles: Uh huh. Well, looks like we're almost out of time. Gavrilo, do you have any last words for my readers before we close out?

Gavrilo: Yeah. Always pay off your debts in cash, and don't think too deeply about the ethical dilemmas that your jobs present to you. Not fun.

T.L. Charles: Right. Well, that's all we have for today. Please turn the page to begin reading *Episode Five: The Phantom of the Jungle*. See you at the next Spacetastic Interview!

Episode Five
The Phantom of the Jungle

I hate the jungle. It's stinky, full of mud, has no bathrooms, and completely lacks chocolate ice cream. It's so hot and humid that I think I am going to die. Why did I even agree to go along on this mission? I should have stayed up in the *Adventure* with Sparky. At least there's ice cream up there."

Galaxy turned over in her sleeping bag to glare at Space. "Because this is a dangerous mission and I need backup. You're pretty quick with a gun, so I thought you'd be useful to bring along."

"But why didn't you bring Sparky instead?" said Space. "Sparky wouldn't mind any of this; after all, he's a robot."

"True, but I don't trust your ability to fly the *Adventure* without crashing it into a cloud and stranding us here," said Galaxy, shaking her head. "Now why don't you just shut up and go to sleep? We're getting up early tomorrow morning to explore those ruins the scanners found and I want to get a good night's sleep so I don't walk through a deadly alien jungle half-asleep."

Grumbling, Space pulled his sleeping bag over his head and muttered, "At least we're in a climate-controlled tent. If we had to sleep in the open, on top of the mud and in the humidity … ugh, I don't think I could make it."

EPISODE FIVE: THE PHANTOM OF THE JUNGLE

Galaxy just rolled to her other side. She reached out and set her com-watch to go off in another six hours and closed her eyes. Her mind didn't shut off, however. As usual when she had a moment to relax, she went over the events of the past day in her mind, mostly because she hadn't gotten the chance to during the day.

About a week ago, Galaxy, Space, and Sparky had arrived on this planet, called Niham, in order to refuel the ship and buy some more supplies at the capital city of Shizor, as they had started to run out and this was the closest world they could stop at where they could buy supplies. While there, Galaxy had learned of some ruins in the planet's southern jungle that supposedly held ancient artifacts of great significance. It was also supposedly 'cursed' and protected by some kind of mysterious shape-shifter, although at the time Galaxy had dismissed that as nothing more than superstitious nonsense, as the Nihamian who had told her the story had offered no proof of this shape-shifter.

Galaxy had, however, confirmed that the ruins existed by consulting the *Adventure*'s computers, though the records on the ruins were scant due to very few archaeologists willing to brave the depths of the jungle, even with modern technology and robots to do it for them.

Seeing an opportunity to make some good money, Galaxy had flown the now-refueled *Adventure* south of Shizor until they came upon the great jungle where the ruins were supposed to be. The ship's radar had indeed spotted a ruined building inside the jungle, which Galaxy wanted to explore in order to find artifacts to sell to collectors and museums for a profit.

It had taken her a while to convince Space to come, however, as he had also heard the rumor of the shape-shifter and wanted nothing to do with it out of the same superstitious fear as the Nihamian from before. But when she described the jungle using poetic, romantic imagery, he immediately agreed to go. Perhaps that had been deceptive on her part, but as she thought that 'the towering giants which blocked out all sunlight' was a valid description of the huge trees that surrounded them on every side, she didn't feel too guilty about it.

Thus far, they had been in the jungle for about a day, sending reports up to Sparky every hour so he would know that they are still alive. They had only seen insects and plants, although more than once Galaxy thought she had seen a gigantic monster hiding in the shadows of the trees. Every time, however, that 'monster' turned out to be either nothing at all or just a strange shadow. Space seemed convinced that some kind of shape-shifting monster was stalking them, but as there was no empirical proof of the creature's existence, Galaxy saw no reason to worry.

Especially now, when I need to sleep, Galaxy thought, listening to the chirping of unknown insects just outside the tent. *Time to get some rest. Think tomorrow is going to be a long day.*

Galaxy closed her eyes. She soon drifted off to sleep ... or thought she did, because she now found herself standing in an empty, inky black darkness that felt like an oppressive force clamping down on her head. It was like she was suffocating, but she wasn't underwater or in the vacuum of space.

She struggled against the oppressive force, but it was overwhelming. Finally, she broke free and found herself flying through the sky before landing on a sandbar at a beach.

Shaking her head, Galaxy looked around and noticed that the

sea was bubbling. Puzzled, she watched the ocean curiously until something began to break the surface. Yet it wasn't a thing, but a monster, a behemoth that dwarfed Galaxy. It looked like a snake, except for the moth-like wings and spikes running the length of its back, like a hedgehog.

Galaxy's heart almost stopped at the sight of the monster. She wondered what it was going to do to her when it disappeared, replaced by a small, turtle-like being who fell to the sand before her. It looked up at her with sad eyes and said, somehow speaking perfect English, "Run."

As soon as the word left its mouth, a tentacle burst out from the trees and wrapped itself around Galaxy's body. Horrified, Galaxy cried out as she was dragged through the sand, pleading with the turtle being to help her. But all it did was watch her sadly as she was drawn into the oppressive darkness of the forest. She looked over her shoulder as she was dragged into the trees and saw what had grabbed her despite the shadows.

And when she saw what had grabbed her, she screamed.

"Galaxy!"

Galaxy's eyes flew open and, without thinking, she lashed out with a punch. Her fist connected with something soft and she heard someone curse in pain quite creatively.

"Ow! What the hell was that for?" said the voice, annoyed. "My breath doesn't smell *that* bad, does it?"

Galaxy shook her head. She blinked several times and, her body shaking, looked up at Space, who held his hands over his nose. "Space? What happened to your nose?"

"You punched it," said Space, in a voice somewhere between a whimper and a growl (though closer to a whimper). "It's not broken, but it hurts a lot. You know, I always considered the phrase 'You punch like a girl' to be an insult, but in your case, it's quite the compliment."

Angrily, Galaxy raised her fist, but she caught herself. Punching Space again wouldn't help, even if it would make her feel better. She had to calm down.

So, taking deep breaths, Galaxy lay back down in her sleeping bag. She realized that she was incredibly sweaty. So was her sleeping bag, which was damp with sweat. That didn't make any sense, as their climate-controlled tent had been put on a moderate temperature to avoid this sort of thing.

"Sorry," Galaxy muttered. "I … I had a nightmare."

"What kind of nightmare?" said Space. "You wanna—"

Galaxy glared at him, causing Space to hold up one hand defensively, saying, "Okay, okay, I get it. You don't want to talk about it. Fine. Sorry for being a concerned friend."

"Why did you wake me up, anyway?" said Galaxy, wiping the sweat off her forehead. "I didn't ask you to."

"You were screaming and thrashing about," said Space as he dug through his backpack. "I was worried, so I wanted to make sure you were okay."

"I'm fine," said Galaxy. "I'm not a child. It's just a bad dream. It's not going to hurt me."

"That's what Uncle Owen always said," said Space as he pulled out some bandages from his pack. "Then it turned out that he had a disease that replayed his worst dreams over and over again until he lost his sanity. Are you sure you don't have Kana's disease?"

"I'm sure I don't," said Galaxy. "Besides, Kana's disease is hereditary and my family has no history of the disease. I'd be more concerned about yourself."

"Nah, I'm fine," said Space as he started bandaging his nose. "Had a doctor check. He told me I probably won't get it."

"Probably?"

"Probably is good enough for me," said Space as he finished bandaging his nose. "Anyway, gotta go back to sleep. We've got a big day ahead of ourselves tomorrow."

"Glad to see you're starting to look forward to it," said Galaxy as Space crawled back in his sleeping bag.

"Look forward to it? Don't be silly," said Space as he snuggled up in his bag. "I just know that the sooner we get going, the soon we can get back to the *Adventure*, which means the sooner we can return to civilization and ice cream."

Galaxy sighed. "Well, good night again, anyway. Sleep well."

"Good night," said Space.

A few minutes later, Galaxy heard Space snoring loudly, as he usually did when sleeping. She closed her eyes and tried to sleep as well as him, but every time she heard the snap of a twig or the rustling of the tree branches outside, her eyes would snap open and remain that way for several minutes, despite her best efforts to close them.

It didn't seem like she was going to get any sleep tonight.

"Oh, life is so much better after a good night's sleep," said Space as he practically skipped through the jungle, Galaxy following at a more sluggish pace. "Even this icky jungle doesn't seem quite so bad anymore. Why, look at that beautiful butterfly. You know, jungles are really fascinating places when they aren't dark and scary."

Galaxy put one hand on her head and muttered, "Could you stop being so cheerful? It's getting on my nerves."

Space stopped skipping and looked at Galaxy. "You've got bags under your eyes. Did you get any sleep last night?"

Irritated, Galaxy stomped passed Space, saying, "No, and it's because of your incessant snoring. Maybe I should have brought along Sparky instead, as he doesn't snore."

"Hey, I don't snore that loudly," said Space as he caught up with her. "I think it was that nightmare you had."

Galaxy didn't answer. She just trudged on through the undergrowth, using her laser machete to cut through branches and bushes that got in the way. More than once she nearly hit Space, but due to her fatigue it was hard for her to register that unless he pointed it out to her.

Her mind was distracted by that dream. Normally, Galaxy didn't let nightmares get to her, but that one was stuck in her brain like a sword. The feel of the slimy tentacle wrapping itself around her body, squeezing the life out of her … those black eyes … and worst of all was her complete inability to remember what that monster looked like. No matter how hard she thought about it, Galaxy couldn't put a face on that monster. That made her heart race and her face sweat and she didn't like that at all.

So Galaxy tried not to think about it, but it was no use. Every time she heard a twig snap or the trees rustle, it caused her to jump. Whenever she jumped, Space would make some stupid joke about it that she didn't really listen to due to her tiredness, although she'd usually hit him over the head with the hilt of her machete anyway.

EPISODE FIVE: THE PHANTOM OF THE JUNGLE

Of course, that didn't do a thing to calm her nerves. She kept glancing over her shoulder even when she didn't hear anything out of the ordinary, because she still felt like something was stalking them. What made it even worse was that it was not such a stupid idea. After all, in the jungle, there were bound to be all kinds of predators around, many of which were probably more than capable of ripping her and Space to shreds.

In fact, it got to the point where Galaxy asked Space to draw his light-gun, even though there was nothing near them that he could use it against. When he asked why, she simply said, "Because we might need it," but otherwise didn't elaborate. Even she wasn't sure why she felt the need for both of them to be armed. It could only be because of the fear in the pit of her stomach, a fear she tried to ignore as best as she could.

Her pace quickened, but she tried to hide it. That was easy, because their path was still obstructed by branches and brush, although she ended up cutting through it faster than before anyway. The adrenaline pumping through her body made her feel wide awake, but it also made her think everything was out to get her, even though she knew logically that that made no sense.

Not to mention the heat and humidity of the jungle made her mood worse than ever. The huge leaves and limbs of the trees around them blocked out most of the sunlight, but it was still far too hot for Galaxy's tastes. She drank from her thermos more regularly than before, because it was the only way to keep cool, although due to their limited supply of water, she still had to regulate how much and how often she drank.

The two walked through the jungle for some time before coming upon a strange sight. There were tracks on the jungle floor, like those of some sort of wheeled vehicle, heading in the general direction of the ruins that Galaxy and Space were looking for.

"Someone else must have come by here recently," said Space. "Can you tell what kind of vehicle these tracks belong to?"

Galaxy squatted down and peered at them, wrinkling her nose at the smelly mud. Her mind was cloudy and unresponsive, making those tracks look more or less the same as every other tire track Galaxy had seen in her time. This was bad because Galaxy, having been a mechanic and engineer for years, should have been able to recognize these tracks right away.

So Galaxy shook her head and said, "No. Don't recognize them."

Galaxy then stood up and looked in the direction of the tracks, which soon disappeared into the undergrowth of the jungle. "Who else could be out here, I wonder?"

"Let's hope they're friendly," said Space as he and Galaxy walked along the tracks. "'Cause if they're not … well, let's not think about that."

Following the vehicle's tracks led them to a sight Galaxy didn't expect to see in the jungle: A camp, with about a dozen or so people scattered around it, with just as many tents. Sitting on the edge of the camp was two large camouflage Jungle-Slicer Jeeps, although they looked like older models, which Galaxy found odd, as the newer models were better equipped for jungle exploration than older ones.

As they were unsure just who these campers were, Space and Galaxy stayed hidden within the trees and brush just outside the campsite. They watched as the campers cooked food and sat around and talked, although the campers were speaking too quietly for them to make our what they were saying.

"Who do you think they are?" Space whispered. "Explorers, maybe?"

Galaxy shook her head. "Doubt it. We're the only two dumb enough to explore this jungle on our own. No, they must be here for another reason."

Space gulped. "Do you think they're guerilla fighters? I don't want to get involved in any government revolutions or anything."

Again, Galaxy shook her head. "Do you see any guns? Do they look like they've been out in the wilderness for months? No. Besides, there aren't any guerilla fighters on Niham, since the government here is pretty stable. They're obviously doing something else out here, though what, I don't know."

Space scratched the back of his head. "So … do you think we should go and talk to them? I mean, if they're not violent, then maybe they could help us."

"Maybe," said Galaxy. "If, that is, they know anything about the ruins. If not, then there is no reason to … no reason to …"

Galaxy blinked and shook her head. She knew what was happening. Her sleep-deprived mind was making it hard to think straight and she was losing her train of thought as a result. So she didn't even try to finish the sentence, instead letting it drift off, as she thought Space would understand her meaning.

"Since I'm not much of a risk-taker in these kinds of situations, I agree that we should avoid them," said Space, nodding. "Why don't we continue searching for those ruins? I'm starting to get sick of the jungle again."

Galaxy gestured at him to wait. "Wait. I want to observe them a little while longer."

"Why?"

"Because there is still a chance they could help us. By observing them, we might be able to learn if they are friend or foe."

Sighing, Space sat back down on the soggy jungle floor and folded his arms. "And how long do you want to observe them?"

Galaxy didn't answer that question. In her sleep-deprived state of mind, she could only nod and look back at the camp. Of the dozen campers she saw, most appeared human, although there were a couple of burly Zaronians with them. The campers appeared mostly peaceful, standing around talking or studying the trees and plants around them with scientific interest. A couple were cooking lunch in the primitive campfire in the center, although Galaxy could not tell what they were cooking from her current position.

Just then, Galaxy felt the tip of a gun press against the back of her head. Out of the corner of her eye, she saw a gun tip pressed against the back of Space's head as well, causing him to yip briefly.

"Get up," said a slithery voice behind her, akin to a snake's. "Or I'll blow your brains out."

Galaxy glanced at Space, who shrugged. They both stood up, as per the snake voice's orders.

"Now march," the voice behind them said. "March, and don't stop until we reach the camp. It's been a while since we've gotten to kill anything and my trigger finger is starting to slip."

Space and Galaxy marched out of the jungle and into the

campsite. As they did so, the campers looked up at the newcomers with a mixture of surprise and confusion. One of the campers, a tall human with a skull tattoo on his right cheek, walked up to them as they approached. He looked more like a soldier than an archaeologist, with dark green battle armor that matched the colors of the jungle around them. Underneath that armor, Galaxy caught a glimpse of powerful muscles that made her look like a stick figure in comparison.

"Well, well, well," said the human in a light French accent, stopping in front of Space and Galaxy. He was at least a head taller than both of them, which added to his menacing appearance. "Look what we've got here. What are you, a couple of thieves waiting for us to let our guard down so you can steal from us?"

"Actually, we're space adventurers," said Space, though he stumbled over his words a little, probably due to the gun still pressed against the back of his head. "Not thieves."

"Space adventurers?" the human repeated. He looked around and said, "Gee, I don't see outer space around here. Maybe you're lost."

"Technically, we're always in space if you think about it," said Space. "I mean, all planets hang in the vast void that we call outer space, like the puppets of some giant puppet master. Therefore, there is space all around you and thus it is perfectly appropriate for us to be here."

The human scowled, which distorted the skull tattoo on his cheek. "Enough with the wisecracks. Who are you two and what are you doing out here?"

"We were going to ask you the same question, skull-cheek,"

Galaxy replied. "We didn't know there was anyone else this far away from civilization."

The human smirked. "My name is Nathan Pierre Sauvage, but cute nickname. Now tell me your names."

"Lower your weapons and we'll talk," said Galaxy. "I don't like speaking when there's a gun to my head."

"But of course," said Sauvage. He gestured over Space and Galaxy's heads. "We're all civilized beings here. Skio, Nif, lower your guns. These two are harmless."

A moment later, Galaxy no longer felt the gun tip against the back of her head. She glanced at Space and saw that he, too, was free of the gun. She glanced over her shoulder to see their captors, but to her surprise there was nobody there.

Galaxy looked back at Sauvage. "Where did they go?"

Sauvage, again, smirked. "Skio and Nif are Kendonians. They can move faster and more silently than any human can, so I imagine they just slipped into the forest before anyone realized."

"You mean you didn't see?" said Space in amazement. "But you were standing in front of us the whole time looking over our heads at them."

"Skio and Nif are just that good," said Sauvage. He put his hands on his hips. "Now a deal's a deal. Tell me your names and what you are doing here."

Seeing no reason to lie, Galaxy said, "I'm Captain Helena Galaxy and this is my friend, Mr. Jason Space. We're space adventurers from the starship *Adventure* and we've come here in search of some ruins we heard about back in Shizor. And you?"

Sauvage turned and gestured for them to follow. "Come with me into my tent, Captain Galaxy. We can talk more in there. I dislike talking out here with all of these annoying insects buzzing in my ears."

Galaxy did not know what he was talking about at first, since she didn't hear anything, but then she heard some buzzing sound in her ears. She swatted at it, though she didn't think she'd hit the stupid insect, whatever it was, because she still heard it buzzing.

"Can I come, too?" said Space. "'Cause you didn't say my name and so I thought—"

"Yes, you can come too," said Sauvage, nodding. "Although, I will have to ask you both to leave your weapons out here with my friends."

Galaxy reached for her light-gun, which was strapped to her leg. "Why should we?"

"I just don't want any of us to accidentally get hurt, you know," said Sauvage. "I mean, guns have an awful habit of going off without meaning to. Besides, I'm a pacifist and can't stand guns even if they aren't being used."

"Fine," said Galaxy. "As long as we get our weapons back after we're done talking, it's not a problem."

"Certainly," said Sauvage. "Now follow me."

They left their weapons with a woman Sauvage simply called Mary. While she lacked the distinctive tattoo or dark green armor that Sauvage had, Galaxy couldn't help notice the way Mary handled their weapons. It was like she was a trained soldier, although Galaxy supposed that perhaps Mary could have been in the army at some point.

When they entered Sauvage's tent, the first thing Galaxy noticed were the stacks of unmarked boxes in one corner. There was at least two or three dozen boxes, but it was impossible to tell what was inside them. They didn't look very large, but what they might have contained, Galaxy could only guess.

On one of the tent walls was a map of the jungle, with notes and markings on it that seemed to chronicle the route the campers had taken to get here. There were photos attached to it, too, but she didn't linger on them, because Sauvage sat down in a chair and gestured for Galaxy and Space to sit down in front of him on two small stools.

"As I already told you, my name is Nathan Pierre Sauvage," said Sauvage. "I'm the leader of a team of archaeologists sent out here to study those same ruins that you two are interested in seeking."

"Who do you work for?" Galaxy asked.

"Excuse me?"

"I said, who do you work for?" Galaxy repeated. "Archaeologists usually work for some university, research group, or sometimes a government. So again, who do you work for?"

Sauvage scratched the back of his head briefly, as if in thought. That would have made Galaxy curious, but she was still too tired to think very critically about the actions of others. "Oh, er, we were actually hired by a man who has asked us to keep his identity a secret. He's a very private, very rich man who has an interest in discovering old ruins and collecting treasures from them. He has given us permission to take what we want—for science, you understand—so long as we get him what he wants."

Space glanced at the boxes in the corner. "What are in those boxes?"

Sauvage smiled. "Just archeological tools, you know. Some are empty, which we plan to use to transport whatever items of interest we find in those ruins."

"I see," said Space. "Well, you guys don't seem like dangerous people to me."

"Hold on," said Galaxy. "Why did your two Kendonian friends have guns?"

"Because the jungle is a dangerous place, of course," said Sauvage. He gestured at himself. "Most of us, including myself, are not very good fighters and lack the training necessary to use weapons without hurting ourselves in the process. We hired Skio and Nif as our escorts and guards. They are the only armed people in this entire camp. The rest of us abhor weapons, especially me."

"Mary back there sure seemed to know how to handle a gun," Galaxy said.

Sauvage looked slightly bemused. "Well, perhaps your mind was playing tricks on you, Captain Galaxy. After all, you have such terrible bags under your eyes. Did you get any sleep last night?"

Though his question seemed innocent enough, Galaxy didn't think it was any of his business. Something about these archaeologists didn't settle well with her, although it could just as easily have been her own lack of sleep making her paranoid.

"It doesn't really matter," said Space, before Galaxy could tell Sauvage that that was none of his business. "So how long have you guys been out here?"

"About a week, I believe," said Sauvage. "Though I will admit, I do not keep track of time very well myself. Mostly, Mary is in charge of timekeeping around here."

"A week is an awful long time to be out here in this jungle," Space said. He leaned on the table on his elbows. "You sure you guys aren't lost?"

"Positively," said Sauvage. He gestured at the map. "We started in the city of Niham and traveled all the way out here. We would have used a ship, but the trees are so thick, you see, that we thought it made more sense to use land vehicles than air or space ones, yes?"

"Wasn't too thick for us," said Space. He gestured at the ceiling of the tent. "Our ship teleported us down here with no—"

Galaxy elbowed Space, causing him to look at her and say, "What?"

She didn't say anything, however, because she didn't want Sauvage to hear her. She just looked at Space and hoped that he understood that she wanted him to stop blabbering, as she wasn't sure it was wise for them to tell Sauvage all about them.

Sauvage, for his part, did not look offended. He merely swatted some kind of insect out of the air and then rested his chin in his hands, watching them both as intently as a tiger on the hunt.

"Yes, Mr. Space?" said Sauvage. "What were you about to say about your ship?"

"He was about to say nothing," said Galaxy. She stood up, although somewhat wobbly due to her sleep-deprived mind. "Thanks for the hospitality, but we're leaving."

"But you just got here and we just started talking," said Sauvage, looking up at her in shock. "Why are you two leaving so soon?"

"Because we're on a tight schedule," said Galaxy. "And we

can't just sit around and talk with you guys. If we don't get to the ruins in a timely manner, it'll mess us up."

That was not entirely true. Technically, Galaxy and Space were on no strict schedule, seeing as they had decided to come to the ruins on a whim and nothing more; still, Galaxy didn't want to stay and talk with Sauvage or any of his friends and was willing to say whatever she needed to in order to get her and Space away from this camp.

Then Sauvage stood up. He towered over Galaxy. "I don't think that is a good idea, Captain Galaxy."

"Why?" said Galaxy. She wished she had her light-gun, even though Sauvage did not seem likely to attack them. "We were doing well out here on our own before we found you. Besides, the ruins aren't far away. It's not like we'll get lost or anything."

Sauvage gestured at the map on the wall again. "Actually, I was just about to use that same reasoning for why we should stick together. The ruins are so close that it makes no sense for us to travel separately. Why not travel together until we reach the ruins? Then we can discuss how to fairly divide whatever treasures we find there among us."

Sauvage smiled as he said that, but all Galaxy could focus on was that skull tattoo on his cheek. When he smiled, the tattoo looked like it was scowling, although that could just as easily have been her own imagination running wild.

Galaxy looked at Space. "What do you think?"

"I think this camp is the closest thing to civilization we've found out here so far," said Space. "So I'm quite comfortable teaming up with these guys until we reach the ruins."

"See? Your friend agrees," said Sauvage. "Besides, in your

current tired condition, you're far more vulnerable to attack than if you travel with us."

"I'm not tired," said Galaxy. "I got plenty of sleep last night."

"You did? Well, then here's your com-watch back," said Sauvage, handing the device back to her.

Galaxy's eyes widened as she took it back. "What ... how ..."

"Even *I* didn't notice him take your com-watch," said Space. He then looked down at his wrist and sighed in relief. "Whew. Mine's still here."

"Like I said, Captain Galaxy, you are very tired," said Sauvage. "But of course, I will understand completely if you do not wish to work with us. It is your choice."

As much as Galaxy hated to admit it, Sauvage had a point. In her current condition, Galaxy wasn't sure she'd be able to travel through the jungle, even with Space at her side. There were a host of unknown dangers that could harm both of them or even kill them. Having some more people looking out for her and Space would be a wise move, even if she still wasn't sure she could trust them completely.

So Galaxy said, "Fine. We'll work with you guys until we get to the ruins and divvy up the valuables between us. After that, we go our separate ways."

Sauvage smile grew even larger. "Excellent, excellent. Now why don't I go introduce you to the rest of the team? We should get to know one another in order to work more effectively."

"Lead the way, then, Sauvage," said Galaxy as she stepped aside. "We'll follow."

It didn't take long for Sauvage to introduce Galaxy and Space to all of the members of the archeology team, although Galaxy only caught maybe half their names due to how tired she was. Even then, none of them really stood out to her except Mary, the woman from earlier, and a Zaronian named Digak, who seemed to know only a little bit of Universal Common, the language spoke of throughout the entire UA.

After that, Galaxy and Space were given their weapons back. Their guns didn't appear tampered with, so Galaxy felt comfortable putting her light-gun back into her holster. She decided that maybe the archaeologists weren't such bad people after all, that all of her earlier fears were unfounded.

When Galaxy asked Sauvage when they were going to the ruins, he waved her off, saying, "Oh, probably later. If I were you, I'd take a nap, since we're not leaving for several more hours."

That idea sounded really good to Galaxy, but she didn't follow it until she and Space set up their own tent within the camp, near Sauvage's tent. She told Space she was going to take a nap and not to wake her until it was time for them to go. Space agreed and said he was going to send a message to Sparky about recent happenings and that he was going to talk to the archaeologists to see if he could find out more about them.

Once Space left the tent, Galaxy lay down on her sleeping bag and, without getting inside it, promptly fell asleep.

Again, she found herself standing in an oppressive darkness that seemed to be trying to crush her underneath its weight. And, like before, she found herself flying freely through nothing until she landed once again at the seaside beach.

Remembering what happened last time, Galaxy withdrew her

light-gun and waited for the giant snake monster to arise from the ocean. She also glanced over her shoulder into the darkness of the trees, expecting any moment now to see a giant, slimy tentacle shoot out and drag her in, just like before.

Nothing like that happened. Instead, a small turtle crawled out of the ocean waves and onto the beach. The turtle then stood up on its hind legs. Once it did so, a white lab coat materialized around the turtle, which it adjusted, as though the coat had materialized around it wrong.

"What ... who are you?" Galaxy asked, remembering how it had spoken to her previously.

The turtle-like being looked up at her again and said, "Escape. Before it's too late."

Annoyed by the turtle being's cryptic talk, Galaxy said, "Speak clearly for once. I'm not in the mood to solve riddles or play games."

"No games," said the turtle being, shaking its head. "Run. Escape. Don't let it get you."

"Not until you tell me what is going on here," said Galaxy, folding her arms. "'Cause if I'm having the same dream twice, it either means I have Kana's disease or someone is messing with me."

The turtle frowned. "You don't understand. It's behind you."

Hearing something rustling in the trees behind her, Galaxy whirled around and saw two tentacles shoot out from the darkness of the trees. She tried to zap them with her light-gun, but she couldn't pull the trigger no matter how hard she tried. The tentacles wrapped themselves around her body and dragged her into the darkness, causing Galaxy to scream when she once again saw the face of the monster.

And, as before, she woke up immediately, her heart beating fast and her hands shaking. She sat up in her tent and reached for her light-gun before reminding herself that she was safe, that it had all been a dream, and that there was no monster in the darkness that wanted to eat her.

In spite of these rational reassurances, Galaxy still felt freaked out. She remained awake until Space returned to the tent a few hours later with the news that the archaeologists were packing up to go to the ruins.

Exhausted, Galaxy asked if Space had learned anything interesting about the archaeologists. Space said no, that most of the archaeologists hadn't wanted to talk with him, and those that did only talked about the most superficial things, such as the weather.

"You know, these archaeologists either have very poor social skills or they just don't like me," Space said with a huff. "Why else would they try to avoid talking to me? I'm not a bad guy, right, Galaxy?"

Galaxy barely listened to his complaint, but she nodded anyway. Her mind was still wrapped up in the fear that that nightmare had driven into her brain. It was an irrational fear, of course, which made her feel very childish, but no matter how childish she thought that fear was, it was still there and she would have to deal with it at some point.

According to Space, the archeology team was going to take down their camp soon because they were now ready to finish the journey to the ruins. Had Galaxy been less tired, she might have questioned why the archaeologists would do such a thing; after all, most archeology expeditions took place over a course of weeks or months, sometimes even years. It usually made sense to keep an intact camp area, where they could return at the end of a long day of work. It was almost as if they intended to go back home soon, rather than stick around and thoroughly explore the ruins over a long period of time.

Still, Galaxy raised no objections and helped Space take down their tent. This took longer than normal, as her tired mind caused her to mess up the procedure more than once. In fact, she was so terrible at it that eventually Space suggested she check on the rest of the archaeologists while he finished the job, an offer which Galaxy agreed to.

In her sleepless daze, though, Galaxy didn't learn much about the archaeologists. She just found a rock to sit on and tried to rest a little. She did notice how quickly the archaeologists broke camp, but she didn't give it much thought. Nor did she stop to ponder why Sauvage showed little concern over how roughly the others were handling the boxes full of what was obviously valuable archeological equipment; her brain just didn't have enough power for it.

A few minutes later, Space approached her with their backpacks and said, "Finished packing up the tent. It was rather hard work, you know, but I did it all by myself. I feel like a real outdoors man now, just like my great-great-great-great-grandfather Jack."

Galaxy nodded without really listening. "Yeah, that's nice, Space."

Space looked at her in concern. "Did you get any sleep during your nap?"

"Yes," said Galaxy. "Now stop shouting. It's getting on my nerves."

"Shouting? I'm talking normally," said Space. "You seriously need to sleep."

"No!" Galaxy said, jumping to her feet and looking at him in alarm. "I mean ... look, I'll be fine. You just worry too much."

Space looked skeptical—probably because, Galaxy realized, he didn't worry nearly as often as she did about anything—but before he could express his skepticism, Sauvage approached them. He wore a camouflage outfit now underneath his armor, like he was in the military, although again Galaxy didn't give it much thought.

"I see you two have finished packing," said Sauvage, his smile distorting the tattoo on his cheek. "How's about you hop in our Jungle-Slicers? It will be much quicker than walking there, you know."

"Really?" said Space. He jumped and punched the air. "Yay! I hate walking through the jungle."

Something in Galaxy's mind, perhaps her subconscious, was telling her not to trust Sauvage or any of his archaeologists, but as that something couldn't give a good reason as to why she shouldn't, Galaxy ignored it.

So the two climbed into the Jungle-Slicers. The only problem was that there was not enough room for both of them on the same JS, so Galaxy and Space were forced to separate. Sauvage did assure them that the Jungle-Slicers would be traveling within close proximity to each other, although again Galaxy's mind was trying to alert her that something was off about this whole thing. And again, she ignored it, because all she wanted to do was sleep and not think.

Due to the cramped space of the Jungle-Slicer, Galaxy was forced to sit near the back, squeezed in next to Mary. She also sat near some of the boxes containing archeology tools from Sauvage's tent. Combine that with the bumpiness of the ride and Galaxy had no chance to catch up on her sleep, like she'd planned.

Despite her drowsiness, Galaxy did notice how tense the archaeologists all seemed. No one spoke; indeed, they were so serious that they more closely resembled soldiers preparing to go to war than archaeologists about to explore ancient ruins. One particular archaeologist kept his hand on the boxes, as though worried that the contents might disappear.

For that matter, Galaxy didn't see the Kendonians, Nif and Skio, in either of the two jeeps. Maybe they were going to walk, which wouldn't surprise Galaxy, because she had heard about the legendary speed of the Kendonian species. Supposedly, on foot they could even outrun a starship, although whether that was legend or fact, Galaxy had never bothered to find out.

It was perhaps five or ten minutes later (Galaxy was not sure, as she had stopped keeping careful track of time after failing to sleep as much as she wanted to) that the jeeps started to slow down and Sauvage yelled, "Get ready, my friends, because the ruins are nearly upon us. Keep your wits about you; that *thing* could be hiding anywhere."

This statement puzzled Galaxy enough to snap her out of her sleep-deprived-induced apathy. She looked at Mary and asked, "What does he mean, 'that thing could be hiding anywhere'? What is 'thing'?"

Mary didn't answer. She just patted her leg pocket, as though that was all the answer Galaxy needed. As she was too tired, Galaxy decided she would ask Sauvage about it later, once they reached the ruins.

A couple of minutes later, the vehicles came to a halt and all of the archaeologists climbed out of the vehicles. Galaxy just barely managed to get out on her own without falling out and soon she met up with Space, whose hair looked a little frizzled and unkempt, no doubt due to the fact that the jeeps lacked any sort of roof or windows to keep the wind from blowing in their faces.

"Galaxy, I gotta tell you something," said Space, his voice a whisper. He looked over his shoulder at the archaeologists, who were gathering around Sauvage, who seemed to be speaking to them about something "Something important I learned while I was in the other jeep."

"And what might that be, Space?" said Galaxy. "That riding in a jeep isn't good for your hair?"

"Besides that," said Space, which he said with such earnestness that Galaxy was forced to conclude that he had not caught her sarcasm. "I found out that there are military-grade assault rifles inside those boxes."

Galaxy blinked several times, yawned, and said, "Assault rifles? That's ridiculous. They told us that those boxes contain archeological tools."

"No they don't," said Space, shaking his head. "When my jeep hit a bump in the road, it accidentally loosened the lid off the box nearest me. I saw a gun inside before that Zaronian, Digak, shut it closed."

"You must have been seeing things," said Galaxy with a smile that she hoped didn't make her look too sleepy. "You sure you're not the one in need of sleep?"

"My eyes are working just fine, Miss 'I-Have-Big-Bags-Under-My-Eyes-But-I'll-Pretend-They-Aren't-There'," said Space indignantly. "Why would Digak want to hide them so quickly if they were just archeological tools?"

"Maybe he didn't want them flying out of the back of the jeep," said Galaxy with a shrug. "Look, even if there were guns in there, what would be the point of it? These guys are a bunch of archaeologists, people who aren't known for their fighting skills. Only Nif and Skio could use them, and maybe Mary, but that's three out of a dozen, so …"

She trailed off, again losing her train of thought.

"Maybe they aren't archaeologists at all," said Space. "You know, I tried to get one of them to explain some of the basics of archeology on the ride here, but he couldn't explain it at all. He just brushed me off like I was an annoying brat."

"You can be rather annoying at times," Galaxy said.

"Are you on my side or not?" said Space in exasperation.

Galaxy shrugged. "We're friends, but that doesn't mean I have to accept every crazy theory you believe. Like the idea that the Universal Alliance is secretly run by Mega Play, the biggest toy company in the UA."

"I never said I *believed* that theory," said Space, folding his arms across his chest. "Only that when you look at the evidence —"

Space was interrupted by the cocking of a gun behind him, causing the two to whirl around in time to see Sauvage standing before them. In his hands was what was unmistakably an assault rifle, just like Space had described. Energy rings ran around its tip, showing that the gun was charged and ready to fire at a moment's notice.

And he was aiming it at them.

"Tell me, Mr. Space, Captain Galaxy," said Sauvage with that same horrible smile from before, "do you like my Kan-300 Assault Rifle? Personally, I think it makes me look sexy."

"See?" said Space, looking at Galaxy in triumph. "Didn't I tell you that they had guns? And that this was a sign that something was off? I told you so!"

Ignoring Space's inappropriate gloating, Galaxy stared at the gun's tip, hardly able to take her eyes off it. "Mr. Sauvage, what is the point of that gun?"

"This gun?" said Sauvage, his aim never wavering. "I'm going to use it to make you two do what I want, of course. And maybe use it to kill the animal we were sent to kill. It has a variety of different uses depending on the owner's intent, you see. That is what is so amazing about guns."

Galaxy suppressed a yawn, because she didn't think that would be the wisest thing to do in this situation. "Wait, so you're threatening us? Why? Aren't you an archaeologist?"

"That was a cover," said Sauvage. "I'm surprised you didn't pick it up sooner; after all, you're clearly smarter than your boyfriend here, and I admit that it was hardly the most convincing deception, too."

"Hey," said Space. "First, we're not dating; that's gross. Second, we're equals in intelligence."

Sauvage snorted. "Yes, I'm sure you are. But whether you are or not, you two will be the perfect bait to send into the ruins."

"Bait?" said Galaxy. "I'm confused. We don't know what's going on here."

"You don't?" said Sauvage. He sounded genuinely surprised, although a little skeptical, too. "Interesting. Well, why don't I explain it to you while I and the others walk you to your doom?"

"Um, couldn't you explain it to us here, minus the doom part?" said Space, putting his hands together in supplication.

Sauvage smirked. "No. I can't very well let you live, not when our employer wanted this mission to remain a secret, after all. Letting you two live would defeat the purpose."

Galaxy reached for her light-gun, but Sauvage said, "I wouldn't do that if I were you. I can probably shoot you faster than you can draw your gun. Trust me, I have a very fast trigger finger. Comes from years of experience, you understand, shooting idiots who get in my way."

Galaxy looked at Space, who shrugged and said, "Guess we really don't have a whole lot of choice in the matter but to go with him, do we?"

"No, you do not," said Sauvage. "Now come with me. If you don't act up, I might walk you to your deaths a bit more slowly."

Based on Sauvage's words, Galaxy had expected only him to lead her and Space into the jungle. But of course, that wasn't going to happen, because the rest of the 'archaeologists' had by now donned thick body armor and were equipped with guns similar to Sauvage's. Mary carried a long, sniper-like gun, which she handled like an expert.

They marched through the undergrowth with Galaxy and Space in the lead. Not that the two wanted to be in the lead, but with a dozen guns aimed at their backs, the two didn't have a choice. Galaxy found it hard to keep walking due to her fatigue and the thick undergrowth making it almost impossible to walk through, but every time she thought about slowing down, she remembered Sauvage aiming his gun at her head and she kept walking.

Soon they came across a clearing and found the ruins … at least, Galaxy thought the building they came across was the ruins, even though it looked nothing like she had expected it to.

Though half-covered in vegetation and obviously abandoned for years, maybe even decades, the ruins looked less like buildings left by some ancient civilization and more like a rundown laboratory. The ruins looked like they had once been a perfectly spherical dome at some point, but with part of the roof collapsed and the door hanging off its hinges, it looked like it was falling apart.

"Welcome to Lab Nine Two Three Five," said Sauvage, stepping in front of Galaxy and Space. "Our destination and your death."

Galaxy yawned, not out of boredom, but due to her lack of sleep. "I don't get it. I thought we were looking for ruins from some past civilization, not a scientist's abandoned lab."

Sauvage looked over his shoulder at the two with a look of annoyance on his face. "My, you *really* don't know anything about this place, do you?"

"Explain it, then," said Galaxy, folding her arms. "Since we're going to die anyway, it won't hurt to tell us who you guys are or what you're really doing out here."

Sauvage scratched his chin. "Well, I did promise to tell you and I consider myself a man of my word. Now where do I start?"

"How's about with who you guys are?" said Space, gesturing over his shoulder at the other pseudo-archaeologists. "That's what I'd like to know, because you guys certainly are no archaeologists, unless archaeologists are trained in military warfare nowadays."

"All right," said Sauvage, nodding. "We are a mercenary squad called the Hunters. We hunt down anyone and anything our clients want us to, which, as of today, includes our current prey, the so-called Phantom of the Jungle."

"You're hunting a phantom?" said Space. He covered his mouth with his hands. "But you can't hunt phantoms. They're—"

"It's not a literal phantom, you idiot," Sauvage said. He rubbed his forehead in frustration. "It's a genetic monster created by the famous scientists Minox Kalo. It was created in this lab ten years ago, but it quickly became unmanageable for Kalo and he left the lab."

"Minox Kalo ..." Galaxy repeated. This time, she did yawn, because there was no reason not to now. "I think I've heard that name before."

"You most likely have," said Sauvage. "Kalo is a pioneer in the field of biological engineering. He has created a variety of biological devices and creatures to enhance the speed, endurance, and strength of soldiers, which is why armies from all over the UA have some kind of connection to him. Quite the intelligent man."

"So this lab was his?" said Space.

Sauvage nodded. "Exactly. Ten years ago, Kalo built one of his labs here in Niham's largest jungle to avoid having to comply with government regulations, as this place is quite out of the way and barely explored even by its inhabitants. He was trying to create the ultimate predator, a monster that would be his finest biological creation yet. And he succeeded."

Space looked at the ruined lab. "Doesn't look like he succeeded to me."

"His success was a double-edged sword," said Sauvage. He jerked a thumb over his shoulder. "The monster became too much to control, so he abandoned it here in this lab in the hopes that it would die on its own without him to feed it. That was approximately nine years ago; however, he caught wind of the rumors of a phantom dwelling deep in this jungle, so he hired us to kill it."

"So he wants it dead because he doesn't want to leave any incriminating evidence behind about his less-than-legal activities, does he?" said Galaxy.

"Exactly," said Sauvage, again nodding. "He worries that it might somehow be captured and linked to him. Considering it was made illegally, that could easily end his long career. Our job is to kill it and destroy the lab so no one could ever stumble upon it accidentally, as you two nearly did."

"Well, what makes you think the monster is still in the lab?" said Space with a gulp. "I mean, what if it's hiding in another part of the jungle or on the other side of the planet?"

"Unlikely," said Sauvage. "Kalo told us that the monster is territorial. He told us that it has likely already chosen the lab as its home; therefore, it has probably not gone anywhere. We should be able to find and kill it easily."

"What are you going to do with us?" said Space. "You mentioned something about us being bait earlier."

"I did," said Sauvage with a wolf-like grin. "You see, before running into you two, we thought we'd have to catch some monkeys or something, strap explosives to their bodies, and then send them into the lab. However, after we ran into you, we changed our plans."

Puzzled, Galaxy was about to ask what he meant when the Zaronian Digak came up behind her and Space without warning. Then he strapped two heavy, tight vests to their bodies so fast that Galaxy didn't even realize it until she felt the weight of the vest on her body. Looking down at it, she realized that the vest had explosives built into it, because she had seen similar vests before on a holofilm once.

"Our plan is simple," said Sauvage. He walked two of his fingers across the air toward the ruined lab. "You two will walk as far into the lab as you can—preferably directly into the center, which is where the explosives will be most effective. Then we will blow you up. The resulting explosion ought to be strong enough to bring down the entire building, as well as anyone—or any*thing*, in the case of the Phantom—inside it at the time. It is quite brilliant."

"Hey, we didn't volunteer for this," said Space. "This is murder, isn't it?"

"Perhaps, but why should we care?" said Sauvage. "These bombs are powerful enough to incinerate flesh. No one will ever know we killed you because there will be no way to connect your deaths with us."

"You're mad," said Space. "Don't you have any robots or something you could use instead?"

"Robots are expensive and unreliable," Sauvage said, turning his back to them. "Organic beings, however, know how to adapt to changing conditions and climates. Therefore, you two will do a much better job blowing up the place than any robot could."

"What if the monster isn't in there?" said Galaxy. "What if we blow up the building and it's not there?"

"It will not have been a waste of time, if that is what you are implying," said Sauvage, gesturing at the lab. "If we take out its home, it will have nowhere to run or hide. Killing it will be much more simple then, as it will probably choose to fight us when its sees its home demolished."

"We'll remove them," said Galaxy. "Did it ever occur to you that we could do that?"

"Yes," said Sauvage, "which is why the vests Digak strapped on you can only be taken off with a special password that only Digak knows. Don't even think about slipping out, either; they automatically adjust their size to be too tight to remove that way."

"This is crazy," said Space. "Besides, what if we refuse to march in there? What's to stop us from pulling out our light-guns and blowing ourselves up right here, right now?"

"You're right," said Sauvage, scratching his chin. "That would be a problem, had I not disarmed both of you when you weren't paying attention."

Surprised, Space and Galaxy felt their holsters, which were indeed empty. They looked up and saw Sauvage carried both of their guns in a side pocket in his pants.

"Although," Sauvage remarked, "perhaps that was unnecessary, because neither of you strike me as the suicidal martyr type; still, better safe than sorry, no?"

Then Sauvage turned to face them again, a smirk on his face, and said, "Well, that's enough explaining. Now get walking. Once you enter the building, the fifteen-minute timer will start. And once that timer finishes … kaboom."

"You mean it'll kill us," said Space. "Right?"

"The effect is the same no matter how you phrase it," Sauvage said. "However you choose to say it, the bomb goes off and the lab is destroyed."

Before Galaxy and Space could raise any further objections, the mercenaries forced them to keep walking toward the lab. The idea of exploding made Galaxy's heart race, but there was nothing she or Space could do to get out of this situation alive right now. After all, if they tried to run, they would undoubtedly be shot and if they went into the building, they would undoubtedly blow up. It seemed like a lose-lose situation for them no matter how she looked at it.

Soon, the party reached the lab's front door, which appeared to have been nearly ripped from its hinges. Sauvage stood beside the door and bowed mockingly as he said to Galaxy, "Ladies first, Captain Galaxy."

She just glared at him as she entered the lab. It didn't seem to bother the mercenary leader at all; if anything, he seemed amused by it.

Once Galaxy and Space entered the lab, they heard the sound of something being fitted in and, looking over their shoulders, saw the torn off door had been put back on its hinges. As soon as the door was replaced, Galaxy heard a ticking sound coming from their vests, which was most likely the timer that Sauvage had told them about.

Space ran up to the door and rammed his shoulder against it, but the replaced door didn't even budge. He then kicked it, but again, the door stood strong.

"Damn it," said Space, stepping away from the door and rubbing his shoulder. "They really don't want us escaping, do they?"

"Not surprising," said Galaxy. She sighed. "Should have seen it coming."

"What are we going to do?" said Space, glancing at their explosive vests. "Do you hear that ticking sound? These things are going to go off in fifteen minutes. Fifteen minutes. That's not even a quarter of the length of your average holofilm. And when they do, we're going to die horrible, fiery deaths."

"Yes, I know," said Galaxy as the ticking grew louder and louder. "We need to disarm them right away."

"I didn't know you knew how to disarm bombs," said Space, looking at her, impressed.

Galaxy bit her lower lip. "Well … I technically can't. But I can learn."

Space stepped away from her. "You know, it might not be such a good idea to have a sleep-deprived person like yourself trying to learn such a delicate procedure like this in this very stressful situation we're in."

"I'm not … not sleep-deprived, Jason," said Galaxy. She yawned and rubbed her eyes. "I'm fine."

Space looked alarmed. "Okay, you *never* call me Jason. This, to me, just proves the seriousness of your lack of sleep, just like when Orkan the Wise referred to his trainee/son Gobac by his real name in the Zaronian holofilm, *A Trouble for Two*."

"Even if I don't try, we're both going to die anyway," Galaxy pointed out. "By giving it a shot, there's at least a small chance we could survive, even if it's tiny."

Space gulped. "Well, okay. I trust you, Galaxy, which is the only reason I will let you do this. But do it quickly; these things don't have timers, so I don't know how much time we have left."

Galaxy nodded and started working on Space's bomb vest. She knew she had to figure this out quickly; in addition to Space's vest, there was still her own to deal with, and there was no telling how long it would take for her to disarm this one. If it took too long, she might not have time to disarm her own, assuming she was successful here at all.

Yet she had to try. It was better than doing nothing, in her sleep-deprived opinion.

Galaxy found some wires that connected Space's bombs to the timer. Unfortunately, she couldn't tell which one would set off the bomb if cut and which one wouldn't. Their different colors—red, green, blue, and yellow—didn't help, seeing as she knew nothing about disarming bombs. She wished she had spent some time learning about disarming bombs in college or, really, at any point in her life.

"Pull the red wire," said Space, raising his voice above the ticking from his and Galaxy's vests.

Galaxy looked up at him, puzzled. "The red wire? Why?"

"Because that's what they do in all the holofilms."

"Space, this isn't a holofilm. It's real life."

"But what if the guys who made the holofilms did their homework?"

Galaxy sighed. "Look, we don't have much time left. I'll just pick a random wire and pull. If it works, you can pull the same wire on my vest, as it's in a location I can't reach on my own."

"Okay, okay," said Space. "Just thought I could help, that's all."

So Galaxy closed her eyes. Every second she spent thinking was another second that brought both of them closer to destruction; therefore, she had to act right away.

Without hesitation, Galaxy reached out and grabbed one of the wires. She opened her eyes and saw that it was the red wire. She didn't look at Space as she pulled the wire, fully expecting it to blow them both and the entire lab sky high.

Yet when she snapped the wire out of place … nothing happened. There was no fiery explosion to incinerate them or send the ceiling flying sky high. In fact, the timer on Space's vest had stopped ticking entirely the very moment Galaxy pulled the wire.

"Oh god," said Space with a sigh of relief. "See? Didn't I tell you it's always the red wire?"

Galaxy wanted to punch Space, but she just stood up and gestured at her own vest. "Whatever. Just pull the red wire on my vest now. I can't reach it."

Space did that without hesitation. As soon as he did, the ticking from Galaxy's vest died off immediately. Not only that, but her vest loosened considerably, as did Space's from what she could see.

A moment later, they had discarded their bombing vests onto the floor. Now they stood together in the empty lobby of the lab, which was eerily quiet without the ticking from the vests.

"Now how do we get out of here?" said Space, glancing at the exit. "The door won't budge, and even if we knocked it down, I bet those Hunters would kill us immediately."

"There must be another exit in this building," said Galaxy. "I mean, if the architects who designed this place were smart, they would have created multiple exits. So we just find one of those and get out of here."

Space looked down the dark hall ahead of them and said, "What about the Phantom that the Hunters are looking for? What if it's hiding in here? Won't it try to kill us for invading its territory?"

"We'll be fine," said Galaxy as she reached for her light-gun. "We've got our … oh, damn it. Forgot that French idiot took them from us."

"And *you're* still sleep-deprived," Space said. "So that's going to make things even more difficult for us."

"How many times do I need to keep telling you that I'm perfectly fine?" said Galaxy. "If I were sleep-deprived, would I have been able to disarm your vest?"

"If you weren't sleep-deprived, you would have noticed that spider crawling up your leg," said Space, pointing at her right leg.

Galaxy looked down and saw a large, hairy black spider—at least as wide as both of her hands put together—crawling slowly up it. Without a second thought, she swatted the spider off her leg. Upon hitting the ground, the spider scurried away into a hole in the wall, although Galaxy had the distinct impression that the spider had glared at her before entering the hole, as though annoyed at her rudeness.

"That was a very stealthy spider," said Galaxy, looking back at Space. "You know how stealthy spiders can be, don't you?"

Space rolled his eyes. "Right. Well, maybe I should call

Sparky. He might be able to help us."

"Doubtful," said Galaxy. "He's up in the *Adventure* right now and doesn't know anything about our current situation. Besides, my com-watch doesn't have any reception in here for some reason. We're on our own for now."

Space sighed. "All right. Then I guess I'll lead. You just take it easy, okay? Try to keep your wits about you."

Walking through the dark lab reminded Galaxy all too much of the nightmares she had been having recently, even though the dark lab was quite different from the beach she had dreamed of. The walls were rusted and beaten, there was vegetation growing everywhere, and a terrible dampness stuffed her nose. They occasionally saw a rat or bug (though it was always too dark to tell what they were exactly), but besides that they seemed to be the only living creatures inside the lab.

Thankfully, the Hunters hadn't taken their flashlights, so both Space and Galaxy had them out and activated. Still, the flashlights did little to calm her nerves. Every shadow made her jump; every skittering or scurrying sound made her stop to listen; and more than once she found herself looking over her shoulder, thinking something was following them, although it always turned out to be nothing but her imagination at work.

Space said nothing to this. She had made it plenty clear to him that she wasn't tired and that she was totally normal. Unfortunately, she was now starting to miss his comments about her health, because she was now starting to see that he had been right. She was sleep-deprived and it was taking a heavier toll on her body than she liked to admit.

The lab seemed far bigger on the inside than it appeared on the outside. It almost felt like they were walking through a maze, where every twist and every turn looked exactly the same. Once they had to retrace their steps when they came across a pool of some kind of unidentifiable chemical mixture in their path that gave off a toxic smell.

The shadows of the lab felt to Galaxy like an oppressive darkness, like the kind from her nightmares, hanging over them like a curtain. More than once she found herself hunched over rather than walking straight, as though something was pushing her down. When she glanced at Space, she saw that he was in a similar position, although whether that was real or just her mind playing tricks on her, she didn't know anymore.

All of a sudden, someone burst out of the side entrance up ahead and stumbled to the floor, moaning in agony. Galaxy and Space stopped and looked at each other before they slowly approached the moaning figure. At first it was hard to see who it was, but when their flashlights revealed a familiar skull tattoo on the newcomer's face, Galaxy gasped.

"Oh my god," said Galaxy, putting one hand over her mouth. "Sauvage?"

The light of their flashlights revealed the mercenary leader lying on the floor in front of them, shivering and quivering like a scared doe. He clung to his Kan-300 Assault Rifle like a child clinging to a security blanket. His shirt was ripped down the front, half of his body armor was missing, a long cut ran down his scalp, and the index finger on his left arm was bent in the wrong way. He looked like he had lost a fight with a space tiger.

"Sauvage is really there, right?" said Galaxy, glancing at

Space. "I'm not imagining him?"

"Yep," said Space, nodding. "That's really Sauvage."

Then, without warning, Sauvage looked up at Space and Galaxy. At first, he didn't seem to recognize them, but then the mercenary's eyes widened and he swore in French.

"You two, still alive?" said Sauvage. His teeth chattered. "Impossible. How did you disarm the bombs?"

"Pulled the red wire," said Space.

Sauvage looked at Space in disbelief. "How did you know the red wire was the right one to pull?"

"Saw it in the holofilms," said Space. He puffed out his chest. "You can learn a lot of stuff from them if you pay attention."

"What are you doing in here?" said Galaxy. "And why do you look like you got in a starship crash?"

Sauvage's eyes widened and he hid his face under his arms, like a child trying to hide from the boogeyman. "No! Get ... get away from me!"

Galaxy and Space exchanged a look. Space mouthed, *Is he crazy?*

Then Galaxy said, "Sauvage, we aren't going to hurt you, if that's what you're thinking."

"Even though you totally deserve it," Space added. "You know, for trying to blow us both to the stars."

Sauvage looked up at Galaxy and Space again, his eyes back to normal. He blinked several times in rapid succession, like he was trying to get dust out of his eyes. "I am so sorry for that, er, my friends. When you spoke, it's just ... I just thought I saw something."

"Tell us what happened," said Galaxy. "We're listening."

Sauvage slowly sat up. He didn't relinquish his control over his gun, which he held on his lap as he looked at them. Despite his cool appearance, Galaxy noticed a fear in Sauvage's body that she recognized all too well, because it was one she felt in her own body, even though hers came more from sleep-deprivation than whatever had happened to Sauvage.

"After we sent you two into this lab, the Phantom attacked without warning," said Sauvage, his trembling lips distorting some of the words. "First it got Nif and Skio, then Digak, then the others, and then ... oh, Mary, why, why ... why."

"But I thought you said you guys were equipped to deal with it," said Galaxy with an involuntary gulp. "Isn't that what those big guns were for?"

"Nothing worked against it," said Sauvage, constantly looking around as he spoke, like he thought the Phantom was hiding nearby. "We shot it with our heaviest artillery, but the Phantom wasn't even fazed by it. I just barely managed to escape into here through a second entrance I found off to the side."

Space scratched his chin. "Did it ... did it follow you in here?"

"I don't know," said Sauvage, shaking his head. "I locked the door, but I have no doubt there are other entrances it could use to get in here. It's going to kill us all. There's nothing we can do to stop it. Nothing, I tell you. Nothing!"

With that, Sauvage hid his face in his arms again and started sobbing hard. Galaxy and Space just stood there awkwardly, because the sight of the large, intimidating man now crying like an oversized baby jangled their nerves far more than anything else had up to this point. Sauvage was practically a living symbol of how desperate their situation was. And even though Sauvage had just tried to kill them, Galaxy couldn't help but feel sorry for him.

"Hey, er, Sauvage," said Galaxy, using a gentler tone, although she kept her distance from him just to be safe. "Do you remember the location of that second entrance you used to get into here?"

Sauvage looked up at her, tears still streaming down his cheeks. He brushed some of the tears away and said, in between sniffles, "What? Oh, yes, of course. Why do you ask?"

"Because I think we can use it to escape," said Galaxy.

"Why?" said Space. "Wasn't the Phantom out there?"

Galaxy shook her head. "Like Sauvage said, the Phantom, if it's in here, probably used another entrance. It probably won't expect Sauvage to go back the way he came, right? Especially with us in tow."

"I guess that makes sense," said Space with a shrug. "Better than just wandering around here getting lost."

"Think you can make it, Sauvage?" said Galaxy, looking at the Hunter.

Sauvage sniffled, but nodded. "I-I think so. But the darkness …"

"It's fine," said Galaxy, trying to sound as encouraging as she could. "It's just darkness."

"It's not just darkness," said Sauvage. "It's the Phantom."

A shrill, biting sound hit their ears just then. At the same time, Sauvage's eyes widened like a frightened deer and he jumped to his feet, screaming, "No! No, you won't get me, you bastard! Eat burning energy! Eat all of it, you sick beast!"

He fired his assault rifle wildly about, forcing Galaxy and Space to drop to the floor to avoid getting holes shot in them. The lasers struck holes in the walls, floor, and ceiling, adding to the cacophony of the shrill roar of the beast and Sauvage's own manic screams.

"Stop!" Galaxy yelled, trying to be heard over the sound of the lasers firing everywhere. "Sauvage, stop! There's nothing there! You're going to kill us!"

Surprisingly, Sauvage seemed to listen, because he did indeed lower his gun. But then his eyes turned wild and then he ran down the hallway deeper into the darkness, shrieking and yelling like a lunatic. Neither Galaxy nor Space tried to follow him. It was clear that he was lost.

"Ow," said Space, grabbing his shoulder. "I think one of Sauvage's lasers grazed my arm. Doesn't seem like a deep graze, though, so I'll probably be okay for now."

"I'm surprised we managed to survive that at all," said Galaxy, shaking her head. "Thankfully the hallway is large."

Space looked after Sauvage. "If only he hadn't run away, then we could have asked him to lead us out of here. And now I won't get to taste my favorite ice cream ever again."

"And we'll both die what will probably be very painful deaths," Galaxy said.

"Yeah, I guess that will be a bummer, too," said Space as he propped himself up on his forearms. "So what now?"

Right now, Galaxy just wanted to lay down, close her eyes, and get some sleep, but she knew that would be suicide in their current situation. Besides, it occurred to her that Sauvage might eventually stumble upon their explosive jackets, assuming the

Phantom hadn't killed him. And in his mad state, what was to stop him from blowing up the whole building if he thought it would destroy the Phantom? He seemed suicidal enough in his current state of mind to try something like that.

"Let's just try to retrace Sauvage's steps as best as we can," said Galaxy as she stood up, though it was a challenge because her tiredness was starting to cover her mind again. "Do you need any help getting up, Space?"

Space shook his head. "Naw. Like I said, it's just a graze, although I kind of wish it had been something bigger and grander in order to make this whole thing that much more dramatic."

"We've got a crazy French guy and a biological experiment gone wild roaming the darkness inside a lab that was abandoned ten years ago in the middle of a mysterious jungle," said Galaxy, shaking her head. We don't need any more drama, in my opinion."

"That's not what I— oh, never mind," said Space as he got back to his feet. "Just lead the way. I don't want to be in here anymore."

Having just seen Sauvage snap like a cracker just added extra pressure to Galaxy's already strained nerves. It was almost too much for her, seeing a monster lurking in every shadow and hearing sounds that could have been her last. Had Space not been by her side, she probably would have broken down like Sauvage; hell, maybe even killed herself.

As it was, Galaxy was forced to pinch herself every now and then to remain awake and aware, although even that became less effective as time went on. Her body was getting used to the pinches and it took longer and longer for the sensation of sharp pain to reach her mind. Space offered to start pinching her for her, but she had denied the request and hit him over the head with her flashlight for good measure.

Not even the adrenaline pumping through her body helped much. It seemed like now she was fighting a one woman war against the sleepiness of her whole body. She wished she could tell her body to hang on a little while longer, just another hour at least, because to sleep here would be to give the Phantom the opportunity to kill her and Space.

It was difficult to retrace Sauvage's steps, because he had not told them the exact route he had used to enter the lab. More than once they entered a room full of broken equipment and furniture, but with no exit that they could find, forcing them to go back and search for another way out. Galaxy was once again reminded of a maze as she and Space made their slowly and cautiously through the building, although she figured that was only due to the darkness and their lack of a map of the building's layout that made it seem so complicated.

"Galaxy," Space said, in a low voice, as they peered into yet another abandoned room, this one full of empty cages that might have at one point held some of Kalo's other biological experiments. "I'm puzzled."

Galaxy looked at him and blinked slowly, her tired brain barely processing his words. "What?"

"I said I'm puzzled," said Space. "I'm puzzled by the Phantom."

Galaxy understood his words this time. "Oh. What about it?"

"Why hasn't it killed us yet?" said Space, scratching his head.

"I mean, it's been here for years. Surely it would have tracked us down and killed us by now, yes? Why waste time going after the Hunters?"

Even answering a simple question like that took most of Galaxy's brain power. "Yes, you're right."

"I mean, we aren't exactly a fearsome force, either," said Space. "I'm wounded, you're sleep-deprived, and we're both unarmed. Maybe it's afraid of flashlights."

For once, Galaxy decided not to argue against the point of being sleep-deprived. "I don't know, Space. Let's just get out of here. There's no point in trying to understand the mind of a creature that isn't even human."

That was where the conversation ended, although Space's questions did haunt Galaxy for some time afterward, despite her apathy toward them.

Finally, after what felt like hours and hours of walking, Galaxy and Space came upon a door at the end of a hallway. Above it was a crooked sign written in Universal Common: EXIT.

"My eyes aren't playing tricks on me, are they?" said Galaxy, looking up at the sign. "Because I think that sign says 'EXIT.'"

"You're right," said Space with a big grin. He pumped his fist. "It does say exit! That means we've found the way out. Yay!"

Just before either of them could dash toward the door to freedom, a laser flew over their heads and struck the exit sign, causing it to fall to the floor in front of the door. The two whirled around and, with their flashlights, spotted Sauvage standing several feet behind them, holding his gun high, his face partially obscured by shadow.

"Sauvage?" said Galaxy, not even bothering to hide the annoyance in her voice. "What the *hell* was that for? Were you trying to kill us? Because I really am *not* in the mood to tolerate any sort of stupidity from a moron like—"

"Um, Galaxy?" Space interrupted her, his voice smaller than usual.

Galaxy glared at him. "What? I was on a roll."

Space pointed a shaking finger at Sauvage. "Look at Sauvage's eyes. There's ... something not quite right about them."

With an irritated sigh, Galaxy looked at Sauvage more closely and saw, to her astonishment, that Space was right. The Hunter's eyes were completely black, without any sort of whiteness around them. That was unusual.

"What happened to you?" said Galaxy. "Sauvage, what's wrong with your—"

"My name is not Sauvage," said the Hunter, his French accent completely gone by now, replaced instead by a droning voice that sent a chill down Galaxy's spine. "Identification: Experiment Nine Two Three Four. Also known as the Phantom."

"Oh great," said Space. "The Phantom possessed him. Just like when my Uncle Isaac—"

"What do you mean, possessed him?" Galaxy said, looking at her friend. "That's impossible. The Phantom isn't a literal phantom. That's just a name the natives gave it because they didn't know what it actually was."

Sauvage lowered his gun, although that hardly calmed Galaxy's nerves. "Negative. I function similar to what you would call a phantom, having no real physical form of my own and relying mostly on taking over the bodies of others to survive. The whole point of my creation was to prove that creating a biological entity that could possess the bodies of others was possible; as you can tell, my existence is proof that it is possible."

"So Sauvage is … dead?" said Galaxy.

The Phantom nodded and patted his chest. "I have eliminated all traces of his consciousness from this body. Therefore, for all intents and purposes, your friend is dead."

"He was hardly what we would call a 'friend,'" Space muttered. "More like a rather deadly acquaintance."

"Well, Phantom, what are you going to do to us now?" said Galaxy. "Kill us, just like you did to all of Sauvage's allies?"

"No," said the Phantom, shaking his head. "Instead, you're going to take me to your ship and off this planet. You will take me to my creator and allow me to finish him off."

Space fell down to his knees and cried out, "Please, Mr. Phantom Monster French Guy, don't kill us, we didn't—wait, what?"

"You heard me," said the Phantom. "You two bipeds have a starship, do you not? A starship that can take me anywhere in the universe, yes?"

"Hey, whoa," said Galaxy, holding up her hands. "Okay, this is confusing. We thought you wanted to kill us."

The Phantom shrugged. "I did, originally, wish to terminate your lives, but I have since rejected that idea. I have since discovered that it is more logical for me to leave this planet with you and find my creator, whom I wish to terminate."

"So you're not going to kill us?" said Space. He stood back up just as quickly as he had fallen to his knees. "Oh, joy! If only I had some chocolate ice cream, then this would truly be a moment to celebrate."

Galaxy tilted her head to the side and wished she had her light-gun with her. "I still don't understand. Why do you want to kill your creator?"

"My creator, to put it in terms you would understand, is a fool and a moron," said the Phantom with a sneer worthy of Sauvage. "He created me, but upon realizing that my programming was too advanced, tried to kill me. And when that failed, he left me here, believing that eventually I would deactivate on my own at some point without anyone to help me."

"So why did you kill all of the Hunters, then?" said Galaxy. "Why didn't you try to bargain with them?"

"I could not trump the money that my creator offered them," said the Phantom. "Besides, we should not forget that they were hired specifically to terminate me, while you two were not."

"Killing them all seems rather monstrous," Space said. "I'm not even sure how you did it, considering you seem to be a spirit of some kind."

"The word 'spirit' is erroneous," said the Phantom, hefting Sauvage's gun. "Rather, I am a biological virus that attained sapience. As for how I terminated them, that was easy: I simply possessed the female, Mary, and had her murder them all. I can assure you that none of her allies saw that coming."

Sauvage's earlier words of sorrow for Mary now sounded much different to Galaxy. "What did you do with Mary?"

"After jumping to Sauvage's body, I left hers to rot, as her consciousness is just as nonexistent now as Sauvage's," said the Phantom. "She outlived her usefulness, as all beings do at some point or another."

"This is insane," said Galaxy. "What will you do after you kill your creator, assuming we let you come with us?"

The Phantom seemed to think about it for a moment. "I cannot say. I am sure it will become clear to me, however, once my creator no longer exists. Anyway, you *will* take me with you, whether you want to or not."

"You can't make us do anything we don't want to," said Space, folding his arms. "What's the worst you could do to—"

A laser struck the floor in front of them, causing both Space and Galaxy to jump. The Phantom had raised his gun without either of them even realizing it.

"I could end your pointless, trivial lives right now," said the Phantom. "That is the worst I could do to you."

"But if you killed us, you still wouldn't get what you want," said Space, somehow managing a smile despite the terrifying situation. "After all, how would you get to our ship if we were dead?"

"For once, organic, you make a good point," said the Phantom, nodding in agreement. He raised the gun up to his head. "Which is why I no longer need Sauvage's body anymore."

The Phantom then pulled the trigger and shot himself in the head, the loud sound making Galaxy and Space start. Sauvage's corpse hit the floor, blooding oozing out of the smoking laser hole in his head.

"What the hell?" said Space. "Why'd he kill himself?"

"I don't know," said Galaxy, shaking his head. "Unless he's —"

A sharp, throbbing pain occurred in Galaxy's head just then, driving her to her knees. Her hands grasped her head, but that did nothing to stop the pain.

"What's the problem?" said Space in alarm, looking at Galaxy. "Are you having a really bad headache? Galaxy?"

"No," Galaxy said through gritted teeth. "It's the Phantom … argh … he's trying to control my mind."

"You mean like what he did with Sauvage?" said Space with a gulp. "What can we do?"

"Not sure," said Galaxy. "I just gotta—"

Then everything went black.

When Galaxy awoke, she immediately recognized the dream she was in. She stood on a beach on a tropical island all alone. She glanced over her shoulder fearfully, wondering if that monster was going to try to pull her back in as it always did. She saw nothing in the shadows of the trees, but that barely reassured her.

Then she heard the crunching of someone's feet walking across the sand and, looking to the right, saw Sauvage walking down the beach toward her. Disturbingly enough, he still had a bullet hole in his head and his face was covered with blood, obscuring even his skull tattoo.

"Phantom," said Galaxy, without hesitation. "You're trying to take over my mind, aren't you?"

The Phantom stopped and folded his arms across his chest. "Of course. I need a physical body to be able to escape this planet and yours will do just fine, as I doubt your robot friend will notice who I really am until it is too late. Seeing as there is only enough room in the human brain for one consciousness, I have no choice but to take your life."

"You're assuming I'm just going to lie down and let you take my body without a fight," said Galaxy.

The Phantom shook his head. "Hardly. I *know* you will lie down and let me take your body."

Galaxy raised an eyebrow. "I'm sorry, but do I really look like a weakling to you? I have a very strong will, you know."

The Phantom nodded. "I know. Your will is far stronger than most people's, which is why I had to weaken you over the course of the last day or so in order to make it easier to take over your body."

"Wait," said Galaxy. "You saying that *you're* the one who caused those nightmares that made it impossible for me to sleep?"

The Phantom bowed. "Of course. Originally, I wanted to take your body right away, but I had no guarantee of defeating a will as powerful as your own. So I tried to deprive you of as much sleep as I could, knowing that you humans do not operate well without enough rest."

"So you're the one who has been messing with my dreams," said Galaxy, her hands balling into fists. "Well, I still won't let you have my body. My will is as strong as ever. Your sleep-deprivation tactics failed."

"I believe they succeeded," said the Phantom. He gestured at the beach they stood on. "Otherwise, how would I even be here, talking to you? No, they're working quite effectively. It will not be long now before you, old program, are no longer in charge of this machine."

"My body is my own," Galaxy said. She pointed at the ocean lapping at the beach. "Go take a swim."

With a growl, the Phantom's form changed. It no longer

resembled Sauvage; instead, it had turned into a giant snake with dragon wings sprouting from its back. Its slimy tentacles extended from its belly toward Galaxy, tentacles that looked exactly like the tentacles that always dragged Galaxy into the darkness at the end of this dream.

The sight of the tentacles was enough to paralyze Galaxy. The memory of those tentacles pulling her into the darkness kept replaying in her head now, this time in high-definition, but she knew she couldn't remain afraid forever. She had to fight back; she couldn't let the Phantom win.

So when the tentacles were close enough that she could see their slimy surface, Galaxy pulled back and punched them as hard as she could. She must have been stronger than she thought, because the blow sent the tentacles retreating back into the Phantom's body.

"A good try," said the Phantom. "But not good enough."

The Phantom lunged forward, causing Galaxy to roll out of the way to avoid being eaten whole by its gigantic mouth. The Phantom's tail came swinging out of nowhere, however, and slammed into Galaxy, sending her flying. She landed at the edge of the jungle, the impact taking her breath away.

The Phantom rose and looked at her, licking its lips as it did so. "I can tell my tactics have been working, because your reflexes are slowing. Now I shall take your life and your body."

Galaxy tried to get up, but she felt so weak and tired that she just couldn't. She was just about to give up and allow the Phantom to kill her when she had a sudden realization.

I am in a dream, Galaxy thought. *Doesn't that mean I can do whatever I want?*

Granted, she did not know if that would work, seeing as this dream seemed to be a creation of the Phantom. Still, it made sense to Galaxy, so she sat up and imagined a bazooka appearing in her hands.

Much to her relief, a massive bazooka did in fact materialize in her hands. It was red and shiny and would have been too heavy for her to wield in real life; however, it felt as light as a feather here, so she held it up and aimed it at the Phantom.

"What?" said the Phantom. "A bazooka? Where did that come from?"

"My imagination," said Galaxy. She was satisfied to hear fear in his voice. "See you later."

With that, she pulled the trigger and watched an oversized black missile fly from the bazooka's barrel.

The missile struck the Phantom before it could dodge, causing it to explode into a million pieces. The force of the explosion was so powerful that it sent Galaxy flying into the shadows of the jungle, only this time, the darkness did not seem so scary.

Galaxy's eyes opened and she found herself lying on the floor of the lab, with a rather frantic-looking Space bending over her as though worried.

"Galaxy, is that you?" said Space, grabbing her face and examining her eyes. "Your eyes *look* normal, but you could still be the Phantom, trying to—"

Irritated, Galaxy slapped him in the face, causing Space to let go of her face and say, "Okay, okay, yeah, it's you, Galaxy. Sorry."

"It's okay," said Galaxy as she sat up, shaking her head. "The

Phantom's gone now. Probably forever."

"Thank god," said Space. Then he glanced at Sauvage's corpse and said, "Er, what are we going to do with Sauvage? And the rest of the Hunters?"

Galaxy frowned. "Not sure. Maybe we can contact Kalo and tell him that his Hunters are dead. We could bury them, I suppose."

"But they probably have families and friends," said Space. "We can't just bury them in a random part of the jungle."

Galaxy stroked her chin. "If we take them with us, it's gonna make us look like murderers. Like I said, we could contact Kalo and tell him what happened. Then it would be his problem, not ours. Or maybe just contact the authorities and let them deal with it."

"I guess so," said Space, scratching his head. "But how do we contact him? It's not like we have his com-watch number or anything."

"I know how we can," said Galaxy. "Come on. Let's get out of here. I'm sick of this place, of this whole planet, and I need to sleep."

Dreaming ... most days, it seemed like that was all Minox Kalo ever did. He would get up at the crack of dawn and immediately hook his brain up to the dreaming machine, a device he had designed to allow him to observe the dreams he had experienced the night before. The dreaming machine allowed him to view his dreams in vivid, full-color detail, which was rare for his species, the Cinonites, who when they dreamed, could dream only in detail-less grayness.

EPISODE FIVE: THE PHANTOM OF THE JUNGLE

His reasoning for doing so was simple. Though a scientist, Minox Kalo had always been a bit spiritual. In his opinion, one's dreams often revealed one's true thoughts and self, more so than any amount of conscious contemplating could. To him, there had always been something mystical about dreams, something worth exploring, because it always seemed to him like there was a vast universe inside the mind of every person, perhaps placed there by God. Most people just didn't know it.

A beeping noise caused Kalo to pause right before he hooked up to the dreaming machine this morning. He glanced around his lab and saw that a message had popped up on his computer.

Puzzled, Kalo put down the dream machine's cord that he had been about to attach to the back of his head and walked over to his computer. He pressed the touch screen with one of his small, stubby fingers to open the message, which read:

Dear Mr. Kalo,

My name is Helena Galaxy. We've never met before, but I managed to get your contact address off one of the mercenaries you sent to Shizor to kill the Phantom of the Jungle.

We didn't know who else to contact, but we decided to tell you that your mercenaries are all dead. They were killed by the Phantom. Ruthlessly; we can't even find all of their body parts it was that bad.

Thankfully, we managed to destroy the Phantom before it could escape Shizor. We apologize for not doing anything to save your hired swords. We were kind of busy at the time. We just wanted to let you know in case you wanted to do something about the bodies.

Yours,

Captain Helena Galaxy.

Kalo's small eyes rested on the final line—"*Captain Helena Galaxy*"—and he muttered, "Now where have I heard that name before?"

Spacetastic Interviews with:

Mr. Jason Space and Captain Helena Galaxy

T.L. Charles: Hello, everyone! Welcome to the Spacetastic Interviews series, in which I, the author, interview characters from the story. Today's interview is with the protagonists themselves, Mr. Jason Space and Captain Helena Galaxy! Mr. Space, Captain Galaxy, why don't you two introduce yourselves to the audience?

Captain Galaxy: Why? Most of the readers have already read all five episodes of Season One. They know us already probably even better than we know ourselves.

Mr. Space: Galaxy! Don't be so rude to the interviewer. Sorry, Charles, but Galaxy's not a good interviewee. She doesn't really know how to conduct herself in these sorts of situations, you understand.

T.L. Charles: I do, seeing as I created her and all.

Captain Galaxy: *sighs* Fine. Hello, everyone. My name is Captain Helena Galaxy, Captain of the *Adventure* and one of the main characters of the series. I'm a starship mechanic by trade and the only one of the crew allowed to touch our bank account.

Mr. Space: And I am Mr. Jason Space, a professional space explorer and adventurer. My mother wanted me to be a lawyer, but the law never appealed to me as deeply as the darkest corners of outer space, where unknown and danger lurk around every corner.

T.L. Charles: Now we're supposed to keep this quick, since I need to get to writing Season Two pretty quickly to make that November release date (laughs). So anyway, what were your favorite memories of Season One?

Mr. Space: My favorite memory was when I destroyed that icebot. I was pretty awesome, wasn't I?

Captain Galaxy: Eh, I've seen cooler.

Mr. Space: (distressed) Was that a pun? It burns.

Captain Galaxy: My favorite memory was when I defeated the Phantom of the Jungle. It was all just a dream, I guess, but that doesn't diminish the fact that I killed an advanced killer virus. I also enjoyed throwing Rocky's prison out into space; the witch deserved it.

T.L. Charles: Whoa now, Galaxy, gotta watch that language. Don't wanna get in trouble with the censors. Otherwise those jerks at Annulus Publishing might not let me do anymore interviews.

Captain Galaxy: You should find a different publisher, then. I don't think I said anything wrong. I just said that Rocky is a witch. How is that anything but the God honest truth?

250

SPACETASTIC INTERVIEWS

T.L. Charles: (nervously looks over shoulder) Well, anyway, let's move on. What do you guys think will happen in Season Two?

Mr. Space: I will become a great holofilm actor and will win the Space Oscars.

Captain Galaxy: Space will keep thinking he's hotter stuff than he actually is. Other than that, I can't say, although I do hope we get a windfall so I can make some much-needed improvements to the ship.

T.L. Charles: What about Sparky? Think anything will happen to him?

Mr. Space: Sure. He'll be my manager when I become a great holofilm actor.

Captain Galaxy: Sparky will probably just keep doing what he's always done, which is to support us in our adventures.

T.L. Charles: Well, I'm sure that whatever Sparky does, it will be great. Maybe I'll interview him next season. Anyway, looks like we're out of time for today. Readers, if you'd like to be the first to know about the release of Season Two, just sign up to my mailing list on my website at www.tlcharles.com.

Mr. Space: Don't do it. It's a scam. His emails are always boring. He always talks about his books and stories and nothing else. He doesn't even talk about chocolate ice cream.

T.L. Charles: But if I didn't have a mailing list, how would I ever let readers know about the release of your newest stories?

You're getting royalties off every copy sold, you know.

Mr. Space: (eyes widen) We get royalties? Galaxy, did you know—

Captain Galaxy: (hurriedly) Uh, look at the time! Guess we gotta go. Bye, everyone, and see you in November for Season Two of *The Spacetastic Adventures of Mr. Space and Captain Galaxy*, available wherever books are sold!

END SEASON ONE

About the Author

T.L. Charles writes comedic action-adventure science-fiction stories such as *The Spacetastic Adventures of Mr. Space and Captain Galaxy* as an indie author. T.L. Charles is the pen name of Timothy L. Cerepaka, who you can read more about at www.timothylcerepaka.com.

Visit T.L. Charles's website at www.tlcharles.com to find out more information and see all of his books.

www.ingramcontent.com/pod-product-compliance
Lightning Source LLC
Chambersburg PA
CBHW031313170626
46807CB00001B/397